WAR

RISE OF MAN BOOK 4

See these other books by E. Wayne Stucki available at your favorite eBook retailer:

Ascendance

Liberty

Betrayal

Mars (Upcoming)

If you enjoy religious works, check out *The Sermon on the Mount: A Leadership Guide*.
If you wish to learn more about upcoming books you can contact the author at ewaynestucki@gmail.com.

WAR

RISE OF MAN BOOK 4
E. WAYNE STUCKI

Second Edition

Copyright © 2024 by E. Wayne Stucki

All rights reserved, including the right to reproduce this book, or portions thereof, in any form. No part of this book may be used or reproduced in any manner whatsoever without written permission from the publisher, except in the case of brief quotations embodied in critical articles and reviews. The views expressed herein are the responsibility of the author and do not necessarily represent the position of the publisher. For information or permission, email ewaynestucki@gmail.com.

This is a work of fiction. Characters and events in this book are products of the author's imagination or are represented fictitiously.

Cover design by MiblArt

Interior print design and layout by Sydnee Hyer

Ebook design and layout by Sydnee Hyer

Published by Red Willow Publishing

979-8-9884608-6-2

eBook 979-8-9884608-7-9

PROLOGUE

Vadim Kazan sat at his console and kept a careful watch on the information displayed in its gauges and readouts. On occasion he keyed for more information about a particular system or contacted people at the launch pad to check a piece of equipment the data indicated needed adjustment.

Vadim was one of almost fifty operators in the mission control room preparing to launch a supply rocket destined for a scientific station orbiting over Earth.

The room's three rows of consoles faced a large wall screen. Displayed was the launch pad containing the rocket booster and the men working to complete preparations for the launch. To the left of the screen a control panel showed the status of close to one hundred systems. All the lights glowed amber as expected. The room hummed with a quiet murmur as other operators spoke with their counterparts at the launch site.

Every time he looked up at the screen, Vadim had to fight the temptation to ignore his console and watch the activity going on around the rocket. All that movement could be mesmerizing. But he knew better than to succumb to that desire. Others who had didn't work here anymore. He'd never heard what had become of them.

Vadim recentered his focus on the data being presented, watching for any problems. A mistake by any one of the console operators, a failure to spot a problem, could cost the loss of the rocket and its payload. He determined that it wouldn't be his fault if the launch failed.

He spared a quick glance at the countdown clock on his console and gave a slight nod. There'd be a final check of all systems in a few minutes before the controller issued the "go" command. The launch was scheduled to occur in just under five minutes. Twenty minutes after that the payload would be in orbit, and Vadim's job would be complete until the next launch. He scanned the displays, dials, and gauges of his console, once again looking for any indication of a problem. Everything remained within the specified parameters.

A nudge to his right arm caught Vadim's attention. Turning, he saw Stepan Koslovsky, the operator at the next console, looking at him with a slight grimace. "What?" Vadim mouthed.

His friend covered his boom microphone with a hand and jerked his head toward the VIP Observation Room situated behind and above the operator floor. "The general's back," he whispered.

Vadim glanced in the direction Stepan indicated. Sure enough, there was General Dmitrii Elin in the seat that gave him the best view of the entire control room through the large glass window. Like Stepan, Vadim made sure his microphone was covered before speaking. "What's this make?" he wondered. "Is this the third or fourth launch he's watched?"

"It's the seventh," Stepan replied. "He's been here for each launch going to this particular space station since its construction." The operator shrugged.

Vadim turned back to his instruments. "What gave the general such an interest?"

The launch controller's voice over the room's speakers and headsets broke through Vadim's thoughts. "Final check prior to launch."

Vadim's eyes confirmed that everything at his console was still nominal, then settled in to wait for his turn to report. He put the generals' presence aside as he focused on his equipment.

In the observation room General Elin, the commanding officer of the Strategic Space Command for the Russian Federation, listened and watched as the final check was conducted. Although there were several rows of seats in the room for observers, he alone occupied the space. This was a routine supply launch to a non-descript research station after all. There was nothing of note to draw a crowd of reporters to this isolated facility -which was fine with him.

To prevent the United States intelligence agencies from becoming suspicious of his activities, Dimitrii Elin had his staff spreading disinformation. Word was being put out he was an eccentric general who was using his position in the space command to indulge in a childhood fantasy to watch rocket launches. He even instructed some of his loyal minions to opine to others that if this behavior continued his superiors may call him in for a reprimand.

General Elin tracked the progress of the final check through the control room below as the seconds to launch continued to tick away. Each time a station reported ready an amber light on the large wall board next to the monitor went green. At last, the announcement came from the controller, "Final check completed. All lights are green. The launch is go in two minutes."

The general looked at the master clock showing in the lower right corner of the large viewscreen. He watched the time switch from 2:00 to 1:59 then 1:58. He shifted to the front of his seat, anticipation building.

His attention riveted on the monitor. It showed the launch pad which held the large rocket that was going to boost the payload into orbit. The clock continued to count down. Vapor could be seen coming from the boosters and streaming down the sides of the rocket.

At one minute to launch a voice came over the intercom counting down the time. The general saw the pad personnel climb into their vehicles and head for their protective bunkers. All the ramps coming from the launch tower released and swung away from the rocket. The console operators kept their attention on their equipment, ready to halt the launch if they detected any problem in the systems they monitored.

When the countdown reached five seconds the engines ignited, sending fire and smoke spreading out from the stern. The controller announced, "Ignition! Good burn confirmed."

The final seconds counted down, and General Elin held his breath. By this time smoke and fire almost blocked the view of the rocket. The grey clouds and red fire increased dramatically when the engines went to full burn. The rocket began to rise on a pillar of flame and smoke then increased in speed. The controller's voice came over the intercom again, "We have lift off."

The rocket cleared the launch tower, continuing to accelerate. Seconds passed, and then the ascending rocket cut through a thin layer of clouds a thousand meters up. A trail of white smoke marked its path from the launch pad.

The general began to breathe again. The launch was a success. The booster selected to send this cargo into orbit hadn't had a failure in the past five years. But there was always a possibility. The controller was continuing to announce the altitude benchmarks the rocket was reaching. "Passing the ten-thousand-meter mark, attitude rolling. Profile is good, no deviation from course."

General Elin settled back into his chair and crossed his legs, still watching the screen. Tension had started to drain from his body. He gave a decisive nod. The rocket's cargo was going to reach orbit. Then its next milestone would be to rendezvous with the orbiting station and dock to transfer its cargo.

A slight smile creased the general's lips. This delivery would complete the inventory for the orbiting station. And when the cargo was transferred from the cargo module and loaded into the magazine the station would be fully operational.

Now that they were coming to the final stages of the preparation, he wondered if the American's had any idea about the station's true purpose. He doubted it because no protests had hit the United Nations agenda.

"Separation of first stage complete," announced the controller. "Second stage burn is good."

Dmitrii Elin glanced at the large screen. The view had switched from the rocket to an orbital schematic. A blinking dot indicated the position of the cargo module along its projected course.

His thoughts continued as he watched the dot ascend toward the orbital track. The general staff had decided long ago when he'd presented the possibilities of this option to keep the purpose of this space station secret. As the items contained in the station weren't nuclear, they didn't come under the international treaty banning nuclear weapons in space. In fact, as inert objects, they weren't covered by any weapons treaty at all. But if the American's discovered what was happening in orbit, they'd come up with plans to eliminate the station or to mitigate the damage. Perhaps they'd put economic pressure on the Federation to disarm the station.

General Elin didn't think President Anatoly Berezin would back down at this point. Their plans had advanced too far for that. Besides, these missiles, for lack of a better term, would have a devastating impact when they hit. They would give the Russian Federation a decisive strike on the United States in any confrontation. Any tactician worth the title would never surrender an advantage like that. The best part would be that there'd be no nuclear contamination to deal with after the war had been won.

By this time, the cargo module was entering orbit. The launch controller had fallen silent after transferring control to orbital command. Console operators were shutting down their equipment and visiting with their neighbors.

General Elin pushed up from his seat and made his way to the exit. The module would take hours to reach the station and dock. With all the paperwork waiting for him on his desk he couldn't stay to see the event. Still, he was confident the mission would succeed.

He took one last glance at the schematic. The screen flashed then shut off. He gave a nod. It was only a matter of time before the Americans pushed Berezin too far. And when that happened the packages on board that station would be a very unpleasant surprise for them.

CHAPTER I

Not many people took notice when Dr. Rod Carue walked into the Senate hearing chamber. At six feet tall, the scientist didn't tower over many people. His hair was light brown, eyes hazel. He bore neither facial scars that would make him rugged nor high cheek bones to help him look exotic. He was merely average-looking.

Only two people were sitting in the observer's gallery as Dr. Carue walked down the center aisle separating the banks of seats. One sat in the back near the aisle on the right side, the other sat in the middle of the left side. Neither bore the trademark tools of reporters.

Rod moved through the small gate in the barrier separating the witnesses from the gallery and stopped by the witness table to scan the room. Between the table and podium where the committee would sit was a carpeted area where reporters could get photos of the witnesses.

In front of him stood the raised podium where the senators of the committee would sit. It was made of polished mahogany stained a dark red with places for nine senators. But the committee he'd be facing today was comprised of only five members. Their name plates were already out.

Rod looked down at the witness table. It was made from the same polished, dark-red mahogany as the podium and the rest of the woodwork around the room. Detailed carving adorned its legs and sides of the tabletop. There was a name plate placed on the table where he was supposed to sit. Two white lace coasters on the table's surface were to protect the polish from the glass and pitcher of iced water that would be provided.

Set into the table a few inches to the right were a monitor with an audio grill. The monitor would display any prepared remarks for the witnesses, while the audio grill picked up and amplified the responses to the senators questions.

Everything would be recorded, of course. Posterity must hear. as well as see, he thought, remembering the words of a senate page from his first hearing for the suspension project. A smirk crossed his face. Like a boring meeting where politicians grandstanded most of the time would be interesting to anyone, anytime.

A mischievous idea brought a spontaneous grin. "This one's for you, Uncle Herman," he thought and placed his burgundy leather briefcase on the table over the audio grill then sat down in his seat. It'd be interesting to see what the senatorial staff's response would be.

Rod glanced up at the ornate, gold-leafed clock on the wall to his right. He'd left his hotel room early so he wouldn't be late for the hearing. The senator's would be more than a little upset if the person they were planning on cross-examining was late. Since Washington, DC, was known for its traffic backups, he'd planned accordingly. But it seemed the anticipated traffic snarls hadn't materialized, or the cab driver had been skillful enough to avoid them. Either way Dr. Carue had plenty of time to kill.

Opening his case, Rod removed a copy of Edgar Rice Burroughs', *A Princess of Mars*. When he'd packed for this trip, he'd included the book on a whim. It was an old paperback version. He'd gotten the entire *John*

Carter series from his grandfather a few months before Papa had died at ninety-five. That was two years ago. Rod hadn't thought of reading any of those books until this trip. Since he was working on a process that could help colonize Mars, reading a series centered on the red planet seemed appropriate.

Fifty minutes later new activity in the room brought his eyes up from the pages. Aides for the senators of the Appropriations Committee were filing into the hearing room through a side door. Rod watched as they made sure the places were arranged the way their senators liked and had water and glasses. They set papers containing, Rod knew, a brief on his project at each place. Then, when they were satisfied that everything was ready, they sat at their designated places against the wall behind the podium to wait for the meeting to begin.

A senate page walked over to the witness table carrying a crystal pitcher of iced water and a matching glass. The young woman placed the two items on the lace coasters in front of Rod without saying a word. The scientist nodded at her and muttered his thanks. She gave no indication of hearing him but retraced her steps and left the room. Rod carefully poured himself a glass of water and ice and took a sip.

Five minutes later the senators entered by the same entrance used by their aides and sat down. Two re-arranged their papers while others made sure their microphones were working.

Rod marked his place in the book and returned it to his case. He took out the original copy of the documents provided to the senators and began to review the highlights of his remarks. He wasn't going to rely on the teleprompter for this presentation. And didn't need to. He'd been over this information often enough he had it memorized.

As Rod was looking through his papers a man in a white shirt and tie entered the room by another door. The badge on a lanyard hanging around his neck identified him as a member of the congressional technical staff. He leaned over to whisper something to the senator chairing the committee.

Senator Ethane Montayne from Iowa nodded his understanding, dismissed the tech with a wave of a hand, and leaned forward so the microphone pickup would work. "Dr. Carue."

Rod stopped his review and looked up at the senator. "Yes, Mr. Chairman?" he responded.

"Please remove your case from the table. It's disrupting the audio recorder."

"Oh, pardon me, Senator," the scientist replied and glanced down at the offending article. "I'll remove it immediately."

Rod was careful to keep the amusement out of his voice and adopt a façade of being contrite. He put the papers he'd been reading on the table then, turning to the case, made sure everything he'd need was already on the table. He secured the lid and slid the case from the table.

"With the technical issues resolved we can begin," announced Senator Montayne after glancing at the wall clock to confirm the time. The sound of his wood gavel striking a small block of white marble on the podium cut through the muted conversations that were going on in the background.

When the room was silent Montayne spoke again. "This hearing of the Appropriations Committee is now in session. In the interest of time, we will treat this hearing as a continuation of prior hearings and forego the usual preliminary statements by members of the committee." He paused long enough to glance at his fellows who nodded their agreement. "This allows us to go straight to our business," Montayne continued. "Dr. Carue, in the prior hearings I just mentioned you were sworn in. You will not have to make the affirmation again but consider the earlier obligation to tell the truth as continuing."

Rod nodded. "I will, Mr. Chairman."

"Thank you, Doctor," said Montayne. "Now to begin! NASA has asked that its budget be increased to expand the scope of your project. This committee has an obligation to the taxpayers to ensure we aren't spending their money on frivolous projects." Rod nodded once again.

"Now, Dr. Carue, please explain this latest funding request," said Senator Montayne.

Rod had been in hearings before and knew how the game was played. "If I may, Mr. Chairman," he began, "the papers in front of you provide a statement of the project's objectives and our intentions for the next phase but I'll give you a summary.

"As you're aware the purpose of my project is to prove out a method for the suspension of human crews on deep-space probes. This method, which uses a combination of lowered body temperatures, drugs, and gasses, effectively reduces a person's metabolism to zero. We can maintain this state indefinitely with no known side effects."

"We understand the objectives and methods of your project Doctor," commented Senator Harlon Pepper, from New York. His tone was condescending. "You've been here before, as the chairman has mentioned. What we want to know is, why the budget increase? That's why you're here, after all."

Rod nodded again to acknowledge the statement but ignored the tone. "Senator, we've completed the first phase of the project," he announced.

"Phase two involves using animals to evaluate the proven equipment, process and drugs under conditions that would occur during a long-term space flight. We need to determine if the mixture of gasses and doses of drugs that were successful in phase one change under low or no gravity. When that's completed successfully, we move into phase three: human trials. We need additional expenditures for the next two phases."

"I see," replied Senator Montayne, "what did you have in mind Doctor?"

Rod took a deep breath. This was the money moment. "For our next phase we need to have two sites; one being the control and the other the real test." He paused again, shuffling his papers to bring a particular sheet to the front. "It's our intent to have the control site at the Nevada Test Site near Las Vegas. The second, the test site that approximates the conditions of space flight, is at the Copernicus research station in a mountain range about ten miles from the Main Lunar Base." There were some exclamations of surprise from the committee although the full impact of what Rod said hadn't registered.

"Two facilities?" asked Senator Montayne. "Is that really necessary?"

Rod shrugged and held out his hands. "It's the scientific method, Mr. Chairman. You have a control group in addition to the test group. This allows us to see if there are any statistical differences between the two groups and prove out the test. In an earlier hearing this committee charged me to follow all proper protocols."

"Dr. Carue, why the 'far out' locations, if you'll excuse the expression?" asked Senator Pepper with a smile. "The test site in Nevada is rather isolated. It'll be expensive to transfer personnel and equipment there."

"The power requirements for the equipment in our new proposal are rather on the high side, Senator," replied Rod. "At present only a fusion reactor can supply those requirements. We've been drawing on the base power at Vandenberg for the limited tests we've done to date. Unfortunately, our increased schedule and additional equipment will quickly exceed what that base can provide. It's our hope that future technological improvements will reduce the power demands of the suspension equipment.

"The Nevada Test Site, an already recognized site for radiation hazards, is a logical placement for the terrestrial control site. It's remote enough that if a mishap happens there will be no threat to large population centers. A survey completed recently by the DOD has shown the site is relatively free of major geologic faults and wind patterns over the area keep to the less inhabited portions of the country. Any incident at the base will be largely confined to the NTS. In addition, the appendix included in the funding request shows the NTS has the necessary equipment to construct the underground base so no construction equipment will need to be shipped in."

"You've mentioned only one facility so far Doctor Carue. Where is this Copernicus base you mentioned?" asked Senator John Collinsworth from Connecticut. "It sounds like an observatory."

Rod looked at him in disbelief. Hadn't he already said "lunar"? And what place on the planet could simulate low gravity? "The second base is on the moon, Senator," he replied.

Senator Pepper had been pouring himself a drink of water when the pronouncement came. The man looked up in surprise and missed his glass, spilling water and ice over the polished wood surface of the podium. Aides rushed to clean up the mess while the senator set the pitcher down, missing the coaster, and stared at Rod. The others on the committee appeared just as surprised. It seemed this was not what they had been led to expect by their staff.

How the senator's couldn't know where the test sites were going to be Rod had no idea. Everything he'd just said was in the proposal. Hadn't they read his brief? He watched as Senator Collinsworth gestured for an aide and began a whispered conversation.

Before any of the senators could get over their astonishment, Dr. Carue continued. "The moon is the logical site for this test. It's as close as we can get to the gravity conditions of a journey to Mars without being in deep space. The observatory that is specified in the proposal has the necessary space which is not being fully utilized at this time. The power plant can be upgraded to manage our needs with little effort or cost. Although the test equipment will need to be transported there and installed, the facility will not require any major modifications."

"After hearing that last location, I can understand the reason for the size of the appropriations increase," commented the chairman.

"Wouldn't it be less expensive to use one of the space stations?" asked Senator Olewanda from Nevada.

Rod smiled as he replied. "Yes, Senator, it would be cheaper. However, the dangers, both politically and environmentally, are much greater."

"How so?" countered the Senator.

"If for any reason the station exploded or fell from orbit the atmosphere could be polluted by the radioactive isotopes from the reactor. The loss of life and contamination in that instance would be extensive. It may even cause an international incident."

"I see." Senator Olewanda seemed thoughtful and somewhat subdued.

"Yes, a fusion explosion on the moon wouldn't have the dangers of that happening aboard a space station," said the chairman. "But will an incident threaten other lunar facilities?"

"No, Mr. Chairman," was Rod's quick reply. "Copernicus is in a mountain range more than ten miles from the closest station."

Senator Montayne gave a slight shake of his head. "That's good to hear Dr. Carue. Now, you have justified the size of the appropriations requested but not why we should approve it."

Translation, thought Rod: What was in it for them?

Rod remained silent for a moment as he collected his thoughts. When he was sure he wouldn't offend the chairman or any of the other senators by making an impolitic remark he spoke. "Consider, Mr. Chairman, the millions of people who have died over the past few decades from diseases we now have cures for. While it's obvious we couldn't suspend all of them it is possible to suspend some. What if one percent, or one percent of one percent, had been suspended until researchers found a treatment? Those lives could have been saved, their potential retained. What contributions to humanity have been lost because of these untimely deaths?" At this explanation, the Senator from Connecticut sat forward in his chair, listening intently.

As he explained his project Dr. Carue felt himself becoming more animated. The notes he'd meticulously prepared were forgotten. He'd lost his grandmother many years ago to a then incurable disease.

Rod wanted to save other families from that pain. NASA was the vehicle that provided the funding to prove out the concept.

He paused to get a drink of water to ease a drying mouth. After setting the glass down on its coaster he resumed his explanation. "Senators, another obvious possibility for this process involves the colonization of the outer planets and asteroids. With suspension, large crew quarters on the ships are not necessary. The money saved by not needing so much life support for the journey could be spent on additional equipment and supplies for the colony. In this way the colonies' chances for self-sufficiency and survival are greatly improved. In addition, if an accident threatens the survival of the colony the colonists simply return to their suspension chambers and sleep while waiting for rescue to come. This process could open the entire solar system for exploration and development."

"But Dr. Carue, our policy has been that no space installation be self-sufficient," objected Senator Collinsworth. "The Russians with their scientists in an orbital station revolting in an attempt to set up a ruling scientific-elite twenty years ago shows the wisdom of that policy."

"Yes, sir, that is true," Rod replied. "The moon and space stations in orbit are potential threats to our planet. But the asteroids and Mars are too far away to be considered a threat or a dependent society. The supply time in that case is years not days. That alone would require a colony to be self-sufficient. . . ."

"By approving this proposal, you will be recorded in history as aiding the outward expansion of civilization, providing a solution to the population problem, and saving large numbers of lives," said Dr. Carue. He looked up at the committee and gave a slight nod. "This project can help guarantee the future of humanity. Senators, thank you for your consideration of our proposal."

Senator Montayne leaned to the people on either side of him, conferring with them for a moment then turned back to face the witness table. "Thank you, Dr. Carue. We appreciate your views and your candor. We will inform you of our recommendation to the Senate within this business week." The committee chairman picked up his gavel. "This hearing is now adjourned," he announced and struck the marble block sitting on the table three times.

With that, the three days of testimony closed. The senators gathered their papers, rose, and left the room by the same door they had entered. Their aides followed moments later after checking to see if anything had been forgotten.

The red light on the audio grill in front of Rod went out indicating that the microphone at the witness table had been turned off. He breathed a sigh of relief and leaned back in his chair. Closing his eyes, he took a few moments to rest, trying to relax from the stress of the hearing. It was only mid-afternoon, yet he was exhausted.

Without warning a hand came down on Rod's shoulder, startling him, and a voice spoke. "Well, do we get it?"

The scientist opened his eyes and turned to see Max Jorgensen, his assistant from NASA, standing next to him. Max wasn't very tall, only five feet eight inches, with jet-black hair and dark brown eyes. Like Rod, he was dressed in a dark business suit. His complexion honestly was light bronze and had the appearance of a permanent tan. He'd come by the complexion because his father was Navajo and his mother white.

"When did you get here?" asked Rod. Then he cocked his head. "Rather, why are you here instead of at Vandenberg overseeing the children?"

Max gave a slight smile. "Children?" he asked and cocked his head in imitation of Rod. "Is that any way to refer to our esteemed colleagues?"

Rod glared at his associate who held up his hands in submission.

"I walked in just after you started your closing remarks," said Max. "The day you left for the hearing I got a call from Houston. The Director of Operations of NASA wanted a personal briefing on the project."

"You had to do that in person?" wondered Rod. "We send them regular progress reports after all." Then he paused and gave his friend a puzzled look. "They've been getting our reports, haven't they?"

Max shrugged. "They have but the DO and his staff are anxious. They know that if we succeed the configuration for the Mars Probe will change drastically. They could minimize the life support, living quarters, that kind of thing, and add equipment and supplies." He nodded at Rod and gave a light chuckle. "Isn't that what you told the committee?" Rod's soft snort of amusement confirmed the statement as Max continued his explanation. "The DO wanted to get a feel for our progress. He prefers the personal touch."

Rod nodded, then reached down to pick up his briefcase. He deliberately set it on the audio grill and opened the lid. "Ok, I can see that," he said. "Again, why are you here?"

"I finished with the DO's staff late last night," Max said and paused. A grin spread across his lips. "It isn't that long of a flight from Houston to here and NASA was buying so I caught a flight out this morning. I thought you could use the moral support."

"Thanks," said Rod smiling back. He glanced at the door the senators and staff had disappeared through. It appeared no one was coming to see about the blocked microphone. The sound and recording systems must really be off.

"Now it's my turn," replied Max and sat down on the witness table facing Rod. "Let's go back to my original question: Will we get the funding? Before I left, I learned the director is planning on it and has issued orders to adjust the Mars Probe design accordingly."

Rod nodded before slowly answering. "I think so; we've got everything going our way."

"Oh, really?" Max asked.

"Yes, really! I think the senator from Nevada will vote for the increase because the additional expenditures on the NTS will bring economic aid to her state."

"What about the senator from Connecticut?" Max asked. "He has a reputation for being skeptical of everything that isn't his idea."

Rod shrugged his shoulders. "He might be anxious to have some money spent in his state, but he'll probably vote for the project."

"Why is that?"

"In addition to his ambitions, he has a granddaughter dying of a presently incurable disease." Rod held out his hands. "There are some promising avenues of research for that disease but nothing definitive yet. If our project works her parents can put her in a chamber and wait for the cure."

"I see you've done your homework, oh fearless leader. And the chairman?"

Rod chuckled and sat up to begin assembling his papers. "He wants to be president," he said and stopped shuffling papers long enough to look over at Max. "If you were running for the highest office in the nation, would you like to be thought of as the progressive who pushed for a new age for humanity? Or as the man who stood in the way of humanity reaching beyond the planet?"

Max shrugged. "I'd want to be the progressive, of course, but there may be more opportune times than right now. The federal debt is growing again and there's talk of a possible recession. With all that bad news Congress may not be willing to spend the money."

"So? There's always a debt with the government, and no one seems willing to do anything about it. Our illustrious political leaders just keep spending." He shrugged showing his indifference. "If they're not going to cut back, why shouldn't Senator Montayne be the one to benefit from the positive political fallout when this works instead of someone else at a later date? At least he'll be doing some good with the funding."

Rod dropped his notes into his case, closed it, and locked it. He looked at Max again and nodded at the committee platform. "Those three senators we've discussed comprise the majority of the committee," Rod said. "With their backing we should get the funding."

He stood and took the case handle. "Let's get out of here," he said. "I want to get something to eat before we fly out for Vandenberg."

Two days after the hearing Rod was walking down a hallway of Vandenberg's research building. His shoes clicked on the polished white tile as he greeted the few people who were coming from the other way. Pictures showing launches of various rockets in NASA's history hung on the light blue walls in between the grey doors of this particular hallway.

He came to an intersection and turned left. There were only two doors in this hallway, one on the left and the other on the right. Rod walked up to the door on the left which had a placard that read "CSC Lab" and swiped his security card to open the door. A test subject had been in the suspension chamber for a year and was due for re-animation shortly. Since there were several objectives for this test, he wanted to be present for the opening.

The scientist went through the small room to enter his office where he put his briefcase on the desk. Yesterday and a good part of today had been spent at that desk working to get the backlog of paperwork caught up.

He shook his head in disgust. The mind set of bureaucrats seemed encased in stone. Some of those reports had to be delivered in person and on paper. They couldn't be emailed.

Rod glanced at his watch. It was almost time. He took off his jacket and hung it on a coat rack standing next to the door. He retrieved his lab coat from another peg on the rack and slipped it on as he went through a side door into the chamber room.

This room was a little larger than the lobby and had no decorations at all. Rather, it had the appearance of a hospital operating room. In the center of the room stood the results of this program: a suspension chamber. The device was seven feet long, four feet wide, and five feet tall. It had a transparent, rounded covering that was frosted by the super-cooled cryogenic gasses contained inside. Off to one side stood the control console connected to the chamber by wires. On the other side of the chamber sat a semicircle of reservoirs containing drugs and gasses for the test. Three people dressed in lab coats were already in place at the console.

Rod walked over and Max moved aside to give the project leader a view of what was happening. "Good timing," Max whispered, "as always. It's due to end in about five minutes."

"I know," replied Rod. "I set the schedule remember. I would have been here earlier but Captain Timberlain wanted to talk about the project exceeding our power allotment for the month."

"Morning Dr. Carue." Emma Rathdrum, a pretty, blue eyed, blonde in her early twenties had just noticed the new arrival. She turned from the chambers' console to smile at him. "How was your vacation?" she asked.

Carter Banner, who had been monitoring the gauges and readouts with Emma started at her voice and looked up from the console. "I'm sorry, Doc," he said. "I didn't see you come in. Did we get the increase?"

Carter was a little taller than Emma and a couple of years older. Because of that, she teased him about being ancient and decrepit. He had auburn hair and brown eyes with a physique more suitable for a wrestler than a lab technician.

Rod smiled as he replied to Carter's question. "My sources in NASA unofficially tell me we'll get the funding. The only hang-up may come from senators and representatives trying to game the system so our equipment will be manufactured in their states or districts. But we're waiting for the official notice."

A tone sounded from the console and a digital display began a two-minute countdown. Everyone quieted to watch the gauges and displays showing the cryogenic suspension chamber's status. Carter started to reach for the controls but pulled back as he remembered all the objectives of the test. Rod stepped closer to the console to watch but was careful not to get in the way or touch anything.

"Chamber temperature is increasing. Gas draw-off commencing," Emma announced and directed Rod's attention to the appropriate gauge with a nod. No one touched the controls because this test was as much about the programming for the chamber as about the results of long-term sleep.

By this time, the mixture of cryogenic fluids inside the chamber was being warmed from an icy liquid to a gaseous state, which was vacuumed from the chamber. The gases flowed through a conduit to a tank to be stored for future examination. As the suspension mixture was being drawn out of the chamber it was replaced with an atmosphere slightly higher in oxygen content than normal. This process continued until sensors inside the chamber indicated all the suspension material had been replaced.

At the forty-minute mark, Carter called, "Draw-off complete, oxygen levels in the chamber are within parameters, reanimation is beginning."

Another section of the console became the center of the quartet's attention. Electrodes placed over various portions of the patient's body sent a low-voltage electrical current into the body to stimulate the brain, as well as muscles, nerves, and tissues. The proper amount of adrenaline was injected intravenously into the subject's bloodstream as the body temperature crept toward normal. Rod could see most of the vital life signs were improving.

"Heart rate increasing, brain activity up," informed Carter.

"Let's not get too excited," warned Emma. "We're not done yet. There's no respiration to speak of."

Rod looked away from the console to the chamber. Its covering of frost had cleared so he could see through its transparent cover to the occupant still asleep on the pad.

"All other systems and life signs are coming to normal," said Emma a moment later. She looked over at Rod again. This time she had a worried look on her face. "There's still no respiration. Are we going to lose him?"

"Wait!" Carter exclaimed, pointing at a particular a display. "There's a slight flutter on the respirator." Everyone turned to watch the display the tech had indicated as Carter continued his narrative. "It's getting stronger . . . stronger . . . , breathing is coming to normal."

"The drug to wake him is being injected now," said Emma. "He'll be up and moving in another twenty minutes."

Everyone gave a sigh of relief. Max gave Rod a slap on the back. "We did it!" he said. "Again!"

Rod rotated and stretched the shoulder Max had just slapped. He gave his friend a fake angry look then turned to the two techs. "While it appears that this test worked in reanimating the subject without assistance, we'll need to check the timing in the programming," Rod said. "We can't have the respiration starting late again." Carter nodded and began making an entry on the console keyboard.

The project leader turned from the console to gesture at the chamber. "Let's get Porky out of there and have the vet examine him. The usual routine. When that's done, send him back to his cage for the usual 48 hours of monitoring. If everything checks out, give Porky the Pig a medal for not giving his all for the cause and return him to the zoo."

"I was almost hoping he wouldn't make it," remarked Carter, and he affected a disappointed face as he turned away from the console. "I haven't had a good set of barbeque ribs since I left Texas." Rod gave him a sideways look and the tech held up his hands in surrender. "Hey, it's true. People here in California can't do ribs." Then he waved a hand at the console.

"All data has been transferred to the main computer for review," the tech said. "The reports will be completed in a couple of hours. They should give us a track on why the respiration came late."

Rod nodded. "That's good," he commented. "I need to know if it was a software or hardware issue that caused the respiration to lag behind the other systems." Rod looked at Carter and Emma. "We've got to guarantee this process is one-hundred-percent foolproof. That could mean long hours before this is solved." The two techs groaned in anticipation of the work ahead of them.

"Don't look so down. NASA is treating us to a celebration." Everyone turned to Max in surprise as he looked up from his phone. "I just received a text from Houston," he announced. "I'm sure you've got a similar message on your phone, Rod. There's a follow-up message from General Brandon."

Rod reached into his pocket to pull out his phone while Max continued to speak to Carter and Emma. "Congress has funded Phase Two completely, no hold backs. Work begins immediately. Dr. Carue is to go to the admin center to meet with the general and his staff."

Rod looked up from his phone, where he'd read the same message. "This can't be right," he said. "It's only been a couple of days. Congress doesn't work this fast!"

Max gave a shrug and held up his phone. "All I know is what it says here. And it says for you to get your illustrious backside to the admin center."

That news coupled with another mostly successful test put everyone in a party mood. Rod, evading his jubilant helpers as best he could, returned to his office with only minor injuries.

As they watched Rod leave Emma turned to Max and asked, "Where do we sign up for Moonwalking 101?"

Two hours later Rod returned to the suspension room, where his staff was hard at work. Carter was reading the statistics from the master console, and Max was using the close-out checklist to make sure everything was closed out properly. At the appropriate time Emma would flip switches. The chamber itself had been cleaned and sterilized for the next test.

"How are we doing?" the project leader asked as he walked over to the console.

The trio turned toward Rod. "We're just about done here," reported Max. "Porky's resting fine. The vet gave him a complete exam and found nothing wrong. There was no sign of frostbite. From the way that pig's moving around you'd never guess he was colder than a slab of bacon in the freezer for a year." He gestured back at the console. "The statistics on the test have been compiled and are ready for review."

"That's good," said Rod as he rolled a chair over and collapsed into it. "Go ahead and finish. I learned some very interesting things from the general, so when you're done, I'll give you a run down."

He watched as his people turned back to the console to complete the shut-down process. Five minutes later all three turned to Rod. "Well?" Max asked. "We're finished. What's your news?"

Rod uncrossed his legs and leaned forward. "If you recall, while I was at the hearing Max was called to Houston. There he learned that the DO had already begun changing the design for the ship taking colonists to Mars."

"You have an amazing talent for stating the obvious," said Emma drily.

"Yeah, we kind of noticed he was gone," added Carter.

Rod ignored the sarcastic comments and moved on. "Well, the DO's done more than that. At the same time, he was changing the ship's design he also commissioned NASA's engineers to begin making the necessary adjustments to Copernicus. He assumed we'd get the appropriation and acted." By this time, his team had pulled up chairs of their own and sat in a rough circle.

"They acted?" questioned Carter. "Before approval? That was risky." Everyone nodded their agreement.

"Yep!" said Rod. "NASA must have some very good contacts in Congress to learn what was going on, or they've got some very influential friends who put in a good word."

"Or maybe the reason is that our project is so good they couldn't turn it down," said Max. "Or you're more persuasive than you give yourself credit for."

"There's that," said Rod with a self-conscious smile. "Whatever the explanation our request not only passed the committee but went through Congress in a day. The bill was introduced in both houses simultaneously and passed without debate. There were no riders or earmarks attached. The president signed it the moment it hit his desk. The speed this happened at is unheard of for DC, but it happened."

He shook his head. "Anyway, NASA has already worked out timetables for equipment shipment and placement on the moon. The first loads for our construction go up in one month." He smiled apologetically. "That's the soonest they could find some open space. There'll be some equipment on each shuttle after that. Our equipment will go to the transfer station and catch the ferry to the moon's main base. It'll go overland from there to Copernicus."

"What about the Nevada base?" asked Max.

"That's another piece of good news," replied Rod. "The architects have already finished the plans for the facility. The construction people at the NTS are accumulating the necessary supplies and will start work within the next two months."

"Two months? The plans are complete? How?" Everyone was looking confused, but Carter had voiced their question.

"Remember those rough sketches we drew up when we were starting to talk about Phase Two?" asked Rod. "That was just over a year ago?" Everyone nodded and he went on. "They were included in the notes of our discussions with NASA's engineers. Using the Freedom of Information Act some professor at Stanford got a copy of those preliminaries from NASA." Carter gave a big smile at the mention of his alma mater. He turned a knowing look on Emma.

"So?" wondered Max.

"He was a professor in design or architecture or something like that."

"And he had his students work on our designs!" exclaimed Emma, almost bouncing in her seat with excitement. "I remember doing things like that when I was at MIT." She gave a slight chuckle. "We always thought they were just some projects the professor came up with to give us a challenge."

The project leader nodded to Emma. "Well, this one wasn't something a professor dreamed up," he said. "It was real. NASA examined the results and picked one. They had their engineers and architects work it over and finalize it. I got to see an artist's rendition of the plans they've got. It's impressive."

"So, when is Nevada estimated to be completed?" asked Carter.

"Inside a year," replied Rod then looked around the room at his people. "Eighteen months, at the latest. It appears to me that we have a lot of work to do with two bases to set up." He paused. "That reminds me."

"More good news?" interrupted Max. "I'm not sure I can handle too much of a good thing."

"I guess the DO is trying to reward us for getting the project this far, this fast," countered Rod. "Several potential sites for the colony on Mars have been selected. Ships full of equipment and supplies are going to be prepositioned in Mars orbit. Once the manned vessel arrives at the red planet, equipment can be landed at the appropriate site and the colony constructed.

"The design of the Mars Probe will include accommodations for our cryogenic suspension chambers. While we're on the moon parts for chambers will be constructed here on Earth. Those parts will be shipped up for us to assemble and confirm the chambers' readiness; then we'll oversee their installation in the ship."

"Yeah, since they're going to all the trouble and expense of getting us up there, they might as well put us to work," complained Carter.

Rod gave the technician a pained look but continued his report. "That means the ship will be constructed in lunar orbit rather than over Earth. We'll get to see it being made."

"Well, for one, I'm glad I'm not going to Mars," commented Carter. "I grew up in Texas, where there are plenty of wide-open spaces." He shook his head and gave a slight shudder. "I couldn't live in domes, corridors, and rooms all the time without seeing trees, grass, and bushes. It'd drive me nuts."

Emma spoke up. "That wouldn't be a long drive." The other tech glared at her. "I don't think you'd be missing the 'wide open spaces' for long, Carter," she added. "MIT has developed a way to generate oxygen from the raw materials Mars has on its surface. NASA has had intentions of terraforming the red planet for some time, and MIT was helping with some of the preparations," she boasted. "The problem they haven't been able to solve yet is how to prevent the erosion of atmosphere due to the solar winds. Mars doesn't have a shielding magnetic field like Earth."

"Not to mention the lower gravity," grunted Carter, "but I bet Edison, Einstein, and Fowlke were at MIT helping out with that little problem."

"Now that you mention it. . . ."

"Lay off you two, we've got deadlines to meet," said Rod, interrupting the friendly byplay. He knew this good-natured ribbing could go on for some time if he didn't stop it before it built up momentum. "Go out and celebrate tonight, because we're going to be very busy people from now on."

"As if we haven't been busy before," retorted Emma. "We work for a slave driver, remember?"

"Go on, get out of here. I'll lock up."

Rod collected his things, turned off the lights in the lab and left. He let the door slide shut and lock behind him.

It took only minutes of walking through the corridors of the building for him to reach the main exit. Rod went past the security station, and the guard sitting in the booth looked up. "Goodnight, Dr. Carue," the man said.

"Goodnight, Ichman," Rod replied and continued through the door into the enclosed passage leading to the first level of the parking terrace.

Rod entered the parking terrace and looked up in surprise. The lights were on. Then he saw the sparsely populated parking structure. It couldn't be that late, could it? He glanced at his watch and started shaking his head. 2000! No wonder most of the vehicles were gone.

A shiver went through the scientist. Now that he was out of the building, he could feel the chill in the air. It was late September, and a cold front had brought unseasonably cold weather into California. Using one hand, he pulled his jacket closed against the breeze blowing through the structure.

Cutting across the empty parking stalls, he hurried over to his pearl white hydrogen fuel cell SUV. Rod placed his right thumb on the locking tab of the driver's door. In nanoseconds onboard computers verified his print against that stored in the vehicles memory. The driver's door opened and the motor came to life. Reaching across the driver's seat, he set his case on the passenger seat and settled in behind the controls. The door swung shut and sealed.

Rod turned his attention to the car's instruments, confirming that all systems were ready. Satisfied, he put the auto-drive on standby and manually maneuvered to the exit, cutting through the empty parking lanes. Once out of the structure, he steered through the streets of the base.

As he approached the main guard station Rod saw a vehicle was already at the gate ahead of him, and he stopped a few feet behind to wait his turn. A moment later the sergeant on duty waved his approval, the barrier rose, and the vehicle moved forward to leave the base. Rod pulled ahead to stop when a red light came on and the barrier dropped in front of his car. He lifted his security badge on its lanyard to the driver's window, where the lights at the gate could catch it. The sergeant walked over, glanced at the badge, then looked in the back seat and cargo area of the SUV. After confirming the scientist wasn't attempting to smuggle secrets or equipment off the base, the guard nodded to his companion, who was still in the booth. The light turned green, and a second later the barrier blocking Rod's vehicle lifted. Rod was waved through.

The scientist nodded his thanks as he passed under the barrier, which dropped back into place behind his car. He maneuvered through the series of barricades designed to discourage car bombers.

Ten minutes after leaving the base he was at the highway intersection waiting for a chance to get onto the road. He pushed the button to activate the auto-drive computer, which would take him home.

Taking his hands off the steering wheel, he watched the displays as the computer cycled through its self-checking routine. Seconds later the system indicated it had control of the vehicle. Then the traffic light gave a green arrow for a right turn, as if it had been waiting for the human inside the vehicle to wise up and let a computer drive. The SUV started forward and made the right turn, increasing speed on a pre-determined course toward home.

Satisfied, Rod reclined his seat and closed his eyes.

The car pulled into the driveway of his house just over an hour later and Rod opened his eyes. The garage door rolled up, and the car pulled into the open space. A light in the center of the garage ceiling came on against the night. Rod looked to make sure the garage door was shut behind his car. Turning back to the control panel, he keyed in the code to send the vehicle into standby mode. A moment later the driver's door opened.

After putting the evening meals dishes into the dishwasher, Rod headed for the living room to catch the news.

The lights came on, and his attention was drawn to the room's large wall screen. Displayed there was the header for the evening newspaper. He'd been so busy there hadn't been a chance to check the news for the last two days. "I wonder what's been happening in the world," he muttered and picked up the remote, then sat in his well-worn leather chair facing the screen. He went through the menu prompts to call up the Tribune Sun.

The front page of the paper came up immediately, displaying pictures and their related articles. He looked through the various options. There was the usual sensational news on vid stars and athletes, an article covering a political scandal, and one about a dog saving a child from a rattlesnake. Rod skipped those.

The first article that caught his attention was the announcement from the Russian Federation. Rather than accusing the Western nations of some plot to destroy the planet President Anatoly Berezin stated his nation's latest orbital research station was operational. It was the latest development in the fight against global climate change.

Rod's lips twitched. Even with the majority of the world's vehicles and power plants no longer using fossil fuels and the atmospheric carbon dioxide levels being reduced, global climate change was still a cause. Of course, if the Greenies could find a way to force volcanoes to curtail their carbon footprint that'd be a step in the right direction.

Next, he homed in on an article of events in South Africa he'd bypassed the first time. "Umph," he grunted. "It seems that fighting between tribes is still newsworthy even for that continent."

The article pointed out that one tribe in South Africa had gained power in that country's parliament and had consolidated its position over the past several years. Now in solid control of the government the tribe began to pass and enforce laws designed to emasculate rival tribes while enriching itself and rewarding allies. Riots by tribesmen protesting the loss of their rights and wealth had left portions of several tribal townships burned, with over a hundred people dead.

Civil rights and NAACP activists in the United States were quoted in statements deploring the South African government's actions and the resulting violence.

An enterprising journalist in a related story reflected that during the mid-to-late twentieth century economic sanctions had been tried by the Western countries to force the white South African minority to turn governmental power over to the Black majority. The sanctions were largely ineffective for years because the U. S. government had banned minor products and services, which left South Africa's main economic base in diamonds and exotic metals untouched.

Rod sighed. History repeating itself, he thought, shaking his head. Couldn't people ever learn from past mistakes? He checked the time in the bottom right-hand side of the screen. Taking the remote control, he shut off the paper and headed for bed.

The next morning Max, Carter, Emma, and Rod met in the main office of his suite. Rod took his staff through an examination of the results of yesterday's test so they could understand what he wanted done. They also needed to know what to expect in the near future.

"Now," said Rod, "once we're on the moon and our equipment's been checked, we'll repeat all experiments performed to date."

"What?" asked Carter. The rest of the small group looked astonished. "We're going all the way to the moon just to redo all the tests we've already done?"

"That's right," the scientist replied with a decisive nod. "We're going to see if the baseline mixture of cryogenic gasses and drugs we've developed for normal gravity will work the same way in low-gravity conditions. When that's confirmed or we've adjusted the mixtures for low gravity, we can evaluate the apparatus and process on a human."

"Uh, okay," Max replied with a nod, "I can see that, but somewhere in all this we need to train some new technicians for the Nevada base. We'll be on the moon during the human trials, and they'll be the ones running the control tests down here."

"Right," nodded Rod. "And that's another reason to rerun the tests. The Nevada techs will have to come to the moon with us and help with the tests. That'll give them valuable experience for when they operate the control portion of the experiment." He shrugged. "Of course, when we're ready for the human trials satellite relays will allow us to monitor the activity that goes on at the Nevada base."

"Does that mean what I think it means?" asked Emma.

"Darn tooting' it does," razzed Carter in his Texan drawl, "you'd better sign up for that moon-walkin' class you were talkin' about yesterday."

Emma looked over at Dr. Carue, eyebrows raised in question. Rod nodded again and a smile appeared on his face. "We're going to the moon," he confirmed. "All of us. And we're going to take the people who're going to run the control base. When the tests are finished and they're trained, the new people will go to Nevada. While being our control, that site will also function as an insurance policy. They can continue the work in case something should happen to us up there." Rod finished his last words in melodramatic fashion.

"Oh, that's so comforting," replied Emma, shaking her head.

"I thought so," smiled Rod. "Our astronaut training begins as soon as our equipment is ready for delivery. Let's make it as quick as possible."

CHAPTER 2

The white van drove up the tree and shrub-lined faux-cobblestone driveway to stop under the large portico of the hotel. A young man in a red uniform hurried over from his station by the entrance and slid open the van door to let the passengers out.

Doctor Rod Carue was the third person to step out of the vehicle. He moved onto the sidewalk and set his bags down next to him. So, this is Florida. He looked around and pulled on his shirt to stop it from sticking to his body.

He'd grown up in Colorado where the humidity seldom, if ever, went over fifty percent. And that was during a rainstorm. After high school he'd gone to Utah State University, where the humidity was about the same at home. Even spending the last few years at Vandenberg hadn't prepared him for the water saturated air of Cape Canaveral. It was like trying to breathe underwater.

"Doctor Carue?"

The question brought Rod out of his thoughts. He turned to face a Hispanic young man who'd come up next to him. The man was dressed in a light-colored polo shirt and jeans. "Yes?" Rod asked and glanced at the name tag on the left breast of the man's shirt. "What can I do for you, Juan?"

Juan gave a slight smile and an acknowledging bob of his head. "I'm here to direct you to your room," he announced, then gestured at the ground with his right hand. "Are those your bags, Doctor?"

"They are," Rod replied and went to pick up the bags but was too late. Juan had swooped in to grab the luggage, tucking one bag under his right arm, and carrying the other in his right hand. The man started for the hotel's entrance.

Rod reached for his wallet to tip the driver, but Juan called back, "Come on, Doctor Carue, don't dawdle." The young man paused and waved with his left hand to get the doctor moving. Shaking his head, Rod hurried to catch up with his guide and they entered the hotel together.

"No need to check in," Juan called back as Rod moved toward the reception desk. "I've taken care of all the preliminaries to save time. We're going straight to your room."

"What's the hurry?" Rod asked Juan as he rejoined the young man.

"NASA wants you on the moon as soon as possible," Juan replied. "That's why you're in an accelerated course."

"Are my people here?" the scientist asked. "They left for training before I did."

"Not that I know of," Juan replied. "There's more than one location for this training."

"Shouldn't I be with them?" Rod wondered aloud.

Juan stopped at the elevator and pushed the call button. "I can't answer that question, Doctor Carue, because I don't know," he said as he glanced up at the numbers indicating the location of the elevator. "What I do know is that you're here."

A few seconds later the elevator doors opened, and Juan entered, still carrying Rod's bags. The scientist followed. "What's your job here, Juan?" he asked.

The young man gave another grin. "Essentially, I'm your steward," he replied as he set the bags down and pushed the floor button.

Rod noticed their destination was the top floor and cocked his head. "Why do I need a keeper. . .excuse me, a steward?" he asked. "I learned how to take care of myself a long time ago." An instant later he grunted. "Wait!" he said. "Is there something unusual about this training?"

"Yes, Doctor," the steward replied. The elevator doors closed, and the car began to rise. "I told you this is the accelerated course. The normal training cycle to prepare a person for a trip into orbit is eight weeks. You get to do it in six. I've been assigned as your steward to help get you through this accelerated schedule."

The elevator doors opened at the top floor, and Juan led the way out. Rod followed as the steward made a right turn and headed down the hallway. After a short walk, the two men stopped in front of a door. Juan set the scientist's bags on the carpeted floor and produced a key card. A second later a green light showed on the lock pad, and the door clicked open.

Juan handed the card to Rod, then picked up the bags again. "This'll be your home for the next six weeks," the steward stated and moved into the room.

The lights came on as they entered. Juan set the bags on the bed, then looked over at Rod. "You've got the rest of the day off," he announced. "Make sure you enjoy it, because once the training begins you won't have much leisure time until leaving for the moon."

He walked over to stand in the open door, then turned to face Rod again. "You'll want to get a good night's sleep," he said. "I'll be back to pick you up at 0630 tomorrow and take you to medical for your pre-training exam. Don't worry about breakfast because the tests require fasting. Please dress comfortably. I believe your instructions included bringing loose exercise clothing?" Rod nodded, and Juan continued. "Good, wear that clothing. I've taken the liberty to arrange a wake-up call for you for 0530."

With that Juan turned and left, pulling the room's door shut behind him. Rod took a deep breath and moved over to the bed where his bags were. He glanced at the room's clock and snorted. Leisure time, huh? Not very likely.

As promised, the attention buzzer sounded in the room precisely at 0630. Opening the door Rod found Juan smiling back at him.

The steward ran an appraising look over Rod and nodded his approval. Dr. Carue was wearing well-worn running shoes with Utah State Aggies sweatpants and a BYU T-shirt. "Have you had any breakfast?" Juan asked. When Rod shook his head, the steward nodded his approval. "I thought you were a good listener," he said, then gestured down the corridor. "Now, Doctor, if you please. Let's get this done so you can get something to eat."

After a short drive from the hotel the shuttle van stopped at the entrance for the Megan Alif Memorial Clinic. Since he had no idea of where to go, Rod let Juan lead the way out of the vehicle and into the clinic. A few minutes later the two men were ushered into a doctor's examination room by a receptionist.

"Just get comfortable," said Juan from the room's entrance. "I'll be back to collect you when the examination's over." He gave a broad smile showing his white teeth as Rod gave a distracted nod.

Then the scientist realized what Juan had said. "Wait!" said Rod as he settled onto the examination table. "You're not staying?"

"Nope," replied the steward. "I'm going for breakfast." Chuckling at Rod's scowl, Juan left, closing the door behind him.

A short time later, the room's door opened, and a woman dressed in powder-blue scrubs walked in. "I'm Melissa," she announced. "Let's get started, shall we? There's a lot to do, and we don't have a lot of time to do it."

The nurse indicated a chair next to the table and continued her instructions. "Please have a seat, Doctor Carue. I need to draw blood and check your vitals."

Over the next hour the scientist was punctured, poked, prodded, thumped, and listened to. Samples of blood, urine, fecal matter, and tissue were taken. When that was done the nurse escorted him to another room, where he was wired to a treadmill. Melissa said it was for a stress test.

When it began the machine had a nice, even pace that gradually increased in speed. After five minutes Rod was going at a fast walk, which became a trot at eight minutes and then an easy run at eleven. By thirteen minutes he was holding onto the bar in front of him, sprinting and gasping for breath. A minute later the test stopped, and the results were updated to the clinics computer system.

The nurse walked him to yet another room for a full body scan. That meant he had to lie inside a white metal tube for over an hour. Before the attendant slid Rod into the tube, she informed him that he had to remain perfectly still. If he moved the test would have to be restarted. Fortunately, besides being strapped down, he was so exhausted by the prior test and the early morning start with no breakfast that he fell asleep.

At last, Rod was back in the original examination room. While lying on the table he glanced over at the sink, tempted to get a drink but he forced the thought away. There was the possibility that taking a drink could distort whatever test was coming next and he'd have to start the entire battery of tests over. His stomach gave a loud rumble, and he shook his head. How much longer was this going to take?

Even though he'd already had a nap the scientist was starting to get drowsy when the door opened again. He turned his head, expecting to see the nurse. Instead, a man in tan khaki pants and a light-blue button-down shirt walked in and shut the door. He held a tablet. Rod groaned and moved to sit up.

The new arrival grinned as Rod worked to get upright. "It's not as bad as all that, Doctor Carue," he said. "You'll recover quickly enough after you shower, dress, and get some food in you." The grin went to a smile when Rod perked up at the mention of food. "Oh yes, you can eat something now." He shrugged. "Or you will when Juan comes to collect you." The man glanced at his watch, then back to Rod. "That should be in the next five minutes. After you've eaten and recovered, we'll go over your test results." He tapped the pad he held. "Everything should be in by then."

Rod nodded his understanding and waved a hand at the credential wall. "I take it you're Doctor Marcus Chambers?" he asked, and the doctor inclined his head in assent.

Rod shook the hand Marcus offered. "I'm glad to meet you, Doctor Chambers."

"And I you, Doctor Carue."

The door opened again, and both men broke the hand clasp. They turned to see Juan enter the room. "Oh good, you're on time for a change," Chambers said, with a mischievous grin.

Juan chuckled. "Don't say that in front of him, Doctor," he chided. "Doctor Carue might think I'm less than dependable and lose sleep."

"Perish the thought," Marcus replied. "Doctor Carue is ready. Let him shower and dress, then take him to the cafeteria and get some food into him. Have him back here at," he checked his watch once more, "1400."

Rod and Juan both nodded their understanding and Doctor Chambers gestured to the door. "Go on, get out of here!" he said. "There are other, more important people I need to see. Just remember to be back here at 1400 hours."

After Rod had showered and dressed, the two men made their way through the corridors of the building. Rod guessed they were getting close to the lunchroom when he started to pick up delicious aromas. "That's coming from a cafeteria?" he wondered.

"NASA doesn't scrimp on its people here," Juan replied. "Although, I think after all that testing, you're hungry enough that anything would smell good." Rod's stomach growled, spoiling any response he could've made.

As Rod ate, he took the opportunity to watch the other people in the cafeteria. At a nearby table, he saw a group of five men in space force uniforms sipping drinks while having an animated discussion. Others sat alone or were in groups of two or three.

Rod was finishing when he noticed a young woman enter the dining room with a food tray. She was petite, about five foot four with long, glossy black hair and was dressed in the standard NASA jumpsuit. The scientist noted that her complexion was dark, but not quite as dark as Max's. In fact, she reminded him of Max. He shook his head, banishing the thought. That'd be too much of a coincidence to be believable.

By this time Juan noticed that Rod had stopped eating and turned to see what the distraction was. It didn't take him long. The center of Rod's attention was making her way to a table on the other side of the room. And she wasn't alone. It looked like she had a steward of her own.

Turning back to wipe his mouth with a napkin Juan glanced at his watch. He dropped the cloth on the table and cleared his throat to attract Rod's attention. "It's time we headed back," he announced.

Minutes after leaving the cafeteria, Rod and Juan were back in the examination room. Rod sat on the table while Juan took the only available chair. As they waited for the doctor to arrive, Rod began examining the diplomas and awards on display.

Rod looked over at Juan and nodded at the awards and diplomas that covered the wall. "Doctor Chambers is very impressive," he said. "With these credentials and awards, he could be at the most prestigious organizations in the world. In fact, he could be running one of those places."

"I was," sounded a voice from the door. Rod and Juan turned to see Doctor Chambers standing in the open doorway. The two men had been concentrating on the wall and hadn't heard the door open.

"I hope I'm not offending you when I ask this," said Rod, "but why are you here?" He held out his hands to indicate the award wall.

Marcus shrugged as he walked into the room and closed the door behind him. A slight smile creased his lips. It was apparent he'd heard this question before yet he didn't seem impatient or frustrated at hearing it again. "It's more fun here, less stress," he replied. "This job's better for family life and I wanted a family. In those 'prestigious' organizations you mentioned there's intense pressure from ambitious people politicking; everyone pushes for power. Every effort is directed toward the furtherance of their career." He shook his head. "There is no joy in the research, just ambition."

The doctor spread his hands out to indicate the training center. "Here I have time to enjoy my research and family without the politics. All I have to do is make sure the candidates for space will survive the trip up. Besides, I've found the people I meet here are more interesting than in those prestigious clinics.

"Can you understand that, Doctor Carue?" he asked.

Rod nodded. "I think I can," he replied. "My dad had a degree in marketing from Columbia, but he chose to be a rancher. He could've been working at any of the Fortune One Hundred companies, sitting in a corner office of a high-rise and bringing down a salary of high six figures. When I asked him about it, he said the money and position weren't anything if you weren't happy."

"Exactly," Marcus said and tapped his pad, signaling a change of subject. "Now it says here that you want to go to the moon, freeze people into popsicles, let them age for a bit then revive them. Is that right?"

Rod nodded. "That's it in a nutshell," he replied with a grin.

"Interesting," the doctor continued. "I don't know how your experiments will turn out, but I've reviewed the results of this morning's tests and find nothing that'll stop you. You're cleared for space." He held up the pad. "I'll make sure the proper authorizations go into your file. So, we're done here."

From the doctor's office Juan took Rod on a tour of the training campus.

After dinner, the two men went to a small auditorium. Standing on the landing behind the back row of seats, Rod examined the room. Two flights of stairs, separated by seats, led down towards the stage. He guessed there were places for at least fifty people on a slope facing the stage below. Maybe ten seats were already occupied. The two men found places in the middle of the top row furthest away from the stage and settled in to wait. "Why're we here?" Rod asked.

Juan glanced at his watch. "We're a little early," he said. "Relax."

Sitting back in his seat Rod reverted to watching people. He saw them enter the room in twos and fours. Within a few minutes close to half the seats were occupied. Almost right on the hour the scientist saw the woman who'd attracted his attention in the cafeteria appear at the top of the stairs to his right. Her steward accompanied her. He watched the mystery woman confer with her companion and start forward. They walked down the stairs and moved into the seats several rows below where he and Juan were sitting. The two women crossed to the center of the row, then sat down almost in front of Rod.

They had just sat down when the lights over the auditorium's seating began to dim. Rod glanced down at the stage. A man dressed in a dark business suit walked out from the wings at Rod's right. As he made his way to the podium the conversations in the room began to stop.

"Your attention, please," the man said into the podium's microphone. When the room was silent, he nodded and spoke again. "Thank you. My name is Doctor Michael Makitis and I'm in charge of this little resort." His remark was greeted with a soft wave of laughter from the audience. "You've had a chance to tour our campus. That walk and the remainder of this evening will be your last leisure time during the training. During the next six weeks you'll be in classes, studying after those classes, practicing what you learned in those classes, doing more studying, and going through physical conditioning."

Makitis glanced around the auditorium. "You'll be up early and go to bed late. Your stewards will be with you the entire time to make sure you're up and to your classes on time. As our campus is new to you, they'll also make sure you don't get lost.

"One note of caution," Makitis said. "You'll be participating in activities that can be hazardous. To date, we've recorded no accidents, and I don't want anyone here doing something stupid to spoil that record. Any injuries or deaths would be very inconvenient for me." He gave a sorrowful look. "You see, there's a lot of paperwork involved with injuries, deaths and accidents." Makitis glared at the audience. "I hate paperwork. It cuts into my nap time. Nobody gets injured or dead! Is that understood?"

Another round of laughter went through the auditorium. "I'm talking about this for a reason," the director continued. "Going into space is dangerous. It's safer now than it was thirty years ago, but it's still hazardous. Being careless in space will get you or someone with you killed. Get in the habit now of being meticulous in your habits. It'll carry over when it counts.

"Now, I'm going to leave the stage for a few minutes," Michael announced, "so you can watch a short video."

The stage lights came back on with the presentations end and Rod blinked to help his eyes adjust. Doctor Makitis returned to the podium. "As you just saw, NASA has had its share of success and failure," the director said. "The successes came from meticulous planning and teamwork. The failures," he shrugged, "mostly came from someone being careless or taking short cuts. Sometimes it's just bad luck. There's always a chance of failure in our line of work, but I prefer deliberate habits that lead to success."

Makitis looked out at the audience and spoke again. "We have probes exploring the moon systems of Saturn and Jupiter, as well as the outer planets." As he spoke, pictures relating to what he was saying appeared on the screen above. "We're preparing to set up a colony on Mars and to send mining expeditions to the asteroids. There are scientists working on ways to terraform both Mars and Venus."

The pictures stopped on an image of Mars, as seen from space and the lights in the auditorium came up without washing out the image. Michael gestured up at the screen. "That's what you've chosen to be a part of. We're taking humanity to the stars."

He nodded at the audience. "Tomorrow begins early. Get some sleep."

The director left the stage to scattered applause and Rod glanced at his watch. It was 2030 hours. He turned to Juan. "What time do we begin tomorrow?"

"I'm coming to get you for breakfast at 0700."

"You're kidding!" exclaimed Rod. "That's 0400 Pacific Time. I'm exhausted from today's early start."

Juan gave a slight smile and shook his head. "I'm not kidding. You're out of your room at 0700 and won't be back until 2200 hours. It's going to be this way for the whole six weeks. I hope you acclimate quickly to new time zones."

He stood and began walking to the end of the row. Rod followed as Juan continued speaking. "After breakfast tomorrow we'll reconvene here in the auditorium, where you'll be divided into cohorts. Then the work really begins."

Once back in his room, Rod put on his pajamas and laid out his clothes for the morning. It wasn't hard to decide what to wear. The jumpsuits NASA provided all looked alike though they did come in two colors—beige and blue. He picked up his alarm clock and made sure it was set for the proper time. After turning on his reading light and turning off the overhead light, he climbed into bed. He adjusted the pillows to support his back as he sat against the headboard. From the nightstand next to his bed, he picked up his scriptures.

When he'd left for Vandenberg years ago his mother was concerned the ungodly people of California would attempt to change her son. She was deeply religious and had worked to instill that sense in him during his childhood. As he was getting ready to leave for California, she'd presented him with a new set of scriptures, then asked him to be faithful in his scripture reading, church attendance, and prayers. He didn't want her worrying about him, so he'd promised to work to keep his faith.

Ten minutes after opening to the Gospel of Matthew Rod's eyelids began to droop. He rubbed his eyes to banish the sleep and began reading again. Five minutes later his eyes closed, and he jerked awake. Trying again, he rubbed his eyes with the heels of his hands and read for a few minutes more. His eyes closed for the second time, the scriptures slipped onto his lap, his head fell forward, and his breathing slowed.

An hour later Rod woke. He worked his neck for a few minutes to ease the stiffness, then marked his place and set the scriptures on the nightstand. He turned off his light and scooted down under the covers. Sleep came quickly.

When Juan arrived, Rod was ready and waiting. The two men left the room and made their way down to the restaurant for breakfast. Then they hopped into the shuttle, which took them back to the medical building. There they joined several people making their way through the halls. Looking around Rod didn't recognize anyone other than Juan.

At 0750 they reached the auditorium. As before, the two men found seats in the back and sat down to wait. To kill time Rod resumed watching people, starting with the closest rows.

Juan noticed Rod's scrutiny and asked, "Looking for anyone in particular?"

The scientist turned to his steward with a sheepish grin. "There was a woman in the cafeteria yesterday."

"Really? I hadn't noticed," mused Juan sarcastically. "You do remember that Director Makitis said there's not going to be any time for leisure activities? I think the term 'leisure' would include dating." He paused, then asked, "Just as a matter of curiosity, why have you singled her out?"

Rod shrugged his shoulders. "She looked familiar," he said, "like someone I knew but couldn't remember her name."

"Well, you won't be finding out who she is anytime soon," Juan said with a smile, "unless she's in your cohort. There won't be any get-to-know-you parties at night. We're going to keep you so busy you'll be too exhausted at night to socialize."

"It isn't anything romantic," Rod protested. "I'm just trying to figure out why she seems so familiar!"

"I see," replied Juan and gave a little shake of his head. "That's your story, and you're sticking to it."

Before Rod could respond the lights dimmed in the auditorium and the director walked onto the stage. "Welcome back," Makitis said. His voice cut through the muted conversations that were still going on. "I hope you had a good night's sleep." A few positive responses were heard and then a louder "no" rang out. Soft laughter rippled through the audience, and Michael smiled back. "In case you missed it or forgot, my name is Michael Makitis, and I'm the director of this place.

"Last night you saw NASA's advertisement. What you're going to get now is a schedule of the torment we're going to put you through. Then you'll be put into your training cohort." He looked stage left and nodded. Two others, a man; and a woman, joined him.

The woman was well dressed in a dark, pin-stripe suit, with her strawberry-blonde hair done up in a bun at the back of her head. Her white blouse was a stark contrast with the dark material. The man was much more casual, in a dark T-shirt and jeans. His brown hair was long, hanging behind him in a ponytail to his shoulders.

"This is Doctor Karen Dewitt," Michael said, and the woman raised her hand in acknowledgement. "I'm not going to recite her degrees and published works to impress you," the director continued. "That would embarrass her and take more time than we've allotted for this meeting. She's responsible for the classroom portion of your training."

Michael gestured at the man next to Karen. "The scruffy looking one's name is Cash Price." Cash smiled and waved a hand at the audience as the director added, "he's in charge of the hands-on, practical application of your training. His expertise comes from actual experience rather than academics. He'll help you become very familiar with what Doctor Dewitt is teaching you."

Rod recognized the man's name immediately. Price had been an astronaut for almost a decade before retiring and had gone into orbit on several missions to help build the lunar facilities.

The director continued speaking. "Cash and Karen are going to take over from here. I'm going back to my office. . .to do some paperwork," he finished with a grimace. After nodding at the two, he walked off the stage.

Cash gestured for Karen to take the lead and found a seat in the front row. The doctor moved forward to the podium as the screen lowered from the ceiling behind her. The lights over the audience dimmed further, and an outline was projected onto the screen.

"These are the topics you'll be taking," Karen said without preamble. "I think they're self-explanatory, so I'm not going to waste your time or mine by talking about them. Besides, you'll hear more about them in your classes. In the first few weeks, each day will be broken into two parts. During the morning you'll have classroom instruction. The afternoon will be the application portion of what you were taught. That'll change as we get past the halfway mark. Then you'll have more time with the practical applications."

She paused and looked over at the audience. "Do not take these classes lightly or treat them like you did classes at the university. There are no unnecessary subjects being taught. What you miss could kill you.

"Your steward will provide you with each day's schedule the evening prior." The outline disappeared as the auditorium lights came on. The screen rose into its ceiling recess.

Karen placed her tablet on the podium, then glanced up at the audience. "You'll go through this training in groups of six. That is your cohort. When I call your name please go to the exit on my right, your left." She indicated the exit she meant. "A staff member will greet you in the corridor outside this room. You'll meet your cohort and be provided with your schedule for the day. From there you'll go to your first class.

"Let's not waste any more time," she said and began to read off names in groups of six. As instructed, those people stood with their stewards and walked to the exit on Rod's left. Karen paused long enough for the people named to leave the auditorium before reading the next six names.

Rod was in the fourth and last group. When Karen gave the twelve remaining people a nod everyone stood and left the room. Rod met his cadre outside the auditorium. Brief. Introductions were made before they were led off to their first class.

The six weeks of instruction began with classes on the environment suit; where to find its components, how to run diagnostics, how to fix its components if something malfunctioned, how to get into and out of their suit, and so on. There were sessions on the various vehicles, rockets, and habitats. They were instructed on how to walk in low gravity, how to eat in low gravity, and how to exercise in low gravity.

In the afternoon came the practical experience of what had been taught that morning throughout the training. Rod couldn't remember how many times he had to climb into an environment suit and then get out. Cash and the other instructors had him and those in his cohort diagnose and repair components of the suit until they could do it blindfolded while in a pitch-black room. If the repairs could've been done one-handed the instructors would've had them practicing that as well.

As the weeks progressed Rod continued to hope for a chance to meet more of his fellow students besides those of his cohort. There was one person he wanted to spend some time with, but there was no opportunity.

As promised, he was out of his room at 0700 each morning and returned at 2200. And the time from 2200 until 0700 was filled with exhausted sleep, more study, or trying to keep up on the progress of the Nevada and Copernicus bases.

Everyone was given Sundays off to attend religious services or to do whatever they desired if they remained on campus. A few attended the nondenominational service that was offered but most of the trainees elected to stay in their rooms to catch up on their sleep. Rod chose to attend the religious meeting. He'd promised his mother, after all.

Three weeks passed before Rod was able to learn the name of the woman who'd attracted his attention. It was Tali Jorgensen. She'd attended one religious meeting and had been introduced to the group. When he heard the name Rod gave a little jerk. She did look familiar and had the same last name as Max. Could it be possible she was related to his colleague? After the meeting he made his way around the room looking for Tali, but she'd already disappeared.

From that point on the pace of their training picked up. There were fewer classes directed by Karen Dewitt and her staff. The classes concentrated on the effects low gravity had on a person's muscles, organs, and bones and how to counteract it. Then Rod's cohort went to the rooms where they continued to practice everything they'd been taught. Cash and his people were relentless. Everything had to be repeated until it became second nature.

After a particularly strenuous day Rod and Juan reached the hotel and were making small talk as they climbed out of the shuttle van. When they passed through the hotel doors Rod scanned the lobby. As usual there were very few people moving around because of the lateness of the hour. It was almost 2300 hours. Both men stopped at the elevator and Rod pushed the call button.

While waiting for the elevator to arrive the scientist glanced over at his companion. "Why was this day different?" he asked the steward.

Juan gave him a puzzled look. "What do you mean?" he replied.

"This day," said Rod and gave a little wave of his hand. He glanced up to see the elevator coming down. "I mean, look at what they had us doing. There were no instructional classes, just PT. Cash and his people had us run five miles—twice! We were going through the exercises to maintain our muscle and bone structure all morning."

He shook his head and snorted. "They even stuck us in the centrifuge." The scientist turned to face Juan and flung out his arms. "The centrifuge, for heck's sake!"

"For 'heck's sake'?" repeated Juan with a laugh. "I haven't heard that word in . . . forever." A chime sounded, and the elevator doors opened. Still chuckling, Juan led the way into the car and pushed the floor button.

"It's my mother," Rod said. He stood next to his friend and watched the doors close. "She doesn't like swearing.

"In the second grade Jimmie Layton pushed me off my chair and laughed. When he didn't get in trouble for hurting me, I got mad. I knew I couldn't hit him like he deserved so I called him some words I'd heard. My teacher, Miss Burton, hadn't seen what Jimmie had done but overheard what I'd said and sent me to the counselors office. He shuddered. "The counselor called my mom. When I got home, she washed my mouth out with soap and sent me to bed without supper."

Juan, who'd stopped laughing, started up again. "When did you grow up?" he asked, "before World War I? That sounds positively archaic."

"Let's not get sidetracked," replied Rod shaking his head. "I was talking about the centrifuge, remember? After getting out of the darn thing I couldn't walk straight for an hour. I thought that contraption was obsolete." He felt the elevator stop and glanced up at the floor indicator. They'd reached his floor. The doors opened.

Juan stopped laughing and left the elevator. "The centrifuge is old," he agreed as he walked down the hallway, "but it's still useful." He gave a shrug of his shoulders. "Besides, it's sort of a tradition. We always have future astronauts endure it as a rite of passage at the end of their training."

Rod stopped at the door to his room and looked at Juan. "What do I have to look forward to? You haven't given me tomorrow's schedule yet," he said. "It isn't Sunday, is it?"

To answer, Juan took an envelope out of his shirt pocket and handed it to the scientist.

Turning his attention to the envelope, Rod opened the flap and removed the papers he found inside. Unfolding the first page, he read the contents, then turned a stunned look at the steward. "They're flight arrangements for tomorrow morning. It says I'm flying back to Vandenberg."

Then comprehension dawned. "Wait! You said people went into the centrifuge at the end of their training. That means I graduated? I'm an astronaut?"

Juan held out a hand, and Rod took it. "Calm down," the steward said as he shook the scientist's hand. "You've graduated and are on your way to the moon. Your arrangements to reach the moon are on the second page. But you're not officially an astronaut until you get into orbit."

The handshake stopped, and Rod shuffled pages so he could look at the second page. "The moon," he said, then glanced back at Juan with a mischievous look on his face. "What?" he asked, "no graduation ceremony? No diploma or certificate of completion?'"

Juan shook his head. "Nope, no ceremony," he replied with a smile. "We couldn't fit it into the accelerated course." He shrugged his shoulders.

"There just wasn't time. A certificate of completion for this course will be placed in your personnel file. Besides, you won't need a certificate to hang on a wall where you're going."

He reached out and keyed Rod's door open. "Get a good night's sleep," he said. "Keep in mind your flight arrangements to Vandenberg. Once back at the base, you'll be taken straight to the shuttle. "

Juan motioned for the scientist to go into his room. "You don't want to miss your flight. If you do, you'll also miss the orbital shuttle. And the next shuttle up won't be for another two or three weeks." With that, he turned and walked down the hall toward the elevator.

Rod watched the man who'd become his friend over the past six weeks leave, then looked at the second sheet of paper.

CHAPTER 3

Rod faced the trip back to Vandenberg with mixed emotions. He was glad to have the rigorous astronaut training over and excited to get into space. But he was also disappointed. Or sad to be separated from the group he'd trained with. He couldn't decide which.

While sitting on his bed waiting for the time to pass, he reached into the left breast pocket of his jumpsuit and pulled out the travel orders Juan had given him last night. A big grin crossed his lips as he read the words again. They said he was going to the moon. The scientist refolded the papers and put them back into his pocket.

The chiming from his watch alarm announced it was time to leave. He shut off the noise, then looked around the small room one last time to make sure he wasn't forgetting anything. But there wasn't much chance of that.

Picking up his bags Rod left the room. He walked down the hallway and turned for the elevator, where he pushed the call button. Moments later the doors opened. He stepped inside and selected the button for the lobby.

To his surprise the elevator stopped on the third floor and the doors opened to reveal Tali Jorgensen. "I didn't know you were in this hotel during the training," Rod said. "You're flying out today?"

"Yep," Tali replied.

Then it hit Rod. "Wait! You've had your room here the whole time?" Tali nodded her head. "How'd we not meet until now?" he asked.

She shrugged. "I usually take the stairs for exercise," Tali replied. "That could explain it. But since I'm going into orbit today, I thought I'd celebrate by taking the elevator."

The two people arrived at the hotel lobby, where Tali excused herself. She wanted to get some reading material and snacks from the gift shop for the flight.

Rod watched her disappear, then walked over to the attendant at the concierge counter. "I'm Dr. Rod Carue," he announced. "I'm scheduled to catch a plane for Vandenberg. Could you tell me where the pickup will be?"

The young man behind the counter looked up, smiled, and began working on a computer terminal. "Carue, that's spelled C-A-R-U-E?" he asked. Rod nodded.

"Good! Your flight for Vandenberg leaves at 0930 hours. That's forty-five minutes from now. The shuttle will be here shortly to get you to your plane." The man indicated the portico in front of the hotel. "You'll board at the front entrance. We'll give an announcement when the shuttle arrives."

"Thanks," Rod said, then turned and headed for the lounge. After a few steps he stopped to look over at the gift shop. Perhaps snacks for the flight weren't such a bad idea.

He walked into the small store to see a few people walking around examining the contents on the shelves. Ignoring the racks of tourist keepsakes Rod went over to the shelf that held snacks. After spending some time browsing, he selected a couple of chocolate bars. This wasn't the most nutritious meal ever purchased, but he guessed those bars would keep a horde of hungries from attacking during the flight.

Rod was at the gift shop register when he heard an announcement coming over the PA system that the airport shuttle had arrived. He finished paying the clerk, grabbed his bags, and hurried for the hotel entrance. The attendant at the concierge station saw the scientist leaving the gift shop and pointed out the vehicle to him. Rod waved his thanks, stuffed the candy bars into the bag with his books, and left the hotel to climb into the shuttle.

"We meet again, Dr. Carue," came a voice as he climbed the steps into the bus.

He saw her in her window seat. "Tali! You're going to Vandenberg?"

"Well, the bus company doesn't have a route to my assignment," teased the engineer. "I did come to get trained to work in weightless conditions, after all, and Vandenberg's got the shuttles to get me there."

When it rains it pours, thought Rod with a slight shake of his head and took the seat facing Tali. Earlier he'd been commiserating over the lack of opportunities to visit with Tali, and now it seemed he'd get a captive audience. For a couple of hours, at least.

The shuttle driver was just getting behind the control panel of the van when the concierge attendant hurried out of the hotel with a white-haired man in tow. Rod didn't know or recognize the man, but it was apparent Tali did. She slid to the far side of her seat and patted the space next to her. The man smiled at the invitation, then scooted onto the seat.

"Brian!" Tali exclaimed. "I didn't know you were here." Then she paused and cocked her head to one side as she considered. "But why? You've been in space before and don't need training."

"I was called in to help with the reactors at Camp Wanna-Get-Into-Space," Brian replied and gave a shrug. "You'd think they'd have someone here to handle their own problems." The van's engine started. "Anyway, that's done now, so I'm heading back."

Rod's lips twitched as he suppressed a smile at the man's name for one of NASA's training facilities. A slight jolt marked the vehicle leaving the hotel. From that point the conversation between Brian and Tali consisted of fusion reactors and the complexities involved.

The scientist gave a resigned sigh, knowing he was outclassed. He leaned back in his seat and closed his eyes.

At the airport, the shuttle drove right up to a Boeing ExecAir jet and stopped. The aircraft's engines were already turning over in anticipation of the flight. A stair ramp had been rolled up to the aircraft, and the rear door was open ready to receive passengers.

Rod, Tali, and Brian Hickson (Rod had finally been introduced to the older man) left the van, climbed the stairs, entered the craft, and selected seats. They placed their bags in the overhead compartments then sat down and buckled their seat belts.

The attendant for the aircraft activated the rear door. It closed and sealed, and she moved forward to check on her passengers. While she was confirming the overhead compartments were secure, a recording came over the intercom to begin the standard passenger orientation. The jet engines were powered up, and the aircraft taxied towards the runway.

Following the instructions coming over the loudspeakers Rod double-checked to make sure his seat belt was buckled, the tray secured, and his seat upright. Looking across the aisle Rod saw that although Hickson and Tali had done likewise, they were still going on about their specialty. He was sure the ills of the world would be solved by the time the aircraft reached Vandenberg.

By the time the ExecAir reached Vandenberg, Rod had taken a nap, eaten his two candy bars, and completed some of his backlogged paperwork. He glanced across the aisle to see Brian and Tali still going strong.

He shook his head. How could there be that much to talk about with fusion reactors?

Rod felt the jet bank as it began to lose altitude and line up for the runway. He looked out his window to see a shuttle. The spacecraft was resting on its launching pad with its nose pointing at the sky. Its shape had the same delta swept-back wings and aerodynamic lines as earlier classes of space shuttles. Gantries and power lines connected the craft to the launch tower as it waited for passengers and crew. It was a beautiful picture of his path to the stars.

The shuttle disappeared from view as the jet finished its turn to align with the runway and begin its final approach.

"After I open the door go down the steps," the attendant told the three people who were lined up behind her. She was speaking loudly enough to be heard over the engines, which were kept at low power. "Follow the yellow line to the terminal," she said. "Once inside, you'll be met and taken to the orbital shuttle." With her instructions given, the attendant activated the door. It swung open, and the noise level increased.

"Thanks," said Rod as he moved into the open doorway.

"And pass our thanks to the captain, as well," added Hickson. "It was an enjoyable flight."

The attendant smiled and bobbed her head. "I'll do that," she said.

With his bags in hand, Rod led the way down the stairs and across the tarmac toward the terminal. Hickson and Tali trailed along.

The trio moved through the automatic door into the terminal, where they were met by a young man in white coveralls. A security badge hung from one lapel, showing his name, picture, and security clearance. Rod noted that the man's name was Henri Greene. Patches and insignia sewn onto his sleeves and chest pockets indicated that he was a member of the shuttle support team.

"Dr. Carue, Ms. Jorgensen, and. . .," the man paused as he glanced at the clipboard he held, "Mr. Hickson. If you will follow me, the launch preparations will reach the final stage shortly. We need to get you aboard the shuttle and strapped in as soon as possible."

Without waiting for a response, their guide turned and headed down the main corridor of the terminal. Rod looked over at Tali and Hickson. Hickson gave a slight smile and a little shrug as everyone started after the young man.

Henri led them through the terminal and into a huge garage. He stopped beside a white van and indicated the open door. "This's your ride to the shuttle," their guide said. "Watch your step, please."

"When is lift off?" asked Tali as she stepped up into the van and sat down. Rod and Hickson quickly followed suit.

Greene climbed in and sat down as the doors slid shut. "The shuttle lifts in one hour," he said as the van began moving.

"That doesn't give us much time to get into our suits," Rod commented.

Greene gave a little smile. "Suits are no longer required in the latest generation of shuttles, Dr. Carue," he said. "The area you'll be riding in is a passenger module protected by three separate hulls. Each hull is made of a special alloy proven impervious to projectiles up to and including armor piercing missiles." The attendant shrugged. "Excluding those of nuclear nature, of course. But we aren't expecting any of those. These modules are designed to withstand a strike from a micro-meteor or space junk."

While the van moved out of the garage and made a right turn Henri continued his instructions. "For your safety, please observe the following restrictions. One: All bags must be placed in their storage compartments prior to lift-off. They will remain there for the duration of the flight. Two: All seat harnesses must remain fastened unless the captain informs you otherwise. Each harness is electronically connected to instrumentation in the cockpit and will inform the crew when it is unbuckled. And three: Smoking or eating in flight is prohibited. Do you have any questions? Your response must be verbal."

He looked over at Tali's friend. "Mr. Hickson?"

"No, you've been very clear, Henri," Hickson responded.

"Dr. Carue?"

"None."

"Ms. Jorgensen?"

"Just one," she announced. "What's the inflight movie?" The somber atmosphere that pervaded the interior of the van evaporated in laughter. Even Greene joined in.

After the laughter stopped, their escort spoke again. "Just sit back and relax. We'll be at the launch pad shortly."

Silence settled over the van as each person was immersed in their own thoughts. Rod kept shifting in his seat to look out the various windows, hoping to get a view of the shuttle.

Hickson noticed Rod's antics and smiled. "This is your first trip into space, isn't it?" he said.

Rod gave an embarrassed nod. "It's that obvious, is it?" he asked.

Hickson smiled. "You're dancing in your seat," he said and gave a little chuckle. "It reminds me of my first flight."

"I've always wanted to get into space," Rod said. "I grew up memorizing the names of astronauts and their vehicles."

"I bet you even read science fiction as a teenager," Hickson said.

With a sheepish look on his face Rod reached into one of his bags and pulled out his reading book. "I got the entire *John Carter* series from my grandfather," he explained. "But I got started long before that. My father introduced me to the 1930 movie serials of *Buck Rogers* and *Flash Gordon* when I was seven. I was hooked from then on. There were also the *Star Wars* and *Star Trek* movies, of course."

Hickson gave a knowing nod. "The classics," he announced. Tali listened with a slight smile but said nothing.

"I remember camping trips in the Colorado Rockies where I could gaze up into the brilliant, starlit sky and wonder what it'd be like to explore the galaxy," Rod said. "Now, I'm going into space." He gave a shrug of his shoulders. "I'm not chasing Klingons or Romulans with Captain Kirk on the *Enterprise*, but I'll be in space."

The van jolted to a stop, bringing the conversation to a halt. A moment later the side door slid open, and two men in white coveralls stepped forward to help the passengers out. Tali left the van first followed by Hickson and Rod.

Once out of the vehicle Hickson, Tali, and Rod looked up to see the launch structure towering over them. Rod stared at the spacecraft rising above him drinking in the scene.

"Dr. Carue?"

Greene's voice took him away from the shuttle. "We don't have a lot of time. Everyone, please make sure you have your bags; the gantry elevator is this way."

Rod nodded and held up his bags, one in each hand, showing he was ready. He couldn't wipe the grin off his face. He was going into space, and the *Enterprise* was taking him!

As the lattice-like elevator doors clanged shut and the car began to rise, Rod's elation started to shift to a sense of unease. He looked through the doors at the expanding spaceport and the surrounding area as they moved upward toward the entry gantry. He easily picked out the building containing the control room for the launch. He also saw the airport with its terminal. Beyond the runway stood the housing and service buildings for the base, with the Pacific Ocean in the distance.

He turned his attention back to the shuttle. The drives attached to the craft were huge. The sense of unease he'd been feeling became a pit in his stomach with the realization that he was going to sit inside a craft propelled into space by three large Roman candles.

Now that he could see the craft up close Rod noticed differences between this shuttle and those of the prior century. While the bulk of the changes were in the electronics controlling the craft, he suspected, others were more visible. The most obvious change was that this shuttle was equipped with a passenger module instead of with a cargo bay. It also boasted three external drives strapped to the vehicle under the wings and fuselage, in addition to the shuttle's internal drives. This craft was larger and had a sleeker, more aerodynamic shape than the first class of shuttles.

The elevator stopped a hundred yards above the ground, and the doors opened to let Rod's group out. They crossed the gantry and moved into the passenger compartment. Standing behind Hickson and Tali just inside the airlock Rod looked up and saw that the passenger seats were anchored to what was now a wall. He counted six rows of four seats climbing toward the ship's nose. The rows were divided into two pairs of seats, with an aisle separating the pairs. Inset into the aisle were metal rungs like a ladder. Two rows of seats near the nose of the craft were empty, while the rows closest to the entry hatch were occupied.

Tali went first. She climbed up the rungs to the topmost row where an attendant helped her into a seat. Hickson followed.

Rod was last. He handed his bags to the attendant in the entry port, who stored them in a compartment. Expecting to sit alone, he climbed the aisle rungs all the way to the top row, then moved into his seat, which was next to the aisle. To his surprise, he found Tali sitting in the seat next to him. Another launch attendant was waiting for him and helped buckle him into his seat with quick, efficient movements.

As the attendant worked her way down to the entry port, she confirmed that all the passengers were ready for launch. The attendant below made sure both doors of the airlock were sealed, and the captain notified. Then the women took their designated seats on the bottom row and buckled in.

With everyone in place, there was nothing for the passengers to do but wait. For Rod time stretched, each minute seemed like an hour. A voice would come over the intercom every five minutes to announce the remaining time to launch.

At last, the final countdown began. The scientist could hear and feel the shuttle engines building to full power. At ten seconds Rod could barely hear the announcer's voice over the roar of the engines.

Glancing over at Tali, Rod could see fear etched on her face. She was gripping the hand rest of her seat so hard her knuckles were white. Without thinking, the scientist pried her right hand free and squeezed it with his left. Startled, she looked over at him, then gave him a tight-lipped smile.

It seemed Tali was about to say something when the solid fuel rocket boosters cut in at full strength. The shuttle started to rise slowly, at first, then accelerating as it gained altitude. Sound cascaded over Rod as his body was pressed back into the acceleration seat. The noise grew to an air-splitting pitch. It seemed to take on a physical presence.

As the craft continued to accelerate toward space, Rod felt as if someone had piled a load of bricks on his chest and forgotten to take them off. It became difficult to breathe. The skin, muscles, and organs of his body were being pulled toward the rear of the craft.

After what seemed an eternity, the sound and pressure began to diminish. There was a sharp jolt, which caused Tali to tighten her grip on Rod's hand even more. Rod closed his eyes and forced away the image of the *Challenger* disaster during the shuttle program's experimental phase. He kept telling himself it was just the depleted booster drives being discarded. Long seconds later the sound of the shuttle engines fell to a dull rumble and then quit. With no thrust, all sense of weight disappeared.

Rod opened his eyes to look around. Across the aisle he saw that Hickson was unconscious. He then glanced to his right and found Tali looking back at him.

He remembered that he was still holding her hand. Embarrassed, he let go. "I'm sorry," he started to say.

"I'm not," Tali interrupted. "It helped. When I was a little girl loud noises frightened me. During the night, thunderstorms would wake me, and my parents would find me in the morning with all the blankets and comforters in the house piled on my bed. I'd hide under them to drown out the sound."

Rod sat and listened as Tali kept the conversation going. It seemed that talking helped ease her fears. On occasion he'd nod and say something noncommittal. There hadn't been an opportunity during the training to learn of anyone's past, and now he was getting a light speed update on Tali. In the background the sound of the life-support system made a comforting hiss.

A few minutes later Rod gave a quick glance over at Hickson to see if he'd rejoined the world. He hadn't. "The blastoff seems to have been hard on Brian," he said when Tali had paused for a moment.

The fusion engineer leaned forward in her restraints to look past Rod. Until now she hadn't been aware that anything was wrong with her friend. "Maybe we should see if he's all right?"

"Can't," Rod said. "We were told to remain in our seats with harness in place until we were told we could get out." He shrugged. "I'm sorry to say I wouldn't know what to do if we could get over there."

Tali's objection was interrupted by a tone coming over the intercom followed by a female voice. "We are now in orbit and will dock with the Transfer Station in little more than sixty minutes. You may remove your harness and enjoy being weightless for a while. When we're ten minutes from initiating docking maneuvers another tone will sound. After the signal you'll be asked to return to your seats and buckle your harnesses. Do not hesitate. The dock maneuvers cannot be delayed. Anyone not in their seats could be injured by the maneuvers."

Rod and Tali were unbuckling their restraints when the hatch in front of them opened and a man swam through toward them. The new arrival wore a blue space force jumpsuit and managed the weightless environment like he'd been born to it.

"You'd better check out Hickson," Rod said and directed the man's attention to where the engineer's unconscious form lay in its seat. "He hasn't moved since we made orbit."

The man nodded his understanding and floated over to check Hickson's vital signs. Rod and Tali stopped fumbling with their restraining harnesses to watch.

After a moment, the man looked over at them. "I'm the crew medic," he announced as he hung in the air above Hickson. He kept a hold on the seat's headrest to remain in place. "While this sort of thing doesn't happen all the time it happens enough that NASA includes someone like me on every launch." The man looked down at Hickson. "He'll be all right."

Then the medic glanced at the other passengers at the stern end of the module and gestured with his free hand toward the cockpit. "Go on into the control room and enjoy the view," he told Rod and Tali. "It looks like you'll have it all to yourselves. No one else seems interested."

Satisfied that their companion was well cared for, Rod and Tali finished releasing their restraints and made for the cockpit of the shuttle. Rod had hoped to appear the seasoned spaceman to impress Tali. But every bump and errant spin brought an embarrassed flush to Rod's face. He shrugged and that was another mistake because it sent him floating off in another direction. Muttering under his breath, he worked to get back to his seat, then moved through the hatch.

The first item in the cockpit that caught the scientist's attention was the control panel. The displays, banks of colored and lit buttons, and digital readouts that surrounded the captain and co-pilot were impressive. Rod began to shake his head in awe but stopped. He didn't want to go flying off again and bump into something he shouldn't. With all those things to look at and manipulate, how'd the pilots know what to do?

Rod glanced out a side port and was stunned by the view. The planet below filled the port showing blue, white, and brown patterns. Oceans, continents, and cloud formations could be seen whirling and speeding beneath them.

"It's beautiful," whispered Tali. She, like Rod, was staring at the sight.

The captain of the shuttle turned from the control console to grin at the two passengers. His white teeth were a sharp contrast to his ebon face. "It always strikes first-timers that way," he said. "But even when you've seen it as many times as we have you never get over it." The co-pilot, a petite Asian woman, nodded her agreement.

Rod continued to stare out the viewport. "I've always wanted to make it to space," he said almost in a whisper. "And now I'm here, and it seems like a dream."

"Would you like to know what the controls do?" asked the shuttle captain.

Rod turned away from the view and gave a slight push with his feet to float up behind the captain's seat for a better view. He held onto the back of the seat as the captain pointed at the readouts, which showed the relative speed and altitude of the craft. While the height they were orbiting was impressive, it was the speed that dazzled Rod. Because there was no sound or gravity, it seemed they were standing still.

Still holding onto the captain's chair, Rod gave a shake of his head. The gauge had the shuttle racing along at tens of thousands of kilometers per hour. As the pilot continued his explanation of the instruments, Rod realized that most of what he could see was the ship's computer. And it was the computer running the ship.

Rod noticed one display that reminded him of a weather radar scope. "What's that?" he asked, pointing.

"That's our radar," the captain replied. "See that blip?" He indicated the white dot on the screen. "That's the transfer station we're heading for."

"How far are we from it?"

"Not far," the co-pilot replied and pointed out the front windows.

Following her direction, Rod and Tali looked out the window. Shining in the foreground, seeming to grow, was their destination.

The station consisted of four rings, like barrel hoops connected. For a moment Rod was reminded of the round Chinese box kite he'd tried flying as a young boy. A large shaft ran through the center of the four rings and housed the reactor and main laboratories. The rings were kept in place by three other shafts running from each circle to the central shaft. Slightly smaller shafts running from one circle to another seemed like barrel slats. The whole structure rotated around the central shaft.

"It looks like a fifty-gallon barrel without the metal, just the frame, rolling around the world," remarked Tali.

"The station doesn't look that big from here," Rod commented. From his position behind the captain's seat, the scientist couldn't see the smiles on the two pilots' faces.

"Distances and sizes are deceptive up here," the co-pilot said. "There aren't any comparisons to use to judge sizes." She gestured at the viewscreen. "That central shaft is the equivalent of four stories wide. The rest of the station is two stories wide. There are more than five thousand people on board, not counting those who are transferring to other orbital stations and the moon."

Rod gave a soft whistle. The station they were discussing was growing larger. He stared at it as more detail became apparent. A tone sounded, startling the scientist.

"Please return to your seats and prepare for docking," ordered the captain as he began to push buttons. The announcement instructing all passengers to return to their seats and strap in could be heard coming through the airlock hatch. A digital readout began to count down the distance to the station.

Aided by an attendant and the medic, Rod and Tali returned to their seats, where they were buckled in. After making sure everything in the compartment was ready, the medic closed the hatch. Rod and Tali heard the pressure seals activate.

"I'm glad you're back," said Hickson from his seat. "I was starting to get lonely."

"How're you feeling?" asked Tali.

"Lousy," he replied. "I feel like a herd of elephants ran over me, stopped, decided it was fun and did it again. But," he shrugged. "I'll live."

"It won't be long," encouraged Rod, "We're almost to the station."

Hickson nodded, swallowed, and grimaced.

Because there were no windows in the passenger compartment Rod couldn't see anything of the docking maneuver. He'd feel the occasional thrust from positioning jets, but the process was left to his imagination. Then a few moments after he'd guessed forward motion had stopped, there was a sharp jolt, and a weird, side-wise motion started.

The forward hatch opened moments later, letting the flight medic back into the compartment. Going to Hickson, he began to release the man's restraints.

"Dr. Carue, Ms. Jorgensen, you may remove your restraints," he instructed. Rod and Tali began unbuckling. Sounds of restraints being released could be heard coming from behind them as the other passengers also rose from their seats.

"Come on," said the medic a moment later as he floated Hickson out of his seat. "Let's get you to the outer ring rec room. Although the simulated gravity isn't up to that of home it'll help you get your legs."

"What about our luggage?" asked Rod.

"Don't worry about your bags," the man replied. "We'll get them moved over to your transfer ships." He gave a little chuckle. "We have a better record than the airlines for getting our cargo to the right destination."

The four people floated through the compartment and out into a large, pressurized hanger. Looking back at the craft, Rod saw that metal braces held the shuttle in place against the transfer station's rotation. That explained the weird side-ways motion he'd felt at the end of the docking. A hatch had been opened near the nose of the ship, and station personnel were removing packages. Other men were moving over and under the craft inspecting its surface for damage before the return to atmosphere.

The medic, still assisting Hickson, led the way through the hanger to another airlock. They floated past people who were going the other way to be rotated back to Earth. People took turns moving through the hatch in a choreographed routine. Although both sides of the lock were pressurized and had atmosphere, the airlock was kept sealed as a precaution.

Once the small party had passed through, the medic approached a station attendant who'd been floating nearby watching the procession. "Get these people to a rec room. They can wait there for the lunar ferry," he ordered.

Then, without waiting for the man to reply, he turned to his charges. "I'm leaving you here," he announced. "I've got to get back to the *Enterprise*."

The three people thanked the medic for his help and watched as he disappeared back into the airlock. When the hatch closed, they turned to look at the attendant. In response, the man pointed up the corridor of the main shaft. "Go forward to the next junction," he instructed. "Take tube 2C to the outer ring and follow the signs from there." Without waiting for a reply, he pushed off to disappear into a side room.

"Looks like we're on our own," Rod said as he watched the attendant leave. Careful to keep his feet anchored in floor sleeves, he pulled his travel papers from a jumpsuit pocket and looked over the itinerary. Then he glanced at his watch, which had adjusted automatically to the new time zone. "My ferry to the moon isn't due to depart for another three hours," he announced. "I'll check out that rec room. Any takers?"

Despite his obvious discomfort Hickson refused. "My ferry is scheduled to dock right after the *Enterprise* leaves," he said. "There's a waiting area nearby. I'll just hang around there until then."

Tali giggled, noting that Hickson was hanging in the air. "Dr. Carue, if you don't mind, I'll float along." The two men grimaced at the pun.

Rod nodded and then turned back to Hickson. He extended his hand to wish the older man farewell.

Hickson refused. He didn't even shake his head. "No handshakes in null G unless you're an acrobat or anchored," he said. "I'm neither. Have a good trip, and luck to you." Before Rod or Tali could say anything, Hickson used a hand to push off and head for a nearby waiting area.

Rod floated a foot above the metal deck with his mouth open. In his surprise, he hadn't noticed that his feet had slipped out of the anchor sleeves placed along the corridor. "He's space-sick, but he talks like a spacer," he exclaimed. "Life doesn't make sense." The scientist shook his head, and the motion sent him spinning.

Tali chuckled as she reached over to stop him before he hit a wall. She'd kept her feet tucked into the sleeves, giving her the leverage she needed. "That's what he is," she replied. "He's been working in orbit for years. Most recently he's been helping construct the science stations over the poles. The reason he was at Canaveral was that he was called down to help with a reactor problem there." She gestured down the corridor. "Shall we go?" She asked before disengaging from the sleeves.

The two people pushed off, floating down the corridor toward the tube they'd been directed to.

"I gather your ferry doesn't leave for a while," Rod said to keep the conversation going. "Maybe there'll be a dispenser in the rec room, and I can buy you a drink?"

"That sounds good," said Tali, "since I have as much time as you do." She gave him a little smile. "My posting is at Copernicus. I'll be helping maintain the fusion reactor for your equipment." Rod felt even better at hearing that news. He was feeling so good he didn't even wonder how she knew about his project.

Arriving at the junction, they read the posted instructions. The transfer tube was divided in half, with the left side designated for traffic heading for the outer ring and the right side, for those coming to the main shaft. Each side could be accessed by ladder.

They positioned themselves so they appeared to be upside down relative to those in the corridor, then used their hands to push themselves down the tube feet first. Tali led the way.

As they progressed from the center shaft Rod began to sense the simulated gravity taking effect. Their bodies began to fall toward their feet. As their speed increased, they used their hands and feet on the ladder to manage their descent. At last, they reached the outer ring and stepped out of the tube.

"This way," said Tali and nodded at a sign on the far wall. She moved down the corridor to the right with Rod following. Now they walked than floated. Ahead of the two, the floor curved upward instead of level like the horizons they were accustomed to on Earth.

A short distance from the tube they came to a hatch with a sign that identified the room they were looking for. Tali keyed the heavy blast door; both people stepped inside, then stopped. The first thing they saw was the outer wall. It dominated the room and was made of extra-thick bullet- or micro-meteor proof transparent Plexiglas. Moving from one part of the wall toward the other was Earth.

"Can you move?"

The voice coming from behind pulled Rod back to his surroundings. He mumbled, "Sorry," and moved off to one side. Tali shook her head as if to clear her thoughts and stepped out of the way as well. A man moved past, and the blast door slid shut.

Now that he wasn't mesmerized by the view Rod took a moment to examine the room they'd entered. The tables were arranged throughout the room so people could sit and watch the ever-changing scene caused by the stations roll. Most of the tables and chairs were occupied. Metal safety shutters, which could be closed over the Plexiglas on short notice, were positioned along the exterior sides of the observation window. Set against the opposite wall were dispensers containing food and drinks.

"I'll get us some drinks if you'll take care of the table," suggested Rod.

"Deal," answered Tali and moved off to find an empty table near the window.

The scientist worked his way through the crowded room. A quick study of the vending machines showed him that the equipment was like any found back home except that there was no method for payment. Apparently, there was no charge for the contents. Or it came down to the fact that no one brought any money with them from Earth.

Rod selected two pints of orange juice, retrieved them from the dispenser, then turned to look for Tali. She'd found a table with a good view. Because of the low gravity he half-skipped, half-walked around the tables and chairs, carrying the containers of juice. When he reached their table, he handed one of the pints to Tali and moved around to sit down.

"All they had were juices and flavored water," Rod explained. "I hope the OJ is okay?"

"Thanks, the juice is fine," she said and pulled a straw out of the plastic that kept it attached to the package.

"I thought we could catch up on current events while we have some free time," Tali suggested. "I picked up some newspapers on the way over." She gave a smile. "They're really on paper."

"Paper?" repeated Rod. "You're kidding!"

She shrugged, then indicated the room. "Perhaps being surrounded by and dependent on all this technology has got people here wanting something to remind them of simpler times." The engineer slid a newspaper across the table to Rod. "Who knows? Anyway, like I said, I don't know what's been going on since we started training and thought we might catch up. That is, if we get tired of the view." She inclined her head toward the window as Earth came back into view.

"Good idea," agreed Rod and reached for the paper Tali had provided.

Silence reigned as both sipped their juice and watched the changing scenery. After ten minutes Rod turned to the paper. On occasion he looked up to glance out the window to stare at the planet below when it came into view.

On the front-page Rod found yet another article about South Africa. "Still in the news," he commented, remembering an article he'd read months earlier. Tali didn't say anything, engrossed in her own article.

The story reported that riots in the Black townships of South Africa were becoming more widespread, with the nation dividing along tribal lines. Whole blocks of houses and buildings had been burned, some of the structures with the occupants inside. People killed or tortured their neighbor on suspicion of collaborating with the current regime. The police and military responded with maximum firepower. A leader had appeared and focused the rioters into a full-fledged rebellion.

Responding to political pressure from activists, and at the request of the president, Congress had placed severe economic sanctions on the strife-torn nation. The legislation required that all U.S. firms in South Africa leave that nation, all investments in South Africa be sold, and any exports to or imports from South Africa frozen. There was one exemption: Congress allowed for the importing of the exotic metals that were vital for the current generation of electronics and crucial for the high-tech weaponry arming the Western world's armed forces. These metals were found in high enough concentrations to be mined profitably in South Africa and some of the Russian Federation states. In addition to the economic sanctions, all embassy personnel at the South African consulate in Washington, D.C., were ordered to leave the United States.

South Africa retaliated and forbade sale or export of the exotic metals to any Western nation involved in the sanctions. Any nation, company, or organization that funneled the specified products to the excluded nations would be added to the blacklist.

"South Africa: A war of nerves," Rod thought aloud.

"What?" Tali asked, looking up from her paper.

"Oh, nothing."

"There's an interesting article on page three," Tali said.

Rod turned the pages. "Doomsday Prophet Predicts Armageddon" drew his attention. A new religious faction known as the Creator's Chosen had appeared in the Bible-Belt of the United States and was growing in numbers. The leader of the Chosen had taken upon himself the name of Elias to signify his role in heralding the Creator's message. Missionaries from this group had been sent out to gather the Chosen and give the world a last chance to repent of its sins for planetary destruction was at hand.

The church had purchased over 20,000 acres of forested land near the town of Seligman, Arizona, and was in the process of building a community.

"There are nuts in every crowd," Rod said with a chuckle.

"I beg your pardon?" Tali asked, glaring over her paper at Rod. "I saw nothing insane or funny in their conclusions."

"You don't mean you believe that mumbo-jumbo?"

"I hardly believe the conclusions drawn by Doctors Cowan and Mendel based on Carl Sagan's work in the middle-twentieth century is to be dismissed as 'mumbo-jumbo.'"

"Wait," Rod said. "Are we talking about the same article?"

"I am referring to the article discussing the nuclear winter model created by Doctor's Cowan and Mendel. Why?"

Rod glanced back at the paper, then chuckled again in relief. "Look next to your article," he instructed then watched as Tali looked at her paper. A moment later he saw her lips twitch slightly.

"You're right, there are nuts everywhere," she laughed. "You're forgiven."

"That's a relief," Rod said, then glanced at his watch. "We'd better start back. The lunar ferry is due to leave in an hour. We don't want to be late for our ride to the moon. Somehow, I don't think they'll wait for us, and hitchhiking isn't an option."

Tali nodded. The two folded the papers they'd been reading, gathered their empty drink containers, and placed everything in the recycle receptacles provided.

During the float back to the transfer bay Rod questioned Tali about the nuclear winter idea, since he'd read the wrong article. She explained that during the mid-to-late twentieth century the eminent astronomer Carl Sagan had created a model predicting the effects of an all-out nuclear war between what had been the USSR and the USA.

In recent years, Doctors Cowan and Mendel, from UCLA, improved upon the model. Basing their figures on a full-scale exchange of missiles between the Russian Federation and the United States, the two scholars determined that the resulting fires and explosions would throw sufficient debris into the atmosphere that the light reaching the planet's surface would be reduced. The entire planet would be cooled by a minimum of ten degrees Celsius. In addition to the extensive spread of radiation, another side effect would be that a sufficient amount of oxygen in the atmosphere would be consumed by the combustion process to make the higher altitudes uninhabitable without life support systems. It would take decades to return atmospheric oxygen levels to normal.

The model further predicted that it would take at least one year for enough of the particulates to filter out of the atmosphere for the sun to resume warming the planet. Of course, the temperature reduction caused by the cloud cover would reduce crop production worldwide. Any crops grown would most likely be found near the equator. The polar ice caps would become larger; glaciers worldwide would expand. Millions would die of starvation, disease, exposure, and radiation poisoning after the initial exchange.

"Sounds like the end of the world to me," Rod remarked to Tali as they arrived at the transfer airlock outside the shuttle hanger. They made sure their feet were anchored in the floor sleeves as they waited. "Maybe that Elias guy isn't as crazy as I thought."

"A few of the better-prepared people away from the blast sites might survive," observed Tali. "But it'll take quite a while for civilization to rebuild."

"From what you've told me, we'd be right back to the Stone Age," Rod said.

"I think you're right," Tali agreed. "Let's hope it never happens. Millions, maybe billions, of people would die."

Their discussion was interrupted as they heard the call to board the lunar ferry. Rod and Tali floated over to join the line of people funneling through the hanger airlock. Once through the hatch they crossed the hanger to the spacecraft that would take them to the moon and joined another line.

This craft was much larger than the shuttle that had brought them to the transfer station and had none of the aerodynamic lines. Rod was amazed that a ship this large could fit into the hanger. It looked like it had five decks. Then he remembered what the shuttle captain had said about this portion of the station being as large as several multi-story buildings.

As each person entered the ferry an attendant floating just inside the airlock assigned a berth for the fourteen-day trip to the moon. Rod was assigned berth 2A on Level One, while Tali's berth was a level down. Everyone was instructed to go straight to their berths and strap in. The ferry would leave as soon as the last passenger was on board and the cargo loaded.

Rod found his room without any trouble. The berth wasn't very big. Nothing adorned the walls; there wasn't even a window so he could look out at the stars. It was just large enough for a bed against one wall, leaving a narrow aisle to walk or float down. There was a closet with four jumpsuits in his size. A sign on the inside of the closet door informed him that a communal restroom with a zero-g shower was down the hall.

As promised, his bags were on the bed. He placed them in the compartment at the head of the bed marked for storage, then stretched out on the sleeping pad to buckle the straps that would hold him in place during any maneuvers.

Soon after he had settled, a tone sounded over the intercom, followed by a recording. "The procedure to leave the Transfer Station will begin in five minutes. Please strap in and remain in your restraints until notice is given that the maneuver has been completed."

Not knowing how long the maneuver would take, Rod stretched and checked the time. It was 0430. No wonder he was feeling a little tired. He'd been up for almost twenty-four hours. While waiting for the departure maneuver to begin, he closed his eyes, and his breathing slowed.

Rod woke with a start and wondered what had roused him. Listening, he heard only the sound of the ventilation system. Then he remembered that he was waiting for the ferry to complete the departure maneuver. He lifted an arm so he could see his watch, and his eyes widened. He'd been asleep for five hours. With that much time gone, he was sure the ferry had left the Transfer Station. In fact, the ship had probably left orbit for the moon. Cautiously he released the restraints that held him to the bed then turned over to reach the storage compartment where his bags were stowed. He'd set up house and then go to check on Tali.

During the flight to the moon, the scientist took advantage of all the free time to rest and do things he hadn't had time to do during training. He spent considerable time with Tali. In the times designated as evening, the two people wandered to the ferry's observation dome to watch the stars, the growing moon, and the receding Earth while discussing their dreams and hopes.

On the ninth evening they sat on a sofa in the observation dome and the conversation moved to Earth and current events.

News reports had the situation in South Africa growing worse. All European and Pacific nations had joined the United States in the sanctions. In response, South Africa expelled all foreign diplomats and shut down all exports, including the exotic metals. It was feared the loss of the exotic metals would push the world into an economic depression.

Eventually, Rod and Tali looked out the observation windows into the vastness of space, gazing at the myriads of stars. Rod felt small, insignificant, and drew toward Tali, as if for reassurance. He put his arm around Tali's shoulders, and she half-turned to snuggle into his embrace. They remained that way until the lights began to dim, signaling the sleep period for the ship.

The fourteenth day came too soon. Neither Tali nor Rod wanted it to. But they both had jobs to do.

Forty minutes prior to the landing maneuver an announcement came over the ships PA system for all passengers to retire to their berths and strap in. Rod saw Tali to her berth, then hurried to his own.

The captain of the trans-lunar ferry watched his instruments. When the last light on the ready board went from amber to green, confirming that the ship's systems and passengers were ready, he toggled a switch, putting the ship under computer control. A monitor came to life and showed a green line with two blinking dots. The blue dot indicated the ship's position, while the red dot marked the point to begin the descent. The gap between the two dots was rapidly shrinking.

Five minutes later, when the two dots touched, nose rockets fired to slow the craft's momentum. A low rumble sounded throughout the craft, and the captain and co-pilot were pushed forward against their restraints as the ship slowed. The moon's gravity began to work, and the ship dropped closer and closer to the lunar surface. Mountain ranges, plains, and craters sped underneath as the craft closed with its objective.

The computer made occasional course adjustments to remain on the correct glide path. Ten minutes after the first rocket burn the ship cleared a low mountain range, and the main lunar base came into view. Again, the computer-controlled nose rockets fired, slowing the craft still more.

The captain kept in close communication with the base controller. Everyone involved in the landing knew the consequence if the ship's approach was too high or too low or its speed was too fast or too slow. One monitor of the captain's control panel outlined the ship's proposed trajectory with benchmarks, as well as the ship's actual trajectory. The computer kept the ferry perfectly aligned with the landing path.

At one hundred meters from the moon's surface, struts extended from the bottom of the ship and rockets further slowed the descent. Dust that had accumulated on the landing pad since the last ferry was blown away in a light cloud by the landing jets. Moments later a slight jolt and the feeling of weight signaled a safe landing.

"Your attention, please."

Rod perked up to listen to the announcement. "We have landed, and the connection to the base facility is being made. All passengers will please gather their personal effects and report to airlock three."

Rod released his restraints, removed his luggage from the storage compartment, and left his cabin. He made his way through the corridors and decks of the ferry to find Tali waiting for him near the airlock. Other passengers were lining the corridor leading to the hatch. Together, Rod and Tali looked through an observation port to see that a pressurized walkway had been extended to the ship's outer airlock from the base terminal.

Farther down the corridor a member of the ferry's crew at the airlock checked his instruments to confirm there was a good seal with pressure in the walkway. He adjusted the boom microphone of his headset and pushed a button on his console. "Luna Base, this is Lunar Ferry *Nimitz*," he said. "Walkway check. I show the walkway green. Do you concur?"

"*Nimitz*, this is base," came the response. "We confirm the walkway is green. Open airlocks is authorized."

"Base, *Nimitz*. Open airlocks is authorized. Opening now!"

The man terminated the communications link, removed his headset, and placed it on a peg, then nodded to another crew member. Moments later the airlock doors at both ends of the walkway opened, and passengers began moving through. Rod and Tali passed through the airlock and down the walkway. After two weeks without any gravity, Rod welcomed the moon's weak pull.

Once inside the reception lounge Rod nodded at Tali and led her off to one side, where they'd be out of the line of traffic. He set his bags on the floor next to a couch and looked around. The lounge had high, five-meter ceilings. Observation windows looked out on the ferry landing pad and the lunar landscape beyond. Couches were placed in strategic positions to give any observers a chance to enjoy the view. Potted plants placed throughout the room provided a homey feel.

"I wonder what we do now?" Rod asked. "Do you see anyone looking like they're looking for us?"

"No," replied Tali and shrugged her shoulders. "I guess we wait?"

Rod reached into his bags for his itinerary. He went to the page showing the trip to the moon. "It says here that we get a ride to Copernicus on a Personnel Lunar Rover," he said.

"Great! Where do we get one?" asked Tali.

"Look for a Bob's Rent-a-Rover sign?"

"I seem to have corrupted you," Tali retorted with a soft chuckle.

Rod grinned then gestured at the far end of the lounge. "Here comes a man who looks like he's trying to find someone."

The person in question had just entered the reception area and was scanning the room. Taking the initiative, Rod and Tali picked up their bags and walked over to meet him.

The man finished his examination of the room and saw the two people heading for him. "Dr. Carue?" he asked when they met.

"Yes, and this is Ms. Jorgensen."

"Good. If you'll follow me, I'll get you to your Rover." With that, he turned and strode off.

Rod glanced at Tali with a wry grin on his face. "Efficient, as always," he said, then indicated for her to lead the way.

Following their guide, they passed through much of the base, which gave them a chance to do a little sightseeing. The base consisted of living quarters for personnel, offices for administrators, laboratories for experiments, hydroponics rooms to help recycle the air and grow food, power rooms, mechanical shops, and observatories. When they walked past a rare window Rod paused to look out at the domed shapes of the surface buildings. The structures were festooned with antennae, radio telescope dishes, and other scientific equipment of unrecognizable designs and purposes.

Their guide explained that the bulk of the base was underground for insulation and safety reasons. The meters of lunar soil and rock above prevented breaches and loss of atmosphere due to small meteor strikes.

Rod noticed the corridor they were in was five meters high, with a padded ceiling. He paused for a moment and pointed up. "What's the deal with the ceiling?"

The man stopped, turned around, gave a little smile, and said, "gravity."

"Could you explain that a little more clearly?" asked Tali.

"The transfer station-to-Luna flight can be made in less than one week," their guide responded. "During the base construction, the flight was made in fewer than three days. The thinking was that the quicker that people made it to the moon the sooner the base would be completed. When they arrived the construction crew hadn't acclimated to the lower gravity. When they went to walk, they jumped." He gave a little shake of his head. "That resulted in head injuries. To prevent further injuries or any fatalities, the ceilings were padded and placed high enough to not get in the way. Now, with the ferry taking two weeks at no gravity, the passengers have become better acclimated. Although these high ceilings aren't necessary anymore, there are no plans to remodel and lower them."

"So that's the reason for the length of the trip from Earth."

"Correct, Dr. Carue."

The trio continued making its way through the base. A half hour after leaving the reception lounge, they came to a door marked "Rover Bay" and entered. It was a large, well-lit room. On their right they saw four Rovers parked in a line. To their left were stations for mechanics. A single Rover was in that area with its engine compartment open. Two men were standing on stools with their heads inside the compartment. Shop lights were positioned to provide better visibility for the mechanics.

"Third PLR on the right," their guide told them. "The passenger compartment door's already open. Find a seat and strap in. I'll let the pilot know you're here."

CHAPTER 4

"Are we the only people going to Copernicus?" Tali wondered. "I don't see anyone else here," Rod said, looking around the hanger. "But if there are other passengers they may already be in the Rover." He held out a hand, inviting Tali to walk ahead of him. "Shall we?" he asked.

She smiled and nodded. "We shall," she replied and started for the vehicle.

As the two moved deeper into the bay, Rod examined the nearest Rover. It looked like a cross between a van and a dune buggy. The van part was comprised of a square gray body containing a cockpit for the pilot and a large compartment for passengers or cargo. The dune buggy features included a whip radio antennae and extra-large balloon tires. Someone had painted a palm tree on the side of the passenger area just behind the cockpit, and below the windows were the words "Thunder Beach."

"That'll be a real hit on the beach," said Tali, nodding at the vehicle. "I wonder if the top comes off."

"Only if I'm in an environment suit," commented Rod, then pointed to a side door in the hanger. "Over there!" A man in a space force jumpsuit had entered the bay and was walking in their direction. "That could be our driver. We'd better get to our ride."

With Tali following, Rod hurried over to the third Rover in line and climbed through its open hatch. "Take your pick," he said to his companion and gestured at the rows of empty seats that filled the compartment. "I'm guessing we're the only passengers."

"Either that, or everyone else is late," Tali replied.

By the time they'd stored their bags under their seats and fastened their seat belts the man they suspected was their chauffeur had climbed through the airlock and sealed the two hatches after him. Without a word to his passengers, he moved down the center aisle, entered the forward compartment, and sealed that hatch as well.

"Real people person isn't he?" said Tali.

"At least with all the viewports in this thing we can watch the scenery," replied Rod.

With a slight jolt, the Rover moved out of its parking space. The lights in the passenger compartment dimmed, then went out as the vehicle turned for the airlock and both passengers settled in for the drive. Watching through a window, Rod saw the hanger's inner door open to let the Rover begin the departure process.

Within ten minutes the Rover was through the airlock and moving across the lunar surface. Dust kicked up by the tires slowly drifted back to the surface in the vehicle's wake. The clustered surface domes of the main base soon gave way to a flat plain.

Rod angled in his seat so he could look through a viewport at the route ahead. It was easy to see they were following a path marked by other vehicles. The terrain they were crossing was marked with craters, gray dust, rocks, and stark shadows. It was a bit depressing. There were no colors but grey and black.

For a moment, a viewport on the other side of the vehicle framed Earth as it appeared just above the horizon. It was like a blue-white jewel set in a velvet-black background. He stared at the sight and gave a slow shake of his head. What could have possessed humanity to leave that beautiful planet for this desolation? Looking at Tali's pensive face, Rod wondered if she was having similar feelings.

Tali glanced his way and smiled. Rod returned the smile, winked, then turned his attention back to his viewport.

A half hour into their drive the Rover left the plain to enter a canyon in a mountain range. Rod estimated they'd covered a little more than fifteen kilometers from the main lunar base. Following the road that had been cut into the rough terrain the PLR moved through the mountains, going from one canyon to another.

With the mountains blocking the sun, it was difficult to watch the scenery since everything was black. Rod shifted in his seat so he could get a better view of the front of the PLR. That way he could see what the vehicle's lights illuminated.

At last, they came to a metal door set in a sheer cliff. The vehicle jolted to a stop about ten meters from the door. A moment later the barrier slid aside.

Rod continued to watch through his view port as the Rover moved into the pitch-black airlock. Without warning, the lights in the airlock came on. The sudden brilliance was painful and Rod had to turn away from the window for a few seconds to blink tears from his eyes. When they had adjusted to the increased lighting Rod returned to his view port and watched as the inner door of the airlock opened to let the PLR move into the lighted bay.

Still looking through the windows, he could see that this hanger was much smaller than the one at the main base. It had room for only a single PLR. The scientist nodded. That made sense. Copernicus was an observatory not the MLB. It didn't need room for a lot of PLRs.

The vehicle stopped, and the engine switched off.

Rod glanced over at Tali. Before either could speak the pilot appeared out of the cockpit. He walked through the passenger compartment and opened the inner airlock door, then the compartment's outer door. Before leaving the vehicle, he paused long enough to look back at his passengers. "We're here, everyone out!" he announced, then disappeared through the hatch.

Tali glanced over at Rod. "At least he said something to us this time," she remarked.

"Yeah, like your said a real people person," Rod replied.

Chuckling softly, the two people retrieved their belongings from beneath their seats and moved for the hatch. Leading the way, Rod stepped out of the Rover into the small bay, where he paused to look around. There was no sign of their pilot, but he did see someone waiting for them. Max stood a few meters, away leaning against a wall. The man had his arms and legs crossed and a silly grin on his face.

"What are you grinning for?" questioned Rod as he moved toward his friend.

"It's merely the pleasure of seeing your magnificence once again," replied Max pushing away from the wall to give Rod a slight bow.

Rod looked at the man a bit distrustfully. What joke did Max have up his sleeve? He set his bags on the hanger floor in a subconscious effort to clear the deck for action.

"Hello, Max," called Tali from the PLR hatch before Rod could question Max further. She bounced down from the Rover, dropped her bags and hurried over to give the man a big hug.

With a twinge of jealousy, Rod watched the two people then asked, "Uh, you two know each other?"

Max's grin got bigger. "Yep," he replied as they broke their embrace. "We're related by marriage."

"Cousins?" Rod was hopeful.

"Nope, her mother married my father."

It took a moment for Rod to work it out. "That means you're brother and sister."

"That's what the people who claim to be our parents tell us." Tali couldn't resist joining in. "But there're times I wonder if they're lying." She gave him a mischievous smile. "I'm sure this one," the engineer nudged her brother with an elbow, "was found in a garbage can near our house."

"But," exclaimed Rod, turning to Tali, "you never told me Max was your brother."

"I thought you knew, since you've been working with him for years," she said with a little chuckle. "I'm sure you noticed the same last name."

"Rod," broke in Max before the scientist could reply.

"Yes?" asked Rod as he turned from Tali to face Max.

"We're on the clock here," Max said. "We need to get you two situated."

Nodding, Rod bent to pick up his bags. In his excitement at seeing his friend again, mixed with the confusion at what he'd just learned, he forgot about the lower gravity and lifted with too much power. The bag containing his books kept going and almost threw his shoulder out of joint. While the bag didn't weigh much on the moon, it still had the same mass as back home. Rotating his shoulder to ease the strain, and ignoring the muffled laughter, Rod followed Max and Tali out of the Rover hanger.

The room Max left him in was larger than his berth on the lunar ferry. But that was to be expected. While this was an observatory, and not a luxury resort for the rich and famous, there was plenty of room available for some conveniences. When he looked inside, he saw a twin bed and a desk with a chair. Stepping into the room to let the door slide shut, he continued his examination. Besides the furniture there was a bookshelf at the head of the bed. Rod moved the reading light on the shelf to a better position. A monitor tied into the observatory net was attached to the wall at the foot of the bed. The monitor remote was placed next to the reading lamp. After dropping his bags on his desk, Rod went through the compartments set in one wall and found the expected jumpsuits.

"They weren't kidding when they said everything would be taken care of," he muttered and held up a jumpsuit to see it better in the light. It was identical to what he'd been given at Canaveral and what he was currently wearing. No fashion statement, but the clothing would do.

At the end of the room, opposite the entrance, he found a bathroom that included a shower. An individual shower in each room seemed a little extravagant after experiencing the austere communal facilities of the ferry.

Then he snorted. What was he thinking? He should be grateful for what creature comforts there were.

Sliding open the shower door, he looked in to see how the facility worked. Rod gave a knowing shake of his head. During the training he'd been told to expect this process. The stall used water to cleanse the occupant, but it was a little different from what he'd experienced back home. Water under pressure would be emitted from sprinklers in the ceiling, and then a fan would come on to push the water to the floor. A suction vent vacuumed the water into a drain. From there the used water would be taken to a reclamation site to be recycled for later use.

Rod had just completed placing pictures of his home and family around the room when an attention tone sounded. His scriptures were set on the bookshelf for his nightly reading routine. Then he glanced over at the phone sitting on the desk, but he didn't see a blinking light announcing an incoming call. That left the door. He moved the short distance to touch the door release. The panel slid aside to reveal Max.

"May I come in, Master?" Max requested, mimicking the accent and stance of a mad scientist's assistant as seen on the late-night wall-vid.

"Ah, Igor, come in, come in," Rod chuckled.

Max entered the room to allow the door to slide shut. He sat down in the room's only chair while Rod made himself comfortable on the sleeping pad.

"Why didn't you tell me about Tali, Max?" Rod asked.

"Me?" Max replied, holding out his hands in protest. "What're you talking about? I told you all about her. You heard about her schooling, her sports, and her drive to get into space. You just weren't interested at the time. Your focus was on the project."

He jerked his head toward the door. "In fact, I just came from making sure she was comfortable. It seems you've made quite an impression on her."

"That's good to hear. She's made an impression on me, as well."

"So she hoped," said Max with a knowing smile. "From what I've seen around here she could do worse."

"Oh, great!" said Rod. "I can't tell you what that does for my ego."

"Don't mention it. I'm feeling charitable today," said Max with a wide grin and a slight dip of his head. "But the real reason I'm here is to find out what our plan of action is going to be. Emma, Carter, and the new techs got here with our equipment about two weeks ago. I arrived a week after they did. Remember, we started our training before you did. Since they didn't have anything else to do while waiting for us to get here, our equipment's been checked, double-checked, and triple checked. Carter and Emma have tutored the new techs, so everyone's familiar with the equipment. Since then, the four techs have worked in the observatory helping repair items the maintenance people haven't had time to get to. That's made them extremely popular with the observatory staff. But now that you're here, everyone wants to start working on the reason we're here."

"Then we'd better come up with something for them to do," replied Rod, moving to the desk, and opening one of his bags. He pulled out a tablet, activated it, then leaned the device against the bags on the desk. Both men moved so they could see the pad's display. They spent the next several hours discussing what tests were and weren't needed.

The two men had just completed setting down a series of tests to determine the proper mixtures of drugs and gasses when the door tone sounded. Max reached over from where he was sitting and released the door.

"I thought so," said Tali as soon as the door opened enough for her to see the two men. "When you weren't at dinner, I thought something was up." She shook her head in disgust, putting her hands on her hips. "Let you two start talking shop, and you forget to take care of yourselves."

Rod looked at his watch. "She's right, Max. It's past the regular dinner time." He glanced over at his companion in surprise. "Now that I think about it, I'm hungry."

"You can tell that now, can you?" asked Tali in sarcastic tones.

"We're finishing up Mom," said Max. "We'll be along in a few minutes. Honest!"

But Tali wasn't convinced. "You'll be along now," she said and reached over to drag Max from his chair.

Once Max was moving for the corridor, Tali turned toward Rod. But before she could reach the scientist he stood, hands up in submission. "I'm coming, I'm coming," Rod said. He went to pick up the tablet and take it with him, but a stern look from Tali convinced him to leave it where it lay.

The next day Rod and Max gathered their people in the conference room assigned to them to explain the agenda. Tali was also there to represent the reactor staff. Max had everyone turn to their tablets and call up the proposed test schedule along with the energy requirements for the equipment.

The first test would be a single-day event involving a rat. Once this experiment ended successfully other tests would follow employing increasing duration and larger animals. The final round of tests for this phase of the project would be on animals having similar physiological characteristics to humans and would last six months.

When there was no more discussion about the process or schedule, Max turned to Tali and gave her a slight bow. "Well, Madame Fusion Engineer," he asked. "Can we do this?"

Tali looked over the data that was showing on her tablet, then turned to Max. "We can manage it," she announced with a definite bob of her head. "We've got plenty of capacity."

"Will we need to give you any notice when we begin so you can increase the power output?" Rod wondered.

Tali glanced at the pad again, then shook her head. "No," she replied. "This test can be managed easily enough with our current output. We won't have to do anything special here."

Excited muttering greeted that news. Rod nodded to Max who nodded back.

"We've covered everything we wanted," Max said cutting through the conversations that had sprung up. "Are there any more questions?"

When there wasn't Rod glanced at his watch. The orientation lasted about three hours. "It's almost lunch," he said. "We'll take a break now. Get something to eat and be in the chamber room at 1330 hours. We'll start the first test then.

It was 1310 when Rod arrived at the lab. He intended to personally examine the control console and chamber before anyone else arrived, but Max was already there. Within five minutes, the rest of the staff walked into the room.

With a knowing smile, the scientist glanced at his people and nodded. "Well," he said, "since everyone's here, why wait?"

One of the new technicians went into the zoo provided by NASA and returned with a rat. Under the experienced supervision of Carter, the new techs Crew Chen and Xavi Schmidt strapped the squirming rodent into a small cryogenic chamber and inserted an IV into the its veins. A sedative drip started to quiet the rat. Monitoring devices were attached to the animal when it had calmed down. At last, the preparations were finished, and the techs closed and sealed the chamber's transparent lid.

"Any change to our plans?" Max asked Rod.

"I don't see any reason to change," was Rod's reply.

"The same it is!" Max announced then turned to Emma. "Repeat the mixture for successful test R-16."

Emma worked the controls on the computer console, confirming the mixtures used in the specified test. "Mixture program set and confirmed," she replied. Then she turned to look at Rod. "We're ready."

Rod looked at the clock on the control console. It showed 1345. "Let's begin," he said.

Emma nodded and pushed a button. The serum to prepare the rat's cells for freezing and reduce its metabolism was injected through the IV. Twenty minutes later instruments showed the animal was ready. With all vital signs nearing flat line, the suspension atmosphere was introduced into the chamber, and the cooling process began.

It was an hour before Emma announced, "Subject in suspension." She continued watching statistics scroll down a display. "Temperature and metabolism as specified."

"Very good," said Rod. "Set the timer at two hours for revival."

Max looked over Emma's shoulder as she started the timer. He read the displays. "It's confirmed," he said with an emphatic nod. "As of 1500 hours, we have a rat-cicle."

Everyone groaned, and Carter threw his pen at Max. The target ducked, and the missile hit a wall. Everyone watched as the pen rebounded in a high arc.

From where he was sitting, Crew reached up and plucked the tumbling missile out of the air. "Here you go," he said handing the pen back to Carter. "Want to try again. Maybe you'll hit something smaller than the building this time."

"Come on Max," said Rod. "We've got less than two hours before we start reanimating this rat-cicle of yours. I'm taking you out of here before someone does you an injury."

"You've got that right," said Carter with an impressive scowl. "He's definitely on my hit list."

Laughter followed Rod and Max as they left the lab. Carter, Emma, Crew, and Xavi remained behind to monitor the chamber's readouts.

When the two hours had passed, everyone gathered around the console. This time the new technicians were at the controls, with Emma and Carter waiting nearby to assist if needed.

Rod gave an approving nod, and Crew keyed in the sequence to activate the revival process. In response, heating elements under the pad the rat was lying on began warming. The technician announced the temperature increasing inside the chamber in increments of ten degrees. Twenty minutes later the suspension mixture began transforming to liquid, then to gas. As the liquid evaporated and was drawn off, the atmospheric mixture was introduced into the chamber. The technicians, new and old, kept careful watch on the equipment readings to see if anything went outside the specified parameters.

"Gas mixture replaced," announced Crew.

"Electrical stimuli administered on schedule," added Xavi.

"How are vital signs?" asked Max.

"Pulse is good. . . . Wait! No! It's slowing . . . slowing. Respiration is almost non-existent," responded Crew.

"Add an adrenaline drip," ordered Rod.

Carter hurried over to a nearby tray and picked out a prepared syringe. The drug was injected through one of the IVs leading to the rat.

"Respiration and pulse are picking up," announced Crew. Everyone stared at the display that tracked life signs. "Getting stronger . . . stronger," chanted Xavi. "Steady."

Then a red light on the console began flashing. Seconds later the heart monitor flat-lined and respiration stopped. The rat was dead. Crew and Xavi hunched over the console in disappointment.

Emma put a hand on a shoulder of each man. She'd been standing behind the two technicians, watching them work. "Don't stress it," she told them as they looked up at her. "We've seen this before. Success will come from the information we get from this failure."

"Please have the computer readings from the test sent over to the main system," Rod instructed.

Xavi straightened and began entering the commands for the transfer routines.

Rod turned to Crew. "Mr. Chen, send the rat for an autopsy," he said. "We'll need the reason for death in the system by 0800 tomorrow."

"Got it, boss," the tech replied. He left his chair and walked over to begin unsealing the chamber.

"We'll plan on meeting in the conference room tomorrow to examine the results of this test," Rod announced. "Rather, make it at 0900." The scientist beckoned to Max, and they left the lab area.

"You don't seem too broken up over the test," observed Max as they walked the corridor outside the lab. "Was this setback expected?"

Rod gave a slight shrug. "Pretty much," he replied. "Anytime parameters are changed, different responses or results must be expected. The reports we get from this test will help determine what went wrong."

That evening Rod and Max had supper together. When they'd finished eating and Max had retired for the night, Rod went to the facilities observation gallery, hoping he'd be able to meet Tali. But after staring at the lunar landscape, Earth, and stars for half an hour he learned that her shift with the reactor wouldn't end for hours.

The next morning Rod and Max met with their staff to review the results of the failed test. They analyzed and questioned each bit of information in the step-by-step process used for the previous experiments. Hours later, when every detail of each report had been reviewed and a plan created, they went back to the chamber room for the next test.

Another rat was readied and strapped into the chamber. The vessel was sealed, and the process continued as before. Rod turned to Emma. "Remember, reduce the amount of Terodine to eighty-five CCs."

Terodine was a derivative of the active agent discovered in bacteria found a mile deep in Antarctica ice. It acted upon the body to protect each cell from being damaged by extreme sub-zero temperatures. With it, treated cells wouldn't rupture when frozen. Earlier tests revealed that an overdose of the drug resulted in weakening, rather than protecting, the cells of the vital organs in test subjects. The autopsy on the dead rat showed the heart had collapsed as its cells ruptured.

Emma nodded without looking up from her controls. She confirmed that all the parameters for the test had already been entered into the system. Then, on Rod's order, she initiated the process to suspend the subject.

The process continued as outlined with the drugs and atmospheric mixtures administered. Then the cryogenic chamber's temperature was lowered to suspension levels, where the gases liquefied and then froze. The timer was set, and technicians followed the readings shown on their monitors. Two hours after suspension had been confirmed the process was reversed. The temperature rose, and the suspension mixture bled off. This time the rat lived.

When the news of the first successful low gravity test reached NASA headquarters, the first phase for the colonization of Mars was put in motion. While the tests continued several drone ships, filled with enough supplies and equipment to accommodate fifty people for two years, left orbit for Mars. Once there they would remain in orbit until boarded and emptied by the colonists who arrived in the *Mars One*. Other shipments were scheduled to follow in six-month increments.

NASA anticipated that the supplies wouldn't be orbiting Mars longer than three years. That's how long it was expected to prove out the suspension concept, finish the colony ship, and travel to the red planet. In fact, a rough framework of the ship had been placed in geosynchronous orbit over the Copernicus facility.

The suspension project began the longer-term tests, which created lots of free time for Rod's people. But that had been anticipated. Everyone in the project was given side jobs in the observatory.

Rod watched as the engineer unrolled the schematics on the conference table. A mischievous grin crossed his lips as a thought came to him.

"What're you grinning for?" Max asked.

Rod grinned even more at his friend and gestured at the engineer.

"Him?" Max asked. "What about him?'

By this time, the object of their conversation had the schematics flat on the metal table with the corners held down with magnets. "He's a rocket scientist," Rod explained. "Literally!"

Max shook his head in disgust. "That is so bad. I can see you've been spending way too much time with my little sister."

The sound of a throat being cleared cut the conversation short, and both men turned to face Westin Chandra, the lead engineer for the *Mars One*. "Sorry," the two men chorused.

Wes nodded and pointed at the schematics. "This is the general plan for the *Mars One*," he announced. He held up an artist's representation of the spaceship. "This is what the finished product will look like."

"That definitely looks better than what's in orbit now," commented Rod.

"It'll take us eighteen to twenty-four months to get there from what we have now," Wes replied as he put the picture on the table next to the schematics. "That's assuming the current economic problem on Earth doesn't create supply issues. As we construct the ship and include your chambers, we need your input."

The engineer paused and gave a little chuckle. "Sorry about that," he said. "I'm better with equipment than people. I'm telling you something you already know."

"No problem, Wes," Rod replied. "Let's get this briefing started."

"If you'll come closer," Wes said, "you can see the ship's layout."

The two men moved up to the table, and the engineer began pointing out the details of the ship.

At the stern of the ship sat the propulsion units with the control room in the nose. Next to the drives was the shuttle bay. Even though there was extensive shielding against the radiation emitted by the drives, the designers wanted an additional safety margin in case of a defect in the shielding. The space of the bay would provide additional insulation for the crew and passengers. Next came the cargo bays for supplies and equipment, rooms where the suspension chambers would be placed, and then the crew quarters. These quarters were being provided for when the crew was awake.

"Because of the travel time and the need to conserve supplies it's anticipated that everyone will be in suspension during the transit to Mars," Wes stated. "NASA intends to place the crew and colonists in chambers while the ship is in orbit around the moon and then wake them when the ship reaches Mars. That means the *Mars One* will be guided by its computers. Once on the way, any course corrections will be made by the internal systems, assisted by tracking personnel from the control center in Houston." He gave a confident nod. "Just like the exploration robots of the late twentieth century.

"Every system will be strenuously evaluated prior to installation and launch," the engineer added. "There are redundancies in place in the event that a system fails. If something goes down, a replacement system will be online in nanoseconds." He held out his hands. "With the crew and colonists in suspension, our systems will be able to handle any situation that arises."

Rod stared at the schematics for a few minutes, then looked over at Wes. "What about contingency plans to wake the crew during the flight?" he asked.

"Excuse me?" The engineer's confusion was evident.

"You haven't mentioned anything about reviving any of the crew during the transit," Rod rephrased.

Wes looked at the scientist for a minute before replying. "Is that necessary?" he wondered.

"I think it is," Rod replied. "No system designed by men can account for every problem that arises." He smiled. "Only God can do that. We need to have an option that will revive the crew during transit. It can be initiated by the control crew in Houston or by the computer if communication with control is lost for a specified period." He shrugged. "Or if something happens to the ship that isn't accounted for in its programming.

"We need to remember that the farther the ship travels from Earth, the longer the communication lag. For the people on board the ship to survive, we need the option to revive them while in transit in the event of a problem."

Wes stared at the schematics as he considered the request then looked at Rod to ask again, "Are you sure this's really necessary?"

Rod didn't hesitate but gave a succinct answer. "Yes! It doesn't impact the construction of the ship, so it won't disrupt the schedule. It's more of a software issue."

The engineer shrugged. "All right." He made some notes on a tablet, then looked at Rod. "As you say, it's a software issue. I'll get the programmers working on it. They'll probably want to talk with you to get a feel for what you've got in mind."

"I'll be glad to meet with them," Rod replied. Max nodded his agreement.

"Good," said Wes. "Anything else?" he wondered. When Rod shook his head, he turned to the next schematic. "This's what we have in mind for the chamber area."

Rod's project continued, with the tests getting longer. Most of the tests were successful. Some weren't. To confirm the effect of the amount of Terodine administered, the test animals were dissected after each failed test so the vital organs could be examined. Rod and his people spent hours reviewing what went right and what went wrong.

When there was a break in the testing, and when he wasn't needed for consulting on the *Mars One*, Rod would take Tali to the observation dome. They'd sit on a couch and watch the ship being assembled. From the bulky, angular shape, it was easy to see that the ship was being constructed for utility and not for beauty or aerodynamic performance.

Eight months after the first successful test, Rod and Tali were in the observation gallery looking at Earth as it hung like a jewel in a black setting. Off to one side the partially completed ship was visible. Phase Three, the phase for testing suspension on humans, was due to start in the next few weeks.

In an exercise of faith by NASA, cryogenic chambers for the ship's crew and colonists had been constructed during the earlier tests' slack time. But none had been installed, leaving the chamber area of the *Mars One* a shell. Once Rod proved that the process worked on humans, NASA would place the chambers in the ship.

After watching the catapult launch components for the ship into orbit for twenty minutes, Rod broke the silence. "Did you hear the latest from home?" he asked.

Tali looked over at him. "Which news?" she wondered. "The disaster that is South Africa, the world-wide economic depression, the riots in cities across the world, or that earthquake in India that killed tens of thousands of people." The engineer shrugged her shoulders.

"It is related to the economy and South Africa. I'm talking about the report on the president's latest Cabinet meeting."

Tali shook her head. "That's politics," she said. "I ignore that stuff." Then the engineer gave her companion an inquiring look.

"Well," said Rod, "it seems that an unlikely coalition of business and union leaders have been lobbying to have President Thorsen rescind the sanctions on South Africa. Several Cabinet members agree with them. Those Cabinet members have expressed their conviction to the president that after the sanctions were lifted the return of the metals into circulation would jumpstart the world's economy. According to the news report, the meeting went for hours."

Tali gave a little chuckle. "I bet that was fun. Did that news report say if there was a decision and what it was?"

"It was a pithy soundbite," Rod replied. "The president is quoted as saying that civil rights trump the dollar."

"I guess that ended that discussion," commented Tali.

"That it did," chuckled Rod then glanced at his watch. "It's getting late. We'd better go to the party, or our reputations will be shot."

Tali looked over and gave him a mischievous smile. "It just depends on what your reputation is."

"What does that mean?" Rod asked.

"The guilty flee when none pursue," Tali replied.

Hand in hand and laughing, they left the observation dome. In the morning those who would be running the test at the Nevada base would leave for the trans-lunar ferry.

The two people found the room where the party was being held without any problems. All they had to do was go where the noise was the loudest.

Cries welcomed Rod and Tali when they walked through the door. Max moved through the crowd of astronomers, technicians, and engineers to hand a packet of fruit punch to his sister. "You've monopolized Tali for too long," he said to Rod. "It's my turn now."

"I can be gracious," said Rod, "since you'll be gone tomorrow, and she'll be all mine."

Max snorted. "That's comforting. I guess that's my cue to ask what your intentions are toward my sister."

"You have a lot to say about intentions," argued Rod. "You're going to be flying into Las Vegas. There'll be wide open skies, grass, palm trees, rain, wind, and slot machines. While you're enjoying all that, we'll be slaving away up here making sure the *Mars One* is ready to fly."

Wiping an imaginary tear from an eye, Max smiled. "I'm touched," he said. "But if past events are predictors of future activity, the techs will be doing all the work. You'll be making passes at my sister."

"Hello," said Tali, holding up a hand to interrupt the banter. "I'm still here, and I might have something to say about what happens." She gave Max a little jab in the ribs. "Maybe you should ask what my intentions are."

Rod motioned to the drinks Max and Tali were holding. "I think now's a good time for me to find something to eat and drink."

"Coward," replied Max, but Rod laughed and headed off through the crowd.

The next day Rod and Tali were in the Rover Bay to give Max, Emma, and Crew a sendoff. Tali gave Max a peck on the cheek, along with a hug. "Remember," she admonished, "take care of yourself, and don't lose your money in Vegas. Mom wants you to buy her a new car."

"I don't think I'll have much chance to lose any money," replied Max and gave a nod of his head at Rod. "Your boyfriend here's arranged things so I can't leave the test site. I'll be too busy."

Tali gave him an impish grin. "What makes you think that was Rod's idea?" she asked.

"Whoa," interrupted Rod, holding up his hands. "Don't get me in the middle of this family fight. Bad things happen to people who get caught in a crossfire."

"Transit for the MLB is now available," said a voice over the intercom, interrupting the conversation.

The trio looked up in reflex to the announcement. Rod slapped his friend on the back and reminded him once again to avoid dropping his paycheck in Vegas.

Tali gave Max another hug. "I'll miss you," she said.

Max turned to Rod. "A year or so ago you asked me why I didn't tell you about Tali. Remember?" he asked.

"Yes?" said Rod.

"And I said I had told you everything? Well, I lied." Max gave a quick glance at Tali. "She cheats."

"She cheats?" repeated Rod.

"Max," warned Tali, moving toward her brother. He began to edge for the Rover.

"She cheats in games," Max said. "Board games, cards, you name it. She has to win. She even cheats when she fights."

Before Tali could retaliate, the final call for the MLB was given. Max gave a final wave, then hurried over to his ride and climbed in.

After being ushered out of the Rover Bay Rod and Tali hurried to the view windows. With a sense of loneliness, they watched the Rover leave the bay and disappear in the darkness.

After a long day working on the chambers for the *Mars One* and monitoring the latest test, Rod lay on his bed watching the news feed from home. A reporter stared at the camera as he thanked the news anchor for the introduction. "The situation in South Africa has grown worse," said the man as he began his report from London. "In the face of universal sanctions, the government has become more intractable. Reports smuggled out of the country indicate the violence is escalating. We've come into possession of video showing some of what's been happening in that war-torn country."

As the reporter continued his narration, the image shifted to show an inferno consuming entire blocks of houses and buildings. "Our sources claim government forces are burning townships occupied by rival tribes. It's reported that the South African military surrounds a targeted population center to prevent any of the inhabitants from escaping. When the encircling cordon is in place fires are set and the town, village, or city is incinerated. Any inhabitant trying to flee being burned alive is hit with flamethrowers or is cut down with machine guns."

The reporter returned to the screen. "There are other reports that population centers aligned with the rebels have been attacked with nerve gas. A government spokesman denies government forces have been employing these measures to suppress anti-government activity. It's his assertion that the rebel forces are guilty of burning townships and massacring populations and then placing the blame on the government."

There was a pause before the reporter added, "With the international sanctions now in place and the retaliatory South African embargo, we cannot confirm any report of atrocities committed by either side. The video you've been watching was provided by the rebels, and they claim the fires were set by government forces. I remind you again that we cannot confirm or refute these allegations."

The news anchor returned to the screen, thanking the reporter, then the news turned to the world's economy. The worldwide depression was deepening. Hundreds of millions of people were out of work, with suicides increasing. Whole countries in Central and South American, Asia, and the South Pacific were disintegrating into chaos. Several countries in Europe were on the verge of collapsing. President Berezin reiterated the Russian Federation's intention to continue its efforts to increase the mining and refining of the exotic metals needed for the world economy. Analysts applauded Russia's announcement but doubted the Russians could move quickly enough to replace the South African exports.

Rod gave a snort of disgust and turned off the screen. It seemed the world was falling apart. At least the economic problems hadn't adversely impacted his project yet. All his equipment had been made prior to the embargo and depression. He keyed on his reading light, pulled out his scriptures, and turned off the overhead lights. He knew there'd be something positive in the words of God.

A week and a half after Max and his people had left the moon, Rod received word that they had reached the Nevada test site. Excitement spread through the lunar suspension staff because the final phase of the project could begin.

To coordinate their efforts, Rod called a video conference with the two teams to consult on the agenda for the next round of tests. The lunar group met in its conference room. Max and his technicians were likewise gathered in a similar conference room on Earth around a similar monitor. This time medical personnel who were charged with the care of the subjects were involved and present at both tables.

"I'm glad you and your people made it Max," Rod said.

"That we did," replied Max a couple of seconds later. "It's taking some effort to readjust to normal gravity. Just walking is exhausting."

"I'm not looking forward to experiencing that," said Rod, then held out his hands. "We don't have much time, so we'd better get busy. Max, is your equipment in place and ready?"

"We confirmed that the day we arrived," Max replied. "I also spoke with our volunteers, and they're ready as well."

"Good," said Rod. "We've done the same here."

He paused to glance around at his people both on the moon and at the NTS, then spoke. "Because we're starting the human tests, we must be extremely careful. While we've done everything we can to make the process as safe as possible for our volunteers, there's always a risk involved. Our subjects are aware of the risks involved and have signed the waivers required by the government.

"I don't want these people endangered because we tried to cut corners or take shortcuts." While he continued his instructions heads nodded. "If there's even a hint of something wrong with a piece of equipment, I want it pulled from service immediately," said Rod and ticked off an item on his checklist. "Mark it as bad and don't use."

"We may have a problem with that," Max said. "When we arrived at the test site, I checked our inventories and found shortages in several components."

Rod looked up from his pad to stare at the monitor. "Will this prevent or slow our testing schedule?" he asked.

"I don't think so," Max replied after a moment's thought. "Of course, that's assuming the items we have in inventory are good. But if there's been a problem with quality control during manufacturing. . ." he shrugged to finish the sentence.

"I see," said Rod. "When we started the lunar testing, we were supposed to have priority in supply. Why haven't our orders been filled?"

"It isn't because our supply officer hasn't tried," Max replied, holding out his hands. "Or that our suppliers are deliberately trying to short us. But with the problems caused by South Africa, there aren't enough raw materials to manufacture what we need. I guess the supply people put priority in getting the supplies up to the moon, and we came in second," he explained. "We've been promised our backorders will be filled in the next two months."

Rod nodded his understanding. "Since it takes so long to get anything up here, the items we needed were laid in before we arrived on the moon.

"Make sure you have one or two good spares of the vital components on hand. Those that fail will have to be reworked, calibrated, and returned to inventory. They can be replaced when the rest of your inventory arrives."

The next day began with Rod, Carter, and Xavi going over the equipment to be used in the upcoming test, looking for any signs of defects. Medical people occupied the room along with the regular suspension staff. While the technicians examined the suspension equipment, the doctor and nurse gave a final examination of the test subject, went over the drug supplies, and instruments, they'd brought with them.

Meticulous care was taken when the technicians checked the chamber designed and built for the human test. In the last stages of a multi-level diagnostic, a red light on one of the monitors began flashing.

"Dr. Carue, we've got an error in the control panel of the chamber," called Carter.

"It could be that a circuit card is loose," Xavi suggested. "Something may have been bumped as we brought the chamber in."

"Possibly," Rod replied. "That's as good a place to start as any."

Walking around to the backside of the chamber console, Rod watched as Xavi removed the back panel. He knelt, pulled a circuit card, reseated it, then checked with Carter to see if there was any change in the status light. When there wasn't, he moved to the next circuit card.

On the fourth card checked the item seemed to come away more easily than the others. After reseating the card, Xavi stood and leaned over the console. "I think that was the one," he announced.

"Lights now show normal," Carter agreed.

"It may have been just a loose card," Rod said. "But to be sure we've found all the problems, restart the test that failed."

It took another hour before Rod was satisfied that everything was in working order. He turned to Xavi and said, "Okay, it looks like we're ready here. Have we heard anything from Max?"

"Nothing yet," replied Xavi from his position at the communications station.

"Is the link to the NTS open?" Rod wondered.

Xavi nodded. "It's been open since we began our diagnostics," he replied. "But I haven't received anything."

"Send a message down the line," ordered Rod. "Let Max know we're ready and ask him when they can begin."

A moment later, the monitor which had been showing the test site logo, shifted to show Max. "It's about time," the man said. "We've been waiting to hear from you for an hour!"

"You've been ready for an hour?" asked Rod. "Why didn't you let us know?"

"We didn't want to rush you Loonies before you were ready."

"Loonies?" questioned Rod.

Max shrugged. "Emma came up with that," he said. "It's quicker than saying moon-people, lunarians, or lunar personnel."

Rod gave a little chuckle. "Whatever," he said. He checked the time, then glanced at Carter and Xavi. "Let's bring in our first volunteer and begin."

At the Nevada site, Emma helped a man into the prepared chamber. Carter did the same with the volunteer on the moon. The two men were wearing comfortable sweat suits. In both locations a nurse inserted an IV into the subject's veins. Then sensors to monitor the life signs were placed on the volunteer and activated. When it was confirmed that both subjects were ready, the chambers on both bases were sealed. The doctors watching the medical monitors checked to see if the subjects' vital life signs were registering as expected, then nodded their approval. Rod glanced over his master console to confirm that data was being received on both subjects.

"Nevada subject is ready," reported Emma, her face showing on the monitor.

"Copernicus subject is ready," repeated Carter from his place at the console.

"Two-hour test," ordered Rod.

Carter and Emma calibrated timers set in their consoles, then announced their readiness. Rod glanced over his master console, checking the data being reported one last time. Satisfied with what he was seeing the scientist said, "The test begins now," and pushed a button set in his console. The anesthetic drug began flowing into the test subjects' veins through the IV lines.

"Let's remember procedure, people," said Rod.

"Copernicus patient is asleep," announced Carter moments later. "Life signs are stable. Suspension drug is being administered." Five seconds later Emma's report from Nevada echoed that of Carter. Monitors showed that the vital signs of both subjects were slowing.

After the prescribed length of time to ensure the subjects were prepared for the deep freeze, the suspension gas mixture was introduced to the chamber. With people clustered around consoles in both locations watching the temperature in the chambers began to lower.

Two hours after confirmed suspension, the timer chimed to signify the end of the test. Rod pushed the button to begin the reanimation process in both places. Once again, everyone gathered around the monitors to watch for any sign of trouble. The temperature increased and the suspension mixture went from ice to liquid to gas and was bled off to be replaced with an oxygen mixture. At the appropriate time and temperature, a light electric shock was administered to get the subject's system started again.

"Vitals are coming up," called Carter. "On strength and per schedule." Seconds later Emma gave the same report.

"Medical teams stand by," ordered Rod.

Excitement and anticipation seemed to increase with the life signs. Then the chambers unsealed and opened. The doctor and nurse at both bases hurried over to begin their preliminary examinations.

Max appeared on the television monitor, "Well?" he asked. "How'd we do?"

"It appears both subjects are alive and well," Rod said. "But I want these men given an extensive examination before I declare this test a success. I'm particularly interested in learning how their vital organs fared. We'll follow our established process." He gave a wry look at his friend. "Without the dissection, of course," the scientist added. "After we have the medical results and review all the reports, we can schedule the next test."

Max nodded, and the screen went blank.

It was five minutes before the lunar test subject stood and left the chamber room with the medical people. "Let's finish up here and go celebrate," the scientist said.

Carter nodded again, a smile almost splitting his face. "I assume you want the reports sent to the system, as well?"

"You assume right."

CHAPTER 5

Everard Thorsen, President of the United States, nodded his thanks to his secret service escort as he entered the Cabinet room of the White House. Ignoring the sound of people coming to their feet, he walked to his place at the head of the conference table. "Be seated," he said and took his own seat.

While everyone settled back into their chairs, the president glanced around the table, mentally noting those who were present. On his left were the four uniformed members of the Joint Chiefs of Staff. Admiral Nboko Kawami represented the Navy. General Tim Matsumo was there for the Air Force and his persona as chairman of the Joint Chiefs, General Aaron Sanderson for the Army, and Mark "Pit Bull" Jeffers for the Marines. Secretary of State, Lisa Edgars, sat on the other side of the table with Martin Harold, director of the Department of Commerce.

"Thank you for coming," Thorsen said. He turned to Edgars and Harold. "I've read your latest reports and your recommendations regarding our nation's situation. Before I make any decisions about those recommendations, I want to hear if you have any further information. I've asked the Joint Chiefs to be here so I can get their perspective on our predicament. Let's start with the economy. Director Harold, if you would."

"Yes, Mr. President," said Martin Harold. He stood and held out his hands. "As I stated in my report, the domestic economic situation is dire and getting worse. It isn't as bad as what's happening worldwide, but it is serious." The director glanced down at a tablet on the conference table in front of him, checking on the information shown there. Then he shook his head and looked up. He already knew what was on the pad. "As you know, our manufacturing sector has come to a complete halt; unemployment is over fifty percent and growing. We have rioting in all our major cities."

"It's hard to miss the nightly news reports of cities burning, people looting, and people being killed, Martin," Thorsen said softly. "I have other reports from Homeland Security that Los Angeles is one-third rubble, San Francisco is one-quarter destroyed, New York almost half gone. The list goes on. The question is: can we recover?"

Martin shook his head and replied. "Not without the South African embargo lifted and the metals flowing."

"What about the Russians?" Thorsen asked. "Aren't they increasing their production of the metals?"

"They are," was the director's immediate reply. "But it's not going to be enough, Mr. President. The Russians are good students of history. They've studied the oil cartel of the Middle East from the twentieth century and assimilated those lessons."

"Which means?" the president prompted.

"The Russians may increase their production slightly, but they're going to keep the supplies of the necessary resources scarce. That will keep prices elevated and maximize Russia's revenues."

"There's a military reason for the Russians to keep production below the demand, Mr. President," spoke up General Matsumo. "The Russians must be aware of our military needs. Most of our sophisticated weapons have components dependent on rare metals. By keeping the supply of those metals scarce, they reduce our supply of replacement parts, and that weakens our military forces." The chairman of the Joint Chiefs held out his hands, palms up. "All they have to do is wait for our supplies to diminish sufficiently, and then they can attack. We won't be able to stop them."

Thorsen nodded. "What's the state of our military right now, General?"

General Matsumo glanced at his electronic pad for a moment. "With the economy in turmoil and unemployment at catastrophic levels, we have an overabundance of volunteers. We're able to pick the best of the volunteers. We could have our military tripled in size within weeks. Our current size is being limited by our budget." The other three officers nodded their agreement.

Matsumo scrolled down to the next page on his tablet and continued his report. "With the manpower issue taken care of our main concern is for the supply of vital components. Prior to the current difficulties, we had an inventory of parts that was expected to last for three years. That inventory is being drawn down due to the wear and tear of normal operations. When the parts are gone our equipment stops, and we become target practice instead of a fighting force."

"Do you have contingency plans ready to seize the resources we need?" asked Thorsen.

"Is that really necessary, Mr. President?" broke in Lisa Edgars. "Shouldn't we continue with diplomacy before entertaining military action?"

General Jeffers glared at the secretary of state. "Having plans doesn't mean they'll be acted upon, Madame Secretary," he said in a raspy voice that was almost a growl. "It's only prudent to have plans in place in the event they're needed."

"Thank you, General," said Matsumo, "I'm sure the secretary is aware of that." Jeffers muttered his apologies but didn't look apologetic.

President Thorsen broke up the exchange. "The contingency plans General?"

"Yes, sir," Matsumo replied. "We do have plans in place. They were developed several years ago when it became clear how important these metals were. I've ordered them updated for today's situation."

"Sir," said Edgars, "I must protest. I know you're aware that South Africa has nuclear weapons. We can't afford to back that government into a corner where it feels it has no choice but to go nuclear." General Jeffers leaned forward to respond once again but Admiral Kawami beat him to it. "I don't think South Africa is the nation we should worry about backing into a corner, Madam Secretary," the Black officer said. His deep voice was almost melodic compared to that of the marine. "Our military is weakening, and the Russians are showing signs of becoming more aggressive as they conduct more military exercises. Our economy is in shambles; our cities are overwhelmed with rioters. I would think that would be your focus, not a country that burns its people alive or uses outlawed weapons of mass destruction on those same people."

"I don't think," began Edgars hotly but was interrupted.

"That's enough!" ordered the president. He stood and leaned over the conference table with both hands on its polished mahogany surface for support. "We have enough problems without fighting amongst ourselves."

When everyone quieted down, he continued. "I've heard and read enough that I've made my decision." He looked around the table at each person to ensure that he had undivided attention. "This is what I want completed before our next meeting.

"I want a plan developed to invade South Africa and seize the mines, stockpiles, and refineries with a minimum loss of life and property on both sides." He glanced over at the Joint Chiefs. General Matsumo looked back at the president and acknowledged the order.

Thorsen held up a hand to forestall Secretary Edgar's coming protest. "I know what you're going to say, Lisa," he said. "But I want all options available to me. Military action is a stick. I'm going to have you send a note to President Titembo for the carrot. Let him know I'm willing to rescind all sanctions and embargoes levied by the United States government. I will also request that all nations with embargos do the same."

He gave the secretary of state a stern look before continuing. "Impress upon President Titembo the fact that failure to resume exports of the needed materials could," he paused, searching for the right words, "have serious ramifications for his nation and the world."

With his instructions given President Thorsen took one last look at the people around the table, then left the room.

South African President Oscar Titembo stood in front of the picture window of his office, staring at the view of Pretoria that spread out before him. He looked over the skyscrapers and streets filled with people going about their business as he considered the situation, he found himself in. His little nation on the southern tip of Africa had the world arrayed against it.

Titembo gave a slight shake of his head. All this trouble because people in faraway lands were dictating to the South African people how to run their country. It was intolerable! When the United States announced its sanctions and recalled its diplomats, there was only one action available to South Africa: its own embargo.

Now, with the world's economy in free fall, people and nations were getting desperate, looking for a way out. A slight smile appeared on the president's lips. Let the other nations threaten and plead for the resources of his people. If they wanted what his people had, they'd have to do what his people—what he wanted.

The South African glanced at his platinum, diamond-encrusted Swiss watch. A special envoy from the President of the United States had flown into the Pretoria International Airport an hour ago and was expected to arrive at the presidential palace any time now. It was rumored that the ambassador carried an overture of peace that would persuade South Africa to resume its shipments of metals. "Like that'll happen," he thought. "The Americans need to be taught a lesson."

As if on cue, the intercom alert sounded. Titembo turned away from the window and walked through the sparse but expensively furnished and decorated room to his desk. Reaching across the cluttered surface, he pushed the accept button on the intercom and asked, "Yes?"

"Ambassador MacDonald from the United States of America is here for his appointment, Mr. President," was the immediate response.

Titembo moved behind his desk to sit in the throne-like chair made of ivory, teak wood, and silk, then said, "He can come in."

Seconds later the office door opened to reveal his presidential aide. "Ambassador MacDonald, of the United States of America," the man announced and stepped aside.

MacDonald moved through the door and walked up to Titembo's desk, where he stopped at the protocol decreed yard away. The South African foreign minister followed the ambassador into the room and walked over to stand on the right side of the president. The aide closed the door then stood behind the ambassador, waiting for instructions.

The ambassador inclined his head in greeting and said, "Mr. President."

Titembo didn't rise to greet the envoy but remained in his seat. "Mr. Ambassador," he said, "I've been told you have a message for me from President Thorsen."

In response, MacDonald opened his briefcase and extracted a letter, which he offered to President Titembo. If the ambassador was affected by the South African's diplomatic slight, he gave no indication.

The aide rushed forward, took the envelope from the ambassador, and handed it to his president.

Titembo looked at the envelope for a moment, examining the presidential seal on the back and how it was addressed. Then the South African took an ivory handled knife from the middle drawer of his desk, slit the envelope, and removed its contents. He leaned back in his chair and read the several paragraphs printed on the expensive paper. No one spoke as the president considered the contents.

Five minutes later he moved forward in his chair and retrieved the envelope from the desktop. He gave a little smile as he carefully folded and replaced the letter. "Your President Thorsen is requesting that my nation," he looked up at the envoy, "that South Africa, a nation ruled by a clique of bigots and criminals, as he so eloquently put it rescue the world."

"Do you have a response, Mr. President?" MacDonald asked.

Titembo considered for a moment, then nodded. "I will comply with President Thorsen's request," he said as he continued to hold the envelope in both hands.

The foreign minister stiffened at the announcement and turned to protest. Titembo noticed the movement, looked over at his foreign minister, and waved the man back.

"I shall do this thing if...." Titembo began again, then gave a dramatic pause as he held up the envelope in one hand. "South Africa will comply with your wishes if South Africa receives its due, Mr. Ambassador," Titembo resumed turning his attention back to MacDonald. "Our status and importance entitles. . . no, requires that South Africa be given a permanent seat on the United Nation's Security Council. We must have the same veto power as the United States, which leads this unwarranted attack on South Africa's sovereignty. That is my condition to resume exports and rescue the world."

The common room for the Copernicus observatory was crowded. An announcement from the White House had been made that President Thorsen would be addressing a joint session of Congress at 1400 hours that day. This speech was billed by the news media as the most important event of the century. As a result, every chair in the room was taken, and people lined the walls. Since the suspension project was between tests, Rod and Tali had gotten there early and were sitting at a table with Xavi and Carter.

While everyone but the on-duty personnel were crowded into the room, no one was talking. Their attention was on the large monitor taking up most of one wall showing the President of the United States move into position behind a podium. "President Thorsen is about to address a joint session of Congress," announced the news anchor covering the speech.

"That's stating the obvious," commented Xavi drily. "The networks have been hyping this speech all day."

Rod waved for the technician to be quiet as the anchor continued speaking. ". . . reported to cover the nation's current economic situation and South Africa." There was a pause, then the man spoke in hushed tones. "Everard Thorsen, president of the United States." The camera closed in on the president.

Thorsen began his speech by thanking the Speaker of the House and the Senate majority leader for allowing him to address both Houses of Congress. When he finished the platitudes, he began to rehash the the economic woes facing the nation and world.

After twenty minutes of not hearing anything new, Rod turned to Tali. "Would you like me to get you a juice?" he asked.

Tali shook her head, motioning to the monitor. "Quiet!" she hissed.

The scientist turned his attention back to the screen in time to hear President Thorsen say, ". . . reason for my request to address both Houses of Congress today. We can no longer sit by and let the atrocities in South Africa continue. Nor can we allow the current economic situation in our nation to remain. I have made a reasonable offer to President Titembo, of South Africa, to resolve the differences between our two nations."

With a sorrowful face, Thorsen shook his head. "Unfortunately, his response was not constructive and leaves me with no other recourse." He took a deep breath, squared his shoulders, and glanced around the packed hall of Congress. "In my capacity as president of the United States and commander-in-chief of its military, I request that this august body of people's representatives vote for a declaration of war against the nation of South Africa."

"What?" The question burst out of Rod as he sat upright in his seat. He was echoed by others in the room. "Did he really . . .?"

Tali interrupted the scientist. "Quiet! There's more!"

"We will not be alone in this endeavor," said Thorsen. "I have been in contact with our allies, and they have expressed their support for this action. In fact, there is a reason I am here at this unusual hour of the day requesting this action. The prime minister of the United Kingdom, Rebekkah Brown, is addressing her Parliament as I address you. She is asking her people to rally with our forces to bring an end to this state of world affairs."

Thorsen paused for a moment as he looked at the camera. It was as if he was looking past the equipment to the people watching his speech. "To the American people, I say, 'Hold on!' You have endured many trials and much suffering. These problems are not of your making, but you've felt their effects.

"We have a military struggle in front of us, but it will end, as will our economic trials. We face a time of strife and turmoil but have courage. We will prevail and emerge from this trial stronger, more united than before. As to my request, you and I await the decision of Congress. God bless you, and God bless the USA. Thank you."

The sounds of clapping coming from the halls of Congress were muted as the announcer came back on to recap the president's speech.

"Oh great!" Rod complained. "Now he's going to tell us what we've just heard and what it means for us."

Tali ignored Rod as she stared at the news anchor on the monitor. "War," she said. Her posture reflected the sadness in her voice. "Are we really going to war with South Africa?" The engineer faced Rod looking for reassurance.

"It sounds like it," Rod replied. "I don't see why Congress won't vote out the declaration."

"What'll happen to us?" she wondered and turned to look at the monitor again. A panel of experts had taken over and was dissecting the president's speech. "Will they evacuate the moon and the orbital stations?"

The scientist shook his head after a moment's thought. "No, I don't think so," he said. "This'll be a localized fight, mainly in South Africa. If there was a threat of the conflict becoming worldwide, I could see the government bringing us home."

Admiral Sinclair Barton, task force commander for the Allied Nations Expeditionary Force, was on the flag bridge of the super aircraft carrier *Enterprise*. He was careful in what he said and did, as this scene was being broadcast worldwide. With a camera crew and pool reporter on the bridge, it required effort to concentrate on his task and not play to the camera.

Stepping up to the plot Barton checked the formation of his fleet. His force was comprised of naval and ground elements from the United States, the United Kingdom, Germany, Italy, France, Spain, and Japan. It had taken a year since the declaration of war had been voted out to plan this operation and assemble the ships, equipment, men, and supplies.

Thirty missile destroyers and twenty submarines were screening the fleet's perimeter watching for hostile submarines. Naval intelligence had no record of South Africa acquiring or constructing submarines, but Barton wasn't going to underestimate his foe. Inside the destroyer and submarine screen were twenty-five cruisers, then fifteen battleships. At the center of this impressive amount of firepower were ten super-aircraft carriers, thirty troop transports, and forty ammunition/supply colliers.

Barton moved from the plot to the radar screen. After examining the console for a moment, he nodded. The Combat Air Patrol of forty aircraft was a hundred miles out, watching for any hostile aircraft or missile boats that could threaten his fleet. A Sentry control aircraft with its powerful radar circled high above the fleet, ready to direct the CAP to any threat.

As he contemplated his fleet and the firepower it contained, he smiled grimly. If he were the commander waiting to engage a force this large, he'd be in a very deep, very armored bunker waiting for the sledgehammer to fall.

"Coming up on zero-hour, Admiral," announced Captain Gareth Smith-Hyde, his chief of staff, from his station.

"Status of the fleet?" the admiral asked.

"All ships report ready," responded Smith-Hyde. "Do you have any orders?"

"We'll proceed as planned," said Barton as he settled into the admiral's chair.

Ten minutes later, at the stroke of 0500 on May 6, the preparatory barrage of missiles and artillery shells began. Paratroopers flown in from Diego Garcia dropped behind the holocaust on the beaches to cut the defenders' communications. Others parachuted in to capture the mining and refining sites for the exotic metals, since there would be no point to the war if the allies captured destroyed facilities and collapsed mines.

The plan devised by the Pentagon didn't go as outlined. Battle plans seldom did. The attempt to capture the mines and refineries had been anticipated and defenses prepared without the allies knowing. Most of the paratroopers were cut to pieces as they descended. Those who survived to reach the ground tried to regroup and complete their missions but were wiped out by the defending forces. There were no survivors to be taken prisoner.

Two hours after it began the preparatory barrage lifted, and landing craft headed for the beach. Defenders in hardened positions launched missiles and fired artillery against the invaders. Vicious dogfights covered the sky as allied aircraft moved to defend against South African fighters and bombers attempting to harass the support fleet and hinder the flow of supplies and men to the beaches.

It was the end of Rod's shift keeping watch on the suspension equipment. Carter had just entered the suspension room and was checking the status of the equipment. "Is there anything I need to be aware of?" the technician asked.

Rod paused his log entry and looked over at Carter. "Nothing of note," he said, then finished his entry. "I've just logged out."

Carter nodded and sat down after Rod had left the console. His fingers rattled on the keyboard for a moment before he announced, "I'm on. You're free to go."

As Rod headed for the door Carter glanced back at his boss and asked, "You going to do anything exciting during your off-shift?"

The scientist shrugged, then answered, "Nothing much. Tali's got this shift, so I'll probably go to the common room and watch the news feed with everyone else."

"Who'd have thought the South Africans would be so tough?" wondered Carter. "They've held us off that beach for two weeks now."

"Well, something's got to break," said Rod and moved for the door. "Good night. If anything unusual happens, call me."

"Of course," Carter replied. "Get a good night's sleep. I'll see you tomorrow."

"Field Marshal Orlov is here for his appointment."

The announcement came over the telephone speaker on President Berezin's desk. Anatoly closed the computer application he'd been working on and turned to face the door. "Have him come in."

A moment later the door opened, and Daman Orlov walked in. The elderly man had a full head of white hair. Even though he was over seventy he walked with a soldier's erect posture and confident stride. His uniform was immaculate and impressive. The left breast of the uniform blouse was covered with campaign service bars and medals. Orlov had risen to the supreme rank in the Russian military through a combination of skillful maneuvering and raw talent.

"Thank you for agreeing to see me on such short notice, Mr. President," the field marshal said as he came to a stop in front of Berezin's desk. He flashed a quick salute.

"You said it was important, Field Marshal," Berezin replied.

"Of course, Mr. President," Orlov replied. "I realize your time is important, so I'll be brief. We need to push the Americans!"

"And how do we do that without starting a war?" Berezin asked.

"The war is coming, and we all know it," Orlov replied. "But when it comes it'll be to our timetable."

"So how do we do it?" the president repeated. "How do we push the Americans?"

The field marshal shrugged and held out his hands. "We push the Americans through a surrogate," he replied. "We've been grooming friendly nations in the Middle East for decades. Turn Iran and Syria loose on Israel!"

Berezin pondered the suggestion for a moment then asked, "Will they do it?"

Orlov gave a light chuckle. "They've had their forces in place for a year now," he said. "The only reason there hasn't been an attack is that we've held them back."

"Can they succeed in taking out Israel?" Berezin was clearly skeptical.

The field marshal shrugged. "Who cares?" he said. "What I want our allies to do is push Israel to activate its mutual defense pact with the United States."

"Ah," was all that Berezin said. A slight smile crossed his lips, and he reached for his telephone. He pushed the button to call his aide.

"What can I do for you, Mr. President?" was the immediate response.

Berezin glanced at the general and said, "Contact Foreign Minister Duskin and have him come to my office."

At the end of three weeks of fierce fighting and high casualties the allies had gained a small beachhead. By this time, they had eliminated South African air force. During the fighting, several teams of SAS and Navy Seals found a way to move through enemy lines, where they worked to eliminate observation posts and disrupt communications. One team stumbled across the defending general's headquarters and called in an air strike. A single explosion did what weeks of fighting had failed to accomplish.

Before a new commanding general could be appointed and rushed to the front, a German armored brigade broke through the battered South African lines and moved inland. Mobile infantry poured through the breach. The defenders had no choice but to pull back to establish another defensive line or risk being enveloped and destroyed.

While the allied ground forces continued their advance, a single, stealthy cruise missile was launched from an inland missile battery. It skimmed a few hundred feet above the terrain, crossed over the advancing ANEF army and then the beachhead before anyone could react. Acting on reports from their ground forces, allied aircraft reacted to intercept the missile but were too late.

A nuclear explosion and the resulting shock wave obliterated the fleet protecting and supporting the forces that had landed. When the general commanding the allied army on the beach saw the forces arrayed against his command, the lack of air cover, and his landed supplies being depleted, he knew there was nothing else to do. A relief force couldn't reach his army in time to do any good. There was also the question of the

South African's launching another nuclear strike against the ANEF army. He sent a message to the South African commander asking for a truce.

It was the third month into the current test, and Rod and Xavi sat in the common room watching the news. Carter was back in their laboratory monitoring the suspension equipment. The three men took shifts in the chamber room as the latest test continued. Rod had established this requirement at the beginning of the longer human trials to help guarantee the safety of the human subject. So far, all their human volunteers had revived without any serious problems.

It had been a week since the Allied Nations Expeditionary Force had been routed, and now the room's monitor showed a news commentator who was interviewing a military expert.

"I guess I'll call it a day," Rod announced and stood to leave for his room. "I've got the later shift."

"Wait!" exclaimed Xavi. "Something's happening!" He pointed at the monitor, where the interviewer and guest had disappeared, and an alert banner was showing instead.

"We interrupt this program for a breaking-news bulletin," the announcer said. The scientist resumed his seat and waited, watching the monitor.

A moment later a reporter in Jerusalem appeared on the screen. "We've just received word that war has broken out in the Middle East," the woman said without preamble. "There are reports that the Russian backed regime of Syria has attacked Israel. Our network analysts tell us the Syrians have been preparing for years for this opportunity. Their Russian sponsor has equipped and trained the Syrian military to use the latest and most sophisticated Russian battlefield weapons."

The reporter vanished from the screen to be replaced by a map of northern Israel. As she continued her report graphics showed the movement of the armies she described. "Two Syrian divisions swept into Israel at dawn this morning, without warning. One army, designated by the Israelis as Army Group A, has moved to seize the Golan Heights, while Army Group B is headed for Tel Aviv. The Israeli military is racing to mobilize its reserves to reinforce the units already engaged in the fighting. All of Israel's units throughout this tiny nation of fifteen million people are on alert, watching for additional attacks from the Gaza Strip, Lebanon, and the West Bank."

The woman returned to the screen. "We will break in as new developments occur. You will now be returned to your regularly scheduled program still in progress."

Ignoring the resumed program, Xavi looked over at Rod and shook his head. "Is the world going mad?" he asked.

"It looks like it," replied Rod, also shaking his head. "But since I can't do anything about it, I'm going to bed." With that, he stood and left the common room.

It took more than a week of fierce fighting, with heavy casualties on both sides, before Israel blunted Syria's advance. Aircraft on both sides fought and burned as the two air forces attempted to assist ground maneuvers while hindering the enemy. The Golan Heights had held and was still in Israeli hands. The Israeli air force was -dropping supplies to prevent the forces there from being overrun. Syrian Army Group B had penetrated deep into Israel, almost reaching Tel Aviv before it was stopped. While the loss ratio was heavily in favor of the Israelis, the more-populous Syria could take the losses longer and easier than the less populated Israel.

As the reserves were activated, with more troops and equipment committed to the war, Israeli leaders grew worried. It wouldn't be long before they would run out of soldiers to replace those who fell in battle. The Israeli prime minister sent an emergency request for aid to the president of the United States.

Shackled with a mutual defense treaty, President Thorsen dispatched a carrier strike force, supplies, and reinforcements to aid Israel. The Americans now had two wars to supply and fight with a devastated economy.

Long before the allied invasion began, and in the face of government atrocities, large numbers of people had fled South Africa for sanctuary in the northern countries. It was during that time that the Western world had sent humanitarian aid and arms to the refugees.

When the allies broke out of their beachhead, the South African military had to pull reinforcements from wherever they could be found to prepare a second defensive line. Many of those reinforcements came from the forces guarding South Africa's northern borders.

Once the allied force had been obliterated or captured, South Africa's attention centered on rebuilding its forces and beach defenses against a second invasion. That was when the rebel tribes in exile chose to attack. They were going to reclaim their lands and exact vengeance for the people who'd been killed or tortured during Titembo's regime.

The weakened South African forces guarding the northern borders were overwhelmed on the first day. They were slaughtered to a man. Then it was the rebels' turn to massacre villages and towns as they advanced. Large numbers of people fled south to avoid torture and rape at the hands of the invading army. Knowing the South African army was adjusting to this new attack as quickly as it could, the rebels plunged headlong into their advance. There was little fear of attack or observation from the air.

As the rebel forces raced south toward Pretoria, scouts ranging ahead detected a lone, antique, single-engine high-wing spotter plane. Little attention was paid to the craft because there were no visible armaments. It appeared sluggish, unable to reach its optimum altitude, as if it were carrying a load its designers hadn't planned for. Commanders decided not to waste the few stinger missiles they had on a craft that obviously wasn't a threat. Jeering tribesmen attempted to shoot down the craft with small arms fire as it flew overhead.

Just short of the advancing army's main body, a blinding flash seared the optic nerves of those shooting at the craft. The flash was followed nanoseconds later by sun-like heat. Soldiers closest to the nuclear furnace were incinerated without being aware of their deaths. Those farther away were conscious of death as their vehicles and ammunition exploded around them. They felt the heat sear and scorch the flesh from their bodies seconds before they died. Farther away still, men who survived the blast suffered agonizing deaths from radiation sickness and burns. The rebels, or what was left of them disbanded, and fled back to the nations bordering South Africa to regroup.

General Tim Matsumo was in his office reviewing reports when the attention tone on the intercom sounded. He glanced at the desk clock his wife had given him as an anniversary present and snorted in disgust. There was never enough time. It looked like another long day, and it wasn't even 1000 hours yet. Just yesterday his wife had been complaining about him never coming home. The boys missed him, she said. With a resigned sigh, he reached over to key the acceptance. "Yes?" he asked.

"Colonel Winston is here for his appointment, sir," replied the receptionist.

"Send him in," ordered Matsumo.

A moment later the office door opened to let the colonel enter. Matsumo indicated a conversation nook to his left containing two burgundy overstuffed leather chairs. "Have a seat, Colonel," he said as he rose from his desk.

The general sat in the chair opposite Colonel Winston and looked at his chief of staff. "What have you got for me today?" he asked.

Winston leaned forward to hand the general a computer chip. "All the details are there, sir," the colonel replied. "My report covers the conflict in the Middle East and there's an update for the next invasion of South Africa. The South African report is supplemented with our latest intelligence of how our targets are being protected." He paused for a moment as he considered. "Oh, and there's a concerning report from Europe," he added.

"Europe?" asked Matsumo. "What's happening, or what does someone think may happen there?"

Winston shrugged and gestured at the chip to indicate it was all there. "The Russians are staging a large-scale war-game maneuver in western Russia near the Baltic States, Ukraine, and Belarus," Winston said.

"I seem to recall they've provided all the required notifications prior to the commencement of their maneuvers," commented Matsumo. Winston nodded. "Then what's the problem?"

The colonel gave a shrug, holding out his hands. "A German intelligence officer was studying satellite photos of the staging area for the maneuver," he replied. "He claims the Russians are mobilizing thirty percent more units than those mentioned in the official notification, most of them armored units."

"That's not unusual," commented Matsumo. "They've understated before."

"True," replied the colonel. "This officer, Lieutenant Adam Ackermann, thinks there's more to it this time. The units involved in these maneuvers comprise forty percent of Russia's Class A combat units. With the world's focus on South Africa and the Middle East, it'd be the perfect time for an attack."

"Really?" Matsumo rolled his eyes. "He thinks the Russians are going to attack Europe?"

"Yes, General," Winston replied, "He says it's a distinct possibility. Those additional armored units I mentioned contain the Russians' most powerful battle tanks."

Matsumo pondered for a few seconds. "We exercise our troops with the best equipment we have all the time," he said. Then he paused and looked at the chip in his right hand. He remembered warning President Thorsen about the Russians being tempted to be more adventurous before the first invasion. Then he shrugged as he put the chip in his right breast pocket. "I'll go over your reports in more detail," he said. "What's your opinion of Ackermann's concerns?"

Colonel Winston held out his hands again. "Who knows?" he said. "It's possible. This would be a good time for the Russians to attack. The European nations have experienced losses in the first South African invasion, as we have and are working to replace those losses."

He shook his head. "Personally, I don't think the Russians are going to attack. They know, or should know, NATO has contingency plans to use small tactical nukes to stem any breakthroughs. If there's an attack and NATO uses its nukes the Russian advance will be blunted, with its original force destroyed. At that point, the fighting would come down to a war of attrition, like World War I." He shrugged. "The Russians have more men and equipment than we do, but we've got better men and equipment."

"Okay," said Matsumo. "As I said, I'll review that report later. Tell me about Israel."

"It isn't pretty," Winston said. "When word got out that the US military was getting involved, Iran and Iraq started sending reinforcements to Syria. Jordan's staying neutral for now, as are Lebanon and Egypt. Some missiles were fired into Israel from the Gaza Strip. This time the Israelis didn't hold anything back since their existence as a people and a nation is at stake. They didn't send in ground troops, because they don't have the manpower, but their air force pounded the entire area. Tere was no advance warning for the civilians to evacuate. To collapse any tunnels the Israeli's used their own version of the mother-of-all-bomb. Since the air attacks, there have been no more missiles. I don't think the Israelis left one brick standing on another when they were done bombing. We have no idea about the casualties in the Gaza Strip, but they've got to be massive.

"There's been fierce fighting by the Consolidated Islamic Forces, that's what they're calling themselves now. The CIF has been pushed back to the Syrian border. Air strikes by Israeli jets and drones have been able to reduce the fighting ability of any of their reinforcements before they can reach the front. The Israeli force holding the Golan Heights should be relieved within the week."

"So, the Middle East is stabilizing," commented Matsumo. "That's good. Now, tell me about the upcoming invasion of South Africa."

The South Africans felt confident in their ability to defend their nation. Nevertheless, they didn't stop working to strengthen their coastal defenses. No one in the South African leadership believed the allies, let alone the United States, had given up. When intelligence agents learned of another invasion force being prepared the defenders worked harder and longer on their preparations.

A new, more powerful force from the Western allies appeared off the coasts of South Africa. This time the fleet kept well back from the coast.

If another nuclear cruise missile was launched against the fleet there'd be time to shoot it down.

As aircraft from the allied carriers neared the beach, the defenders' SAM battery radar operators tried to track the craft. With the allied stealth technology, it was difficult. Infantrymen and construction workers toiling feverishly to complete the new, more extensive beach defenses, ignored the aircraft flying overhead.

Prior to the assault, allied satellites had photographed the South African coasts, so the defenses were anticipated by the allies. Using the SAM battery's radar for targeting, Wild Weasels fired missiles that homed in on the radar sites. More allied aircraft searched for the SAM batteries themselves.

Surface-to-air missiles from the surviving defensive batteries were fired at the overflights to take out the aircraft. A few allied planes were shot down, but most returned to their carriers.

In preparing the plans for this attack, the Allied Planning Board remembered what had happened to the first invasion attempt. Part of their offensive included two E-3 Sentry planes. While one watched for hostile aircraft, the other scanned for terrain-skimming missiles.

An additional point added to the invasion plan was that CIA contacts in South Africa had been able to pinpoint that nation's nuclear arsenal. Satellite photos showed that all nuclear sites had been camouflaged as manufacturing facilities in or near large population centers. Intelligence had also confirmed that the mines and refineries which were the object of the war, had now been rigged for demolition if the South African leaders determined the war was lost.

On the second day of the assault, just as dawn broke over the South African beaches, the allied fleet erupted with cannon fire and missile launches. Observers watching from the sentry aircraft overhead reported seeing an area behind the beach, several miles in length, disappear in explosions. At the same time airports and military bases throughout South Africa were bombed from the air.

Six hours after it began the bombardment stopped. Expecting landing craft to be inbound, the defenders moved out of their hardened shelters and took up position in what was left of their prepared trenches. Armored covers were retracted to expose artillery and missile batteries.

Allied Wild Weasels swept in over the beaches once again. Their job was to detect and eliminate any surviving missile batteries and radar installations. Surface-to-air missiles fired at the craft were lured off course by decoys. The radar attempting to target allied aircraft was used to lead missiles back to the radar installations. With the South African air defenses pared down even further, the allied fighters banked and headed back out to sea. A cruise missile launched from the command ship passed below the formation of fighters heading for their carriers.

The forces defending the beaches, along with their reserves and equipment were turned to radioactive slag as the cruise missiles' nuclear warhead detonated and cleared the beach. This time the Allies were playing to win and weren't holding anything back.

When the fireball dissipated troop ships closed on the coast, and the assault force, outfitted for operations in a radioactive combat zone, advanced toward the beach. The South African leadership was unaware its defenses had been obliterated because the presidential command post had been destroyed by another nuclear explosion.

Since the nuclear weapons storage sites, as well as the exotic metal storage, mining, and refining sites were needed undamaged, thirty allied high-altitude bombers from Diego Garcia swept toward South Africa. Two hundred miles from the South African coasts, the allied aircraft released cruise missiles, and turned back for their home base. The missiles flew the rest of the way and detonated five thousand feet above their objectives.

This attack occurred at the same time that the beach defenses and national leadership were obliterated. Radiation from the neutron bombs killed or disabled those defending the targets so no one could activate the self-destruct. Two hours after the detonations, airborne troops from Diego Garcia dropped in to occupy the refineries and mines.

With the bulk of its armies and all of its leadership incinerated, South Africa surrendered. Additional troops landed and began to occupy the major cities. The general commanding the occupation forces declared martial law and had restricted areas cordoned off. Decontamination teams began the rehabilitation of the existing metal stockpiles, refining plants, and storage areas.

CHAPTER 6

General Tim Matsumo leaned back in his office chair and propped his feet up on his desk. For once, its surface was clear of computer chips and hardcopy reports. With the South African War successfully completed, most of his stress was gone; not to mention a decent amount of his workload. All that remained was to help Israel wrap up the war with Syria.

He glanced over at the picture sitting on his desk that showed his wife and three sons. It'd been months since he'd been able to spend any significant amount of time with them. At the height of the South African War there were days when he hadn't been able to go home. Now that he had more time, maybe he could take his family camping for a week or two. A smile crossed his lips, and he gave a slight nod. Yes, that was it! They'd go to Yosemite or Yellowstone for a couple of weeks. While his wife wasn't a big fan of sleeping in a tent, she'd go for her sons. Those three boys couldn't get enough of the outdoors, and the break would do him some good as well.

An attention tone disturbed the general's thoughts. Leaning forward, he keyed the accept button on his desk phone. "Yes?" he asked.

"Colonel Winston is here for his appointment," said his receptionist.

Matsumo glanced at his desk clock and nodded. "Send him in," Matsumo ordered.

A moment later the office door opened, and Winston walked in. He came to a halt just in front of the general's desk and saluted.

Matsumo acknowledged the salute. "What've you got for me today, Colonel?" he asked.

The colonel dropped the salute, reached into the left breast pocket of his uniform blouse, and retrieved a computer chip. He placed the device on the clean surface of the desk in front of his commander. "Everything's there," Winston announced.

The general had heard that phrase thousands of times over the years he and the colonel had been working together. He didn't pick up the chip or even look at it but nodded at an overstuffed chair facing the desk. "Take a seat, Winston, and give me a summary."

Winston sat in the indicated chair. "I'll start with South Africa," he announced. "The first shipments of the exotic metals from the South African reserves are being loaded onto cargo ships and should reach their destinations within two weeks. The first load is being divided between the U.S. and Europe. The next shipment goes to Asia and the South Pacific. The mines are being opened and the refineries readied."

Matsumo nodded, and a broad smile crossed his lips. Maybe the much-needed leave and camping trip was more doable. "That's better than I'd hoped," he commented, then asked. "How's the occupation going?"

"We've a different story there," Winston replied. "Most of the major cities are under control. But the problem we've got is in the rural areas and mid-sized population centers. With the prior regime gone, the oppressed tribes that had left South Africa are returning to take revenge on their oppressors. Patrols have found evidence of massacres where the victims have been tortured, murdered, and mutilated. We don't have enough troops in the country to cover the entire nation."

The general shook his head. "Why can't these people leave well enough alone? They've experienced oppression and persecution so now they have to become the oppressors and persecutors." Before the colonel could respond he asked another question. "How large of a troop size do we need?"

This time Winston consulted his tablet. "What's left of the national and provincial police forces can't be used because they were associated with the deposed regime," he said. "We estimate an additional force of 250,000, including support troops, will be able to keep the peace."

Matsumo's eyes widened. "That large?"

The colonel nodded.

"Tell me where we are in replacing our South African losses," the general ordered.

"There are 60,000 men at boot camp, with another 100,000 waiting for their training to begin," Winston replied. "It'll take six months to a year to bring our manpower back up to pre-war levels. We need at least three to five years to replace the equipment that was lost."

"I see," said Matsumo, then fell silent for a moment as he considered. "The extra troops for South Africa will have to come from NATO and our other allies," he said a moment later. "We provided most of the troops for both South African campaigns, and our earlier losses won't be made up in time to do any good. Couple that with our commitment to support Israel, we simply can't send any more troops to South Africa." He worked on the keyboard built into his desktop. "I'll ask the SecDef to send the request to the appropriate parties."

When he finished a reminder, he looked up and said, "Now tell me about Israel."

"After heavy fighting, the Consolidated Islamic Forces have been forced back into Syria," Winston replied. "The Golan Heights have been relieved."

"Are Iran and Iraq continuing to send reinforcements?" Matsumo asked.

"They're trying, but without success," the colonel replied with a satisfied smile. "Using drones and satellites, we're able to spot any sizeable group of vehicles or men heading for Israel. Once those reinforcements are discovered, we use our air superiority to take out that force." He gave a little shrug. "We've experienced some losses in our equipment but no loss of life. The Syrian reinforcements are shattered before reaching the front.

"The Israeli missile defense is knocking down any missiles sent against it from Iran," Winston added. "Nothing's getting through. They're concerned the Iranians are trying to nuke Israel."

"I see," said the general with a nod. "Taking out reinforcements before reaching the front should cause any other nation that wants to join the jihad to reconsider." He looked down at his desk and picked up the computer chip. "Is there anything else?"

Colonel Winston looked down at his tablet and fidgeted for a moment. Then he turned back to his commander. "There's another report and a request from Germany about the Russian war game maneuvers."

"You did the same thing to me months ago," chided Matsumo with a pained look on his face. "Is this from Lieutenant...," he paused as he tried to remember the name. "Addermann?"

"It was Lieutenant Ackermann," Winston reminded.

"Right, Ackermann," amended the general. "Is this from him?"

Winston shook his head. "No, sir," he replied. "This time it's from his commanding officer. The Russian war game exercise had been scheduled to finish two weeks ago. It didn't!"

"Did the Russians provide a notice of the extension?"

"They did," the colonel replied. "They announced that, in addition to the extension they'd be expanding the maneuver's scope."

"And that's got the German's nervous?" asked Matsumo.

"Yes, sir," the colonel replied. "In fact, they're worried enough to request that two NATO armored corps with equipment and supplies be stationed in Germany."

"Two corps?" Matsumo's stomach dropped. "That's sixty thousand men!" He gave an emphatic shake of his head. "There's no way we can do that! We're going to be robbing Peter to pay Paul for any additional troops to occupy South Africa!"

"I understand that General," replied Winston. "In light of this request, I don't think the Germans will be sending any more troops there either."

"I agree." Matsumo looked down at his desk for a long moment. "Tell you what. We won't be taking any more troops from Germany, and we'll send those in South Africa home. That should give them their two corps. The other European nations will have to make up the difference in South Africa."

The general made a few additional notes on his desk system then looked up. "I'll get the word to the SecDef," he said. "Was there anything else Colonel?"

Winston thought for a moment then shook his head. "We're good."

President Anatoly Berezin was not happy. His carefully prepared schedule for the day had just been blown up. Damon Orlov, had requested an emergency meeting, and he was so influential it was impossible to refuse. Berezin looked at his desk clock and grimaced. The field marshal was late—again!

Ten minutes later Orlov entered the presidential office. Berezin left his desk and crossed the room to greet the field marshal. A false smile was on his face. "It's good to see you again, Damon," Berezin said and conducted the man to a chair. He was careful to hide his chagrin at the man. "What is so vital to my military that I had to rearrange my entire day?" he asked in a half-chiding, half-joking tone as he sat in a chair facing Orlov.

The field marshal inclined his head in an apology as insincere as Berezin's smile. "My apologies, sir," he said. "I wouldn't have made the request if this opportunity wasn't short-lived."

"Opportunity?" prompted Berezin. "What opportunity?"

"I have just learned that in order to pacify South Africa the Western allies are sending in additional troops," he replied. "Between what's already in South Africa and the Middle East, the Americans have very few troops left to send. As a result, the bulk of the additional troop strength will be coming. . .from. . .Europe." He gave his commander-in-chief a knowing look. "This just happens to be while our latest war-games exercise is being conducted in our western regions."

The president gave a silent ohh. "I see," he said, then gave an emphatic nod. "Very well, you have authority to proceed with Operation Throne."

Without a word, Field Marshal Orlov stood, gave a short bow to the president, and left.

Two weeks after Orlov's meeting with President Berezin, Russian fighter-bombers altered course from their announced flight plan and violated NATO's air space. At the same time corps spearheaded by columns of tanks invaded the Baltic States, Belarus, Ukraine, Finland, and Poland. The Russian military had gone through an extensive overhaul since the debacle in Ukraine, and it showed. NATO airbases and the planes on the ground were destroyed by long-range cruise missiles before any response could be organized. The allied aircraft already in the air put up a valiant fight before being shot down by the overwhelming Russian forces.

NATO ground forces were outnumbered and grossly unprepared for battle. The commanders soon found their alternatives were to surrender, be destroyed, or retreat. They chose to fight a delaying action, which would allow the allies a chance to regroup at a secondary defensive line near the German border with Poland. Once the Russian advance had been stopped, the allies could prepare counterattacks staged from Belgium, Holland, France, and the United Kingdom.

General Heinrich Zimmer, NATO's supreme commander, walked the corridors of his headquarters in Brussels, Belgium. He turned down a side hall, then moved past the guards stationed outside a conference room. Once through the open door, he saw the representatives of NATO surrounding the polished Bavarian pine table. A few of the ambassadors watched as Zimmer moved to the head of the table. Others continued their muted conversations until the general rapped his knuckles on the table's surface to gain their attention.

"Thank you for coming on such short notice," he said.

"Your 'invitation' said it was of the utmost importance," the British ambassador said as he stroked his graying goatee.

General Zimmer nodded. "It is," he replied. "I'll be brief. This is your official notice of my intention to utilize my nuclear arsenal."

"Your what?" Only the French and Austrian ambassadors had the presence of mind to speak and were on their feet. The rest of the ambassadors were too stunned by the general's announcement to respond.

Zimmer waved the two men back into their chairs. "Your military advisors will confirm what I am about to tell you.

"As a result of the South African campaign, a large portion of NATO's forces are elsewhere. I'm assuming that's why the Russians attacked when they did. What this means is that the forces available to fight this new war are outnumbered ten to one. That includes material and equipment as well as men. Unless those odds are improved NATO will . . .."

A brilliant flash interrupted General Zimmer's briefing. The general, his staff, and the assembled ambassadors in Brussels joined Paris, Amsterdam, Rome, Athens, and other capital cities of Europe as radioactive dust, incinerated by preemptive nuclear strikes. Most of the military bases where NATO's tactical nuclear weapons were housed had been targeted as well; the NATO weapons added their own destructive force to the devastation of the surrounding countryside. Russian cruise missiles launched from missile boats in the North and Mediterranean Seas had flown in under the radar.

A few surviving NATO commanders and missile crews, acting without authorization, launched their own nuclear missiles at several Russian armored corps. The forces targeted were destroyed, but the overall Russian advance was not halted.

In their planning, the Russians paid special attention to England. Not wanting to leave a refuge from which an invasion of the mainland could be staged, the entire country was barraged with nuclear explosions.

Two weeks after the attack began, the fighting stopped, and the results were impressive. Europe had been conquered. The British Isles were a mixture of mounds of radioactive slag, plains of melted rock where cities had once stood, contaminated countryside, and a small population dying from radiation poisoning.

Switzerland was the only unconquered country in all of Europe. President Berezin made a personal call to the president and gave the

Swiss government twenty-four hours to open its borders to "liberating" Russian forces or face obliteration. There were no terms given, only the opportunity to surrender. The Swiss government agreed to the Russian demands and opened its borders, ending that nation's long history of independence and neutrality.

Rod and Tali sat alone on the observation gallery sofa. The engineer leaned against the scientist, her head on his shoulder. Both people stared at the planet hanging above the moon's horizon. The lines in that blue-white jewel appeared less distinct, the colors muted from debris thrown into the atmosphere by nuclear detonations. The darkened room seemed to match the dejection of the two people.

"When do you think we'll be evacuated back home?" Tali asked, breaking the silence at last.

The scientist gave a sigh and shook his head. "Who knows?" he replied. "I heard that Harry MacDonald, from the radio telescope section requested space on the ferry to the Transfer Station a few days ago."

"Harry's leaving his project?" Tali asked in surprise and Rod nodded. "According to the schedule, he's only got a month or two left!"

"Yep," Rod said. "He told me that he didn't want to wait for the rush of a last-minute evacuation."

"I see. When does he leave?" Tali asked.

Rod shook his head again. "He doesn't," he replied. "His request was denied."

"Denied? Why?"

"For the time being all traffic is being restricted to essential personnel only." The scientist shrugged. "Whatever that means."

"So, what do we do?" Tali asked.

"I guess we keep doing what we've been doing," the scientist replied, holding out his left hand. "I've put the year-long test on hold until the situation back home is resolved. It takes at least an hour to reanimate a suspended person, and we may get less than an hour's notice to evacuate the observatory. Instead, my people are working on the sleeper modules for the *Mars One*."

"Do you think the ship will ever be finished?" Tali wondered. "Will anyone survive to go to the stars?"

"Who knows?" was the reply.

An awkward silence fell between the two people. They returned to watching the Earth. Hanging in the sky off to one side of the planet was the *Mars One*. Most of the construction on the ship had been completed, but with the war in Europe the finishing work had stopped. The ship needed its sleeper modules and controls installed before it could be sent to Mars.

"Just before my shift ended Ger told me the Russian president had made an announcement," Tali said at last. She kept her gaze on the injured planet. "It seems we have a new nation—the Greater Russian Republic."

Rod didn't say anything, but Tali continued talking. "The Russian State Duma and Federal Assembly have approved the annexation of all European countries to form this Russian republic. It stretches from the Bering Sea to the Atlantic Ocean and from the Arctic Ocean to the Mediterranean Sea."

The scientist sighed in disgust. "Hitler conquered most of Europe in six weeks," he said quietly, almost to himself. "But the Russians got it all in two." He glanced over at Tali. "I don't know how we can free Europe this time. It seems we're all alone in this fight."

President Everard Thorsen glanced around the conference table at his Cabinet. After Russia's light speed conquest of Europe, the mood in the room was somber. There wasn't the usual, easy-going banter that preceded a meeting. A quick glance at the room's clock told him it was time.

"Okay, people," Thorsen said. His words seemed shocking in the silence. "Let's begin. We've got a lot to cover, so I hope you've cleared your calendar." A low rumble of assent went around the table. "Good," remarked the president before turning to General Matsumo. "Tell me about South Africa."

The general took a deep breath, looked at the president, and began his report. "We've secured all the mines, refineries, and existing stockpiles of the essential metals," he announced. "The mines and refineries are being put back into production as quickly as possible. Shipments of the metals from stockpiles have begun." He paused, then added, "All major cities have been occupied and are under martial law."

"What about the fighting in the rest of the country?" Lisa Edgars asked.

The general glanced over the table at the secretary of state. "The rest of the country will have to take care of itself," he replied.

"But we . . ."

"We don't have the manpower, Madame Secretary," Matsumo said interrupting Edgars. "We were pulling additional NATO troops to stop the fighting. Those troops were at various NATO bases waiting for transport when the Russians attacked." He held out his hands and shrugged. "That solution is no longer available."

"But the fighting, the atrocities?"

"We can't do anything about that," Matsumo said again. "We have to worry about our own survival right now."

"Isn't that a little melodramatic?" asked Martin Harold. "Not to mention paranoid?"

"Tell that to the now-extinct European nations," the general replied in a harsh voice. "The Russians took advantage of our weakness. If we don't recover swiftly, we'll suffer the same fate. You've heard what's been happening in occupied Europe, haven't you?"

The director's face went white, and he gave a jerky nod. Matsumo couldn't tell if Martin's reaction was rage or fear.

At this point, the president broke into the conversation. "We've already received several shipments of the metals, Martin," he stated. "What're we doing with them?"

The director of the Department of Commerce took a deep breath, coughed as if to clear his throat, then glanced at his tablet before answering. "The metals we've received have been injected into the economy," he said. "We started with vital areas such as energy production." He looked at the president and shrugged. "It'll take some time and more of the rare metals before the economy fully recovers."

President Thorsen noticed General Matsumo raising his hand for attention. "Yes, general?" he asked. "You have something to add?"

"I have a request, Mr. President."

"Let's hear it."

"Thank you, Mr. President." The general glanced over at the director of Commerce. "Right now, our country is vulnerable because our military is experiencing a shortage of parts. And those parts need the South African metals."

"Your request, General?" prompted Thorsen.

"Yes sir. For the foreseeable future, all the metal shipments from South Africa should go to industries manufacturing the needed military components. We need to close our vulnerability window as quickly as possible."

Thorsen pondered that for a moment, then nodded. "We can do that," he said, then held up a hand to forestall a protest from Commerce.

"The general's right, Martin," he added. "We've got to get our military rebuilt, or we present an opportunity the Russians can't refuse. Is there anything else, General?"

"Two items, actually, Mr. President," Matsumo replied. "For the past twenty years we've worked to eliminate our dependence on oil for our vehicles. We've made progress, but a significant portion still relies on petroleum."

"You're talking about the Middle East," stated Edgars.

The general shook his head. "We need to have a secure supply, Mr. President, and that means our oil cannot come from that portion of the world."

"We could convoy," said Edgars, "just like during World War II."

"That's what we're doing with the metals," replied Matsumo and shook his head. "And it won't be like World War II. We used domestically produced oil then. The convoys were used to transport material and troops from the United States to England. Here we have to go from South Africa to the US. That's a very long distance for the Navy to cover, especially if the Russians decide to make it difficult.

"Then there's the Middle East," he said. "With Syria, Iran, and Iraq in the Russian sphere of influence, our shipments from the oil fields in that region are under constant threat. We don't have the ships to adequately protect both routes."

"That may not be an issue," spoke up the secretary of defense.

"What do you mean, Lucas?" asked Thorsen.

"If the Russians want to stop our oil supply, they don't have to sink ships," Peacock said, "or have their surrogates attack the convoys. All they have to do is bomb the oil fields to take out the rigs and distribution system. Or they could use their military to seize the fields" He shrugged. "It'll be easy."

"There is that," Matsumo commented.

"We have a large number of domestic rigs that've been shut down waiting for the price of oil to rise. We can restart those," suggested Austin Villa, from the Interior Department. "But that won't come close to matching the Middle East production." Then his face lit up as a thought came to him. "We can open ANWAR. The oil reserves there are double those of the Middle East, and it's more secure."

"That's perfect for the long term," said Matsumo. "But we need a secure source producing oil in this hemisphere now. That way we won't have to convoy the oil."

"The only producing fields that," began Edgars, then stopped. "No!" She glared at Matsumo. "You can't mean. . .."

"The Gulf of Mexico and Mexico," finished the president. "Now that I think about it, this can help solve the border problem.

"Lisa, this is your area," Thorsen announced with a widening grin. "Prepare a letter to President Augusto Vincente. Inform him that Mexico is being annexed by the United States. All Mexican citizens will become US citizens with all the rights, privileges, and responsibilities that go with citizenship."

"And if Mexico refuses?"

"You could drop a not-so-subtle hint about South Africa," suggested Matsumo with a knowing smile. "This will also help solve the drug cartel issue," he added. "We can deal with it once and for all."

"You said two items," reminded Thorsen. "What's the second, General?"

"We need the Russian's complacent, Mr. President," Matsumo replied. "With their conquest of Europe, they must know we're going to be rebuilding our military as fast as we can. To complicate things, they need to think we're so badly hurt that it's going to take some time for us to recover." He shook his head. "But we don't want them to think we're so badly off that they'll attack now."

"There's a way we can do that," Thorsen said. "Lisa, after you've drafted the letter to the Mexican president, contact the Russian ambassador. Please relay my request to President Berezin that he and I meet to discuss what happens next. The meeting should take place at a suitable neutral location." He paused for a moment to consider the problem then spoke. "I suggest Reykjavik, Iceland."

Over the next three months President Thorsen embarked on a series of face-to-face meetings with the Russian president. At the end of the negotiations, the two signed a document known as the Icelandic Accord. After several days of debate, Congress ratified the agreement ceding Europe to the Russians, with North and South America going to the United States. The agreement also ended the current Middle East War. Using their influence, the Russians had the Syrians pull their forces back from the Israeli border and stand-down. The Iranians and Iraqis went home, and the American troops left Israel.

With the treaty completed the Russians continued consolidating their holdings in Europe. They rounded up educators, civil and religious leaders, as well as anyone else who appeared intelligent or brave enough to oppose their rule. These prisoners were put into the work gangs assigned to clean up sites contaminated with radiation. Those who resisted were shot without hesitation as an example to keep the rest of the population compliant. It wasn't surprising that the people comprising the work forces died just like those who resisted. It just took longer and was more painful.

A few people, mainly remnants of the obliterated NATO forces, were able to escape detection and organize themselves into small guerilla cells.

Obtaining what weapons and ammunition they could during raids, they began to hinder the Russian conquerors, hoping the Americans would come to free Europe.

As shipments from South Africa continued and factories reopened, the resolve of the American people to oppose the Russians grew and life started to normalize. Commentators pointed out that the accord signed by President Thorsen would give the people of the United States time to rebuild their economy and develop a strategy to free Europe. The more hawkish media pundits said the goal was for the armed forces to be strengthened, and then the treacherous Russians would be removed from the face of the planet. No one really believed the Russians would hold to their side of the accord for long.

President Berezin entered his Kremlin conference room to see his military council standing around the conference table. Junior officers stood against the walls behind their generals, admirals, or field marshals. Berezin moved to his chair at the head of the table and sat down. The officers around the table followed suit.

After keying his tablet for the agenda, the president looked over at Sergey Duskin, foreign minister for the Greater Russian Republic. "Before we decide to begin the next phase in our plan for guaranteeing the security of the Russian people, I want all of us to be informed on the Americans' latest activities. Minister Duskin."

The foreign minister nodded as he stood. "Since the European conquest and the Icelandic Accord, the United States has been working hard to secure its borders and lines of supply," he said. "Mexico, with its oil reserves, has been annexed, although the annexation hasn't gone as smoothly as the Americans hoped. There has been some resistance from formations of the Mexican military and drug cartels. The National Guard has been utilized to stop the vandalizing and sabotage of rigs and refineries. Canada has voluntarily become part of the United States, making its oil shale reserves available. The oil rigs in the Gulf of Mexico have been nationalized. In addition, the president has ordered all idle oil rigs there to be brought online, opened ANWAR, and started drilling, as well as laying pipelines to bring the oil south. The governments have suspended many of their environmental and land-use laws and regulations to allow the activity."

"This means they've secured their oil," commented Admiral Victor Pozniak, chief of naval operations. "I've received word that their shipments of metal from South Africa continue to operate in convoys protected by units of the United States Navy, supplemented with elements from what remains of the various European navies." He shook his head in disgust. "Those navies have proven to be very adept with anti-submarine warfare."

"Not that it'll do them any good," added General Elin, of the Russian Space Command.

"From all appearances, the Americans are working within the accord," finished the foreign minister.

"From all appearances," repeated Orlov. "My sources have learned that the metals from South Africa are building up their military stocks, not to improve the general economy. In a way, our conquest of Europe has simplified matters for the Americans." Confused muttering greeted that observation. "If we'd left Europe alone the Americans would have been required to share the spoils," he explained and shrugged. "Now they're taking it all."

The field marshal stood and leaned forward to rest his hands on the conference table. He looked straight at Berezin. "The Americans are gaining strength; they're preparing their forces. We can't wait any longer, Mr. President. We must act now!"

"But we are still involved in incorporating Europe into our system," was the immediate protest from Duskin.

"And the Americans are dealing with annexing Mexico and Canada," Elin responded.

The debate stopped when Berezin stood. Field Marshal Orlov settled back into his seat. "I've made my decision," Berezin announced. "We will wait one month. Our inaction should give President Thorsen a false sense of security. This soon after our liberation of Europe, all their forces are at highest alert. No force can maintain that level of readiness for long periods of time. Their equipment will continue to become inoperable due to lack of parts. Even with the shipments from South Africa, they won't be able to produce the number of necessary replacement parts within a month. When they are forced to reduce their alert, we will act."

"What if the Americans don't relax their alert?" asked the foreign minister. "They have to know we have a small window of opportunity before their economy and military rebound. What if the American's move first?"

"Their presidents have always asserted that they will never fire the first shot. It's been reiterated numerous times," Berezin replied. "But if the Americans become suspicious and decide to launch an attack we will know well in advance, because we know the process they have to follow." He paused to look over the assembled officers. Then his gaze settled on General Elin.

"As we wait, a judicious thinning of the Americans space defenses seems warranted," he said.

Elin grinned. "It'll take a week to set up, Mr. President," he said. "By the time we're ready to attack, our missiles will have a clear path."

"What about the missile boats?" asked Admiral Pozniak. "It takes time for them to get into position. If we're going to move in a month, shouldn't we be getting them into position, as well?"

"And the army?" suggested Orlov.

Berezin thought for a moment, reviewing the alternatives, then gave a sharp, affirming nod. "We can prepare," he said. "But go slow." Berezin gestured to Pozniak. "Send your boats in at the same time General Elin's people begin their winnowing of the American space shield. Do it slowly, in small packets to avoid raising suspicions."

Berezin turned to the field marshal. "Prepare our forces," he ordered. "And do it under stealth. We want the Americans to reduce their alert, not maintain it!"

Technical Sergeant Doug Webster, of the US Space Defense Network, gave a curse and straightened in his seat from bending over his console. "There's another one!" he exclaimed.

His companion at the next station, Walter O'Donnell, turned from his equipment and looked at Webster. "Another what?" he asked.

"I just lost another satellite," Webster replied. "No warning, nothing intermittent. It just went out!"

"That's, what? Two in the last week?" O'Donnell asked and turned back to his monitors.

"Three," Webster replied. "And that just isn't right! Satellites don't malfunction in groups."

"No, they don't," O'Donnell agreed and made some adjustments to his console.

The two men were at their stations in the Denver, Colorado, control room for the orbital net defending the United States from a Russian missile attack. Their responsibility was to monitor and control the orbital weapons and detection satellites in a particular sector of space.

"I've lost only one," said O'Donnell. "It's been a few months since the Russians took Europe, and now we've begun losing parts of the Net. Seems suspicious, doesn't it?"

"It does to me," Webster replied as he worked his equipment to log the loss of another satellite. "I just hope the general sees the connection." O'Donnell nodded his solemn agreement.

General Chance David, commanding officer of the US Space Defense Network, examined the information being displayed on his monitor. "This can't be a mere coincidence," he muttered. When he finished rereading the entire report he keyed for his chief of staff.

"We've had a series of failures recently," he said when the colonel responded. "And it's opening a hole in our defenses. I want a back plot of known Russian Killer Satellites in the area of our deactivated devices. Check to see if there's any connection." Without waiting for a reply, the general cut the link.

"This line is the orbit of RKS 240," Colonel Timothy Cooper said. He traced the red line for the Russian Killer Satellite with a finger. "This line is USDS 105." The chief of staff for General David traced a blue line for the orbit of the defense satellite.

"And the orbits intersect where?" David asked.

"Back here," replied Cooper and tapped the point at which the two orbits met. "The 105 was here when it was taken out." The colonel tapped the blue line at the appropriate spot some distance before the orbits intersected. "The RKS 240 was here." He marked the spot ahead of the intersection and continued. "From this point, it would be an easy shot with a laser or projectile." Cooper traced a non-existent line from the red orbit to the blue orbit and tapped the end point for emphasis.

The next orbital plot was called to the general's monitor.

David was cursing thirty minutes later. "They didn't even wait three months after signing the Icelandic Accord. They're prepping us for an attack!" He turned to his COS. "What's your take on this, Colonel?"

"It's obvious our satellite failures aren't a byproduct of normal wear and tear," Colonel Cooper replied. "We haven't had a failure in over a year up to this point. Now we've had four in less than a month. Someone is deliberately working to create a hole in our space defense net. I have confirmed reports that all the Russian Killer Sat's are slowly adjusting their orbits to coincide with our orbital units."

"I don't think there's any question as to why they're doing it, do you?" David asked with a wry smirk on his face.

"No question at all, sir," Cooper replied. "So, what do we do?"

"First we implement Case Red," the general ordered.

"General?"

"You heard right Colonel," continued David. "On my authority, implement Case Red immediately!"

"Yes, sir!" Colonel Cooper replied then repeated. "Implement Case Red." After flashing the general a salute, he swung around and hurried from the office.

General David turned back to the orbital schematics Colonel Cooper had provided. In activating Case Red he'd just ordered a covert retaliatory strike on the Russian space net. He would use the Russians' own tactics and open a few holes in their defenses.

Before doing anything else though, he had to sound the alarm. David keyed the intercom. "I need an appointment with the SecDef," he announced when an aide responded. "Today!"

In the first ten minutes of the briefing, it became apparent that Lucas Peacock, the secretary of defense, was skeptical of the general's allegations. With exquisite patience General David persisted and took the SecDef through the orbital schematics and his thinking process in a meticulous, step-by-step process.

Several hours later the general left the secretary's office with orders to take no direct action against the equipment, installations, or personnel of the Greater Russian Republic unless under the explicit direction of President Thorsen or the SecDef. Peacock remained unaware of the present retaliation that was occurring because the general hadn't told him. It must have slipped General Chance David's mind.

Arriving back in his office, David made a call to the director of NASA. Since the space agency was tasked to keep track of everything in orbit, the general hoped its records would provide conclusive evidence that the Russians were attacking his space defense units. As requested, NASA checked its archived records for the specified dates and calculated trajectories, then sent a report back. The entire process took less than two days. Meanwhile, the destruction of defense satellites for both sides continued.

The moment the report from NASA entered David's email list he put aside everything else and opened the file. The commander of the space net swore under his breath as he read the executive summary, then keyed the link specified in the summary and continued to read. According to the appendix, several of those records showed objects leaving the killer satellites on a direct course for a defense satellite. "I should have done this the first time!" he muttered.

Reaching over, he activated a link to call for an orderly. "You are now a courier," the general announced. David copied the NASA report onto a computer chip. He added the earlier presentation he'd given to the

SecDef, along with a few comments, then removed the chip from its slot. He carefully placed the item in an envelope. "This chip is to be delivered to General Matsumo of the Joint Chiefs immediately," he instructed the orderly after sealing the envelope. "No one else."

General David paused and looked at the woman. "It's important he sees this report as soon as you reach him," he explained as he handed the envelope to the orderly, then glanced at his desk clock. It was 1930 hours. "I don't care if he's in bed, in the shower, or with the president. You interrupt whatever he's doing and give him the chip."

Chairman of the Joint Chiefs Matsumo had just finished reading General David's disturbing report when another courier walked into his office. The man's uniform identified him as Navy. Matsumo glanced at his desk clock and groaned. It was 2330. With a sigh of resignation, he signed for the case and began pulling out its contents. Before he got past the second page of the new report, another courier entered the office. This one was from the Army. At that point Matsumo realized this was going to be another all-nighter.

When the general finished the last report, he stood from behind his desk and walked over to look through his office window. Being the chairman of the Joint Chiefs, he had the office with the best view. At 0515 it was still dark, with the new day just starting. Lights from a few vehicles entering the Pentagon's parking lot meant the early risers were arriving to begin their day. It looked normal; business as usual except . . .

"I can't believe they'd risk it," he said, shaking his head.

Then he noticed his reflection in the glass. The image was of a man who hadn't slept in twenty-four hours. It seemed he'd aged years during that time. He almost didn't recognize himself. But he hoped that after he showered, shaved, and got into a new uniform he'd feel better. Matsumo shrugged. He didn't think so. Not with what the Russians were preparing to do.

Turning back to his desk, he called for the night orderly. To his surprise his chief of staff answered. Apparently, the colonel had chosen to remain at his desk while his general was working. "On my authority, I want all bombers and tanker aircraft of the Strategic Air Command in the air," Matsumo ordered. "All missile silos and submarines go to War Alert." He paused and took a deep breath. "We'd better get that alert to everyone. After that's done, get me a joint meeting this morning with President Thorsen and the SecDef. This meeting cannot be postponed or take place later today. It's a matter of national security!"

General Matsumo walked into the Oval Office of the White House. Since his appointment with the president was at 1100 hours, he'd been able to catch some sleep. When he woke, he cleaned up and climbed into a clean uniform. The sleep, a shower, and some food, combined with a large amount of caffeine, had him feeling almost normal.

Before falling asleep, and when he knew his family would be up for the day, he placed a call to his wife. He glanced at a wall clock. Right now, Sharon and the boys would be packing the car for an extended trip to her parents' home in New Mexico. He imagined the boys were ecstatic to miss the last two weeks of school, but they'd wonder why the sudden change in plans. The trip to Yellowstone had been set for July. He imagined they'd be asking why their dad wasn't going with them. By the time this meeting with Thorsen was over, his family would be well away from D.C.

Turning his attention back to the room, he saw the president sitting behind his desk talking with Vice President Monroe Benton-Smith. The V.P. sat in a chair to the right of the president. Lucas Peacock, the secretary of defense, was relaxing on a soft blue sofa facing the presidential seal on the carpet.

"This is highly irregular, General," the vice president said as soon as the door shut behind Matsumo.

Matsumo glanced at Benton-Smith, dismissed him, and then turned to face the president. "Mister President," the general began, "the Russians are preparing to attack the United States."

"Not this again!" exclaimed the SecDef as he sat upright and scooted to the edge of the sofa. "I heard the same nonsense from General David of the Space Defense two, three days ago. We aren't ready for another war." He looked over at Thorsen. "The whole reason for the Icelandic Accord was to give us time to recover and prepare."

"That's the problem with wars, Mr. Secretary," replied Matsumo. "The aggressor never waits for its target to prepare. We may not be ready for war but the Russians are, so we have to go with what we have."

"I don't have a lot of time, General," announced the president. "I've put back several important appointments and meetings to accommodate your request. I'm sure you have some evidence to back up your assertion?"

At the president's invitation the general walked up to the desk and sat in a wing-back chair that matched the sofa the SecDef was sitting on. Matsumo reached into his briefcase and pulled out the hardcopy reports.

At first, Thorsen dismissed the losses in the space defense net to a combination of hits from orbiting junk and the failure of components. Then Matsumo handed over the documentation from NASA. The president spent a few minutes going through the report, turning pages, and examining the accompanying appendices. When he was finished, he looked over at the SecDef. "You didn't think the Russians were involved in our orbital-defense losses when you saw this?" he asked in an accusing tone.

"To be fair to the secretary of defense," interceded Matsumo. "General David didn't have the NASA report to refer to when they met. It was only after being rejected by the secretary that General David thought of contacting NASA for corroborating evidence."

"Very well," Thorsen said and put the NASA report on top of the defense net report. "While destroying our satellites is an act of war, I assume you have more?"

In response, Matsumo passed over the Navy report. Before the president could open to the executive summary, the door opened, and an aide poked her head in through the opening. "I'm sorry for the interruption, Mr. President," she said. "But you have five minutes before your meeting with the Chinese ambassador."

"Thank you, Sally," Thorsen replied. "But I can't meet with the ambassador today. Please express my sincere regrets. Something has come up that I can't put off. Clear my schedule for the rest of the day."

"Yes, Mr. President."

After the aide disappeared and the door shut the president went back to the Navy's report. The report from the army followed, and then the one from the Air Force. When the last report was added to the pile on the president's desk, Thorsen looked at General Matsumo and began asking questions. The group spent the next several hours going over the reports in more detail. At last, the president set the report he'd been re-examining back on the desk. He looked at the three other men in the room, took a deep breath, and let it out.

"You're right, General," Thorsen announced. "All these reports say the same thing. The Russians are preparing an attack. Assembling an amphibious force on their side of the Bering Sea is a clear indication that they're looking to take ANWAR and Alaska from us."

"What do you want to do, Mr. President?" Secretary Peacock asked.

"What steps have you already taken, General?" Thorsen asked instead of replying.

"I've ordered all the bombers of SAC into the air," Matsumo replied. "All our forces are on war alert. Our ICBM silos and missile boats are ready to launch."

"Shouldn't we evacuate the cities first, Everard?" wondered the vice president.

"No, Monroe," replied Thorsen after a moment's thought. "The Russians know our process to begin a war, and they'll be watching for it. In this instance, if we start an evacuation they'll be warned and attack."

"Okay, I can see that," said Burton-Smith. "To repeat the SecDef's question, what do you want to do?"

"General Matsumo has already taken appropriate measures," Thorsen replied. He glanced over at his vice president. "Monroe," he said, "it looks like you're off to your secure location in Cheyenne Mountain."

The man who'd sat quietly during most of the meeting stood and left the room. When the door shut, leaving the three men in the room, Thorsen turned to the SecDef. "Let's get the designated survivors moving to their secure locations, Lucas. Would you see to that?"

"Of course, Mr. President," the SecDef replied. Peacock stood and hurried out of the office.

"It's just us now, General," Thorsen announced.

"Yes, sir," replied Matsumo. "Your orders, Mr. President?"

"I know the Russian submarines are being tracked and shadowed," the president said. "It was in the Navy's report. Our forces are to close in on those submarines. The key here is time-on-target, General. When I give the order to evacuate the cities, I want those missile boats sunk."

CHAPTER 7

The Russian missile submarine, *Korozov*, lay near the sea bottom off the coast of the New England states. She had been in the first group dispatched from Severomorsk and had arrived late yesterday afternoon. Now that his boat was in position, all Captain Victor Korsak and his crew could do was wait the two weeks for the command to launch.

Korsak glanced around the control room, checking to see who was at their stations. There was a subdued murmuring as men talked to their counterparts in other portions of the boat. A slightly cool breeze coming from the ventilators was welcome and should help his people remain alert. He noted that not all the stations were manned; the weapons board was unoccupied, which was good. At the moment, there was no need for the weapons officer and the ratings he commanded. Those men were resting, preparing for the weapons launch and the fight to return home. He didn't think the *Korozov* would have a free ride home after dropping nuclear missiles on the Norfolk Naval Base, Boston, New York City, and other population centers.

Satisfied that everything was as it should be the captain walked through the command center to the sonar suite. "What's the picture?" Victor asked.

"All clear, Captain" was the quick response from his lead sonar man, Ensign Andry Tur.

"You're telling me that we've reached our launch point while eluding the best ASW navy in the world?" the captain asked.

"Da!" replied Ensign Tur. "This is the best boat in the fleet, as you well know, Captain. You made us that." The ensign gave a slight nod at his scope. "The only concern was that destroyer yesterday. But he was thirty kilometers distant and heading away from us."

The Captain shook his head at the ensign's élan. He didn't know whether to be pleased at the man's confidence or concerned about his ignorance. Korsak turned to return to the control room then stopped to face the sonar man once again. During the next two weeks the rest of the missile boats would arrive. In that time, he and his crew had to make sure the *Korozov* remained undiscovered, imitating an unoccupied spot in the ocean.

"Keep watch," Korsak ordered. "I want to know if anything. . .anything happens."

Ensign Tor nodded his acknowledgment of the order without taking his eyes off his scope.

From experience, the captain knew the enemy could be right on top of him and he wouldn't even know it. Their surface ships could be as silent as his boat when their sound-masking technology was operating. But that wasn't the real danger. It was those cursed helicopters and prop-driven planes. They could detect his submarine from the air, where his sonar couldn't give a warning. The only indication he'd have that the Americans had found the *Korozov* was when their weapons had dropped.

His thoughts went back to that destroyer from yesterday. American surface ships could be detected if their crews were lazy, inattentive, or they wanted to be tracked. In addition to that, their passive sonar was so sensitive that the surface ships could locate his boat if his people weren't at their best. And if that happened, the first he'd know about it would be a torpedo, targeted on his boat, hitting the water.

With his instructions given Korsak moved yet again to return to his station. Then Ensign Tur held up a hand to get his attention. The man's other hand pressed an earphone closer to his head to assist his hearing. "Transients," he announced. "We have transients in the water!"

The ensign stared at the sonar screen for a second or two, then turned a disbelieving look at his captain. "Those are torpedoes, sir. The Americans have dropped on us. I swear there was nothing there!"

Cursing helicopters and life in general, Captain Korsak reached over and keyed the intercom from the sonar board. He announced, "Command, this is the captain. All ahead flank speed! Bring the boat to red alert. Prepare for battle. Have communications get word to ATCOM that we're under attack."

Rod entered the cafeteria after another long day going over the sleeper chambers. With no suspension tests in progress, he and his staff had a lot of free time on their hands. To keep from getting bored and depressed Rod, Xavi, and Crew were going over every component in every chamber that had already been constructed, looking for any problems or defects. They also prepared more than enough drugs to complete the remaining tests and the flight to Mars. He wanted to ensure that nothing would go wrong when the spaceship was launched. In fact, they had enough drugs to suspend more than five hundred people, which was three times the capacity of the *Mars One*. But now that things seemed to be calming down back home, Rod was considering starting the final test of the suspension process.

The scientist went down the food line, looking at the various options and putting his selections on his tray. As he neared the end of the buffet line, he noticed the cafeteria monitor was replaying a Do-It-Yourself show someone had recorded earlier. Next to the desserts were copies of *The New York Times*. He added the paper to his tray. Satisfied, he moved to an empty table as far away from the monitor as possible.

It wasn't long after he'd sat down that Tali walked up carrying her food tray. "You have enough room for another tray?" she asked and nodded at the paper spread over the table.

"Sure," Rod said without looking up. "Pull up a chair."

"To do that," said Tali with a smile and held up her tray, "I have to find a place where this fits." She paused and cocked her head. "Unless you don't want company."

"Fine," replied Rod still reading his paper. Then he realized what he'd said and looked up. "I'm sorry," he apologized. "I didn't mean to be rude. Particularly to you." He began shuffling and folding papers to make room for the engineer. "Have a seat," the scientist prompted.

When there was enough space, Tali placed her tray on the table. She gestured at the paper as she sat down to eat. "What's so interesting?"

"Depends on what you consider interesting," he replied, then nodded at the monitor. "It sure isn't that!" The show's host was continuing her instructions on how to install a toilet. Tali chuckled, then took a drink of water from a pouch.

Rod continued his update. "You know that since the South African War is over metals are being shipped home." She nodded. "That means it shouldn't be very long before the economy has fully recovered."

"What about Europe?" the engineer wondered. She set the water pouch on the table to take a bite from her hamburger. Chewing, she waited for Rod to answer.

"That's what I was reading about when you got here," he replied. "What information the Resistance has been able to get out suggests a return to concentration camps and forced labor gangs to clear the contaminated areas."

"No!" Tali stopped eating, her eyes wide in shock. She shook her head in denial. "No! We can't have gone back to the barbarous years of the twentieth century."

"It seems we have. The Resistance has been able to smuggle out pictures and witnesses to give an idea of what's going on."

"How can leaders of a civilized nation be so barbaric?" asked Tali, her eyes flashing in anger.

"It seems they're not that civilized," replied Rod with a shrug of his shoulders. "But things have calmed down a little now that the Icelandic Accord has been signed."

"But for how long?" Tali wondered. "The Russian leadership has shown they're not exactly trustworthy."

"You're not alone in that assessment," agreed Rod. "Harry MacDonald wasn't the only person wanting to go home when the Russians took Europe, you know. And that line hasn't gotten smaller since the accord was signed." He shook his head in frustration. "Those in charge back home still won't let them go."

He turned the page of his paper, then looked back at his companion. "They were told that what they were doing here will help provide resources, so wars won't have to be fought."

"You're kidding me, right?" scoffed Tali. "Wars don't have to be fought! And they're not fighting over resources. They're fighting over control, who wields it and benefits from it."

Before Rod could agree the cafeteria door near their table slid open, drawing their attention. The two people watched as Jan, one of the engineers working in the power room with Tali, rushed into the cafeteria. The woman paused just inside the entrance, glanced around the room, then stopped when she saw Rod and Tali. She almost flew to their table. "Tali!" she gasped, trying to catch her breath. "You won't believe what's happening!"

Tali stood to leave. "Has something gone wrong with the reactor?" she asked and reached down to check the communication unit attached to her standard-issue jumpsuit. "Why wasn't I beeped?"

Jan shook her head. "The reactor's fine. It's back home!" she announced. In her anxiety, she almost shouted the news. Other people sitting at nearby tables started to look in their direction, trying to figure out what all the excitement was about. "Word's just come in that New York, Chicago, Seattle; all the large cities are being evacuated."

At first conversations in the room stopped as diners started to process the news. They looked at Jan, then at each other. Five seconds passed before the import of her words hit then the room erupted as people rushed for the monitor remote to switch the program to a live news feed. Rod and Tali headed for the control room, their food and paper left forgotten on the table.

Russian spy satellites were in position over the United States, transmitting images of that country to their receiving stations. The pictures that had any transmission errors were cleaned up and sent to the Ministry of Intelligence for evaluation. The first pictures of the day showed the cities in the United States bustling, people coming and going, conducting business as usual. But the latest photos showed people boiling out of the cities like ants in a disturbed anthill. All roads leading out of urban centers were bumper to bumper, and that included both sides of freeways. Because the activity was well outside normal parameters, a notice was sent to the commander of the analysis department, who passed the information on to the minister of defense who made an appointment with President Berezin.

The Russian president sat behind his desk and finished reading the report. "The initial conclusion made by our analysts is that the Americans are preparing a first strike," the minister said when Berezin looked at him.

"But that conclusion contradicts the statements of many prior presidents," argued Berezin as he lowered the tablet. "They've always maintained they would never use nuclear weapons first." He stood and walked around his desk. He handed the device back to Minister Volkov.

"I must have verification of the Americans' intentions before moving up our plans," Berezin said. "The early stroke oft goes astray," he said, then turned to look at a painting hanging on the wall behind his desk of an ancient battle. It showed a historic event where valiant Russian knights prevented a village's massacre by German invaders. "Mistakes may be made if we rush to launch. Our intelligence analysts know the process Thorsen must follow to use their nuclear weapons." He turned back to face the minister. "We need to find out if that process has been implemented."

"I'll see to it, Mr. President," the minister said then left.

While he waited for Volkov's report, Berezin worked through his regular paperwork. But other reports were brought to his attention that Russia's communications, defense, and killer satellites were becoming inoperative. There were too many deactivations, coming too fast, too close together to be a product of collisions with meteorites or other space junk. Holes were being opened in the space shield in a deliberate manner.

The Russian president began to feel uneasy. Would Thorsen attack without following the format prescribed by American law? He shook his head. The American president had shown he was a person who followed protocol and procedures to the letter. Berezin gave a slight, decisive nod from his head. He would wait for confirmation of an attack before ordering the Russian strike.

An aide rushed into the presidential office, disturbing his thoughts. A report from an operative in the Pentagon was handed to Berezin. It outlined Thorsen's order to evacuate all major cities. The report also included the instructions to sink all unfriendly submarines within two hundred miles of the coastline. That action was an act of war. Berezin's unease increased when he came across the orders sending all American armed forces to their highest alert. Was the man really going to attack?

At this point, Minister Volkov rushed back into Berezin's office without being announced. "President Berezin," he called. "Mr. President! All the submarines along the American coasts have been asked to check in. None have responded," he announced.

"The American's have sunk them all?" Berezin asked. The minister nodded. "How sure are we?"

Volkov held out his hands in ignorance. "There's no way we can know for sure without the Americans announcing it Mr. President."

"Of course," Berezin said. He took a deep breath then gave an almost imperceptible shake of his head. This was it! His confirmation. "Notify all commands," he ordered. "We are now on a war footing. The command staff are to report to the war bunker." He stood, moved around his desk, and headed for the door. "They can meet me there!"

The president left his office and moved through the reception area. "Yuriy," he said as he passed his aide's desk. "Have the driver bring my vehicle to my entrance."

The facility the Russian leader was heading for was located twenty kilometers outside Moscow under a complex of hardened factories. An elevator shaft ran three hundred meters down to where the command post, living quarters, storage rooms, and communications center were located—all the items necessary to conduct and survive a nuclear war. Besides its secret location and its depth, the bunker's main defense consisted of three-meter-thick concrete walls and a ceiling reinforced with four-centimeter metal plates placed every twenty centimeters. Its designers guaranteed that if the Americans learned of the bunkers existence and sent missiles, it would withstand multiple direct hits by the largest nuclear weapons.

As the Russian command staff rushed to its war bunker President Thorsen boarded Air Force One, heading toward a similar bunker.

According to procedures established decades earlier, crews in American missile submarines worldwide were arming and targeting their missiles for Russian cities and military installations. Bombers of the Strategic Air Command were in a holding pattern just off the radar screens of the Russians.

The crews in the missile silos were finishing their pre-launch countdown. From time to time a missile tech would look up at the ceiling, worried about incoming Russian missiles. Then he'd shrug his shoulders and go back to work. His job was to get his missile off before the Russian missile hit. When that was done, he could hunker down and hope the bombproofing worked.

Several congressmen tried to contact Thorsen, wanting to know why cities were being evacuated, but were told the president was unavailable. Reporters were busy interviewing many of those who were being uprooted, which added speculative ideas to the many fantastic rumors that were already rampant. Trying to leave the cities was a nightmare, because all the roads were clogged.

To make matters worse, when the evacuees reached their destinations, they found the locations crowded and disorganized. Many people, upon hearing the evacuation notice, left their homes assuming an attack was on the way. They didn't take food or water, just the clothes on their backs. Some people, after experiencing a prior emergency where evacuation was necessary, took prepared packs of clothing, food, and water, along with other items, and were better off than most. Other people felt that the evacuation was just a test of the Civil Defense System and that everyone would return home in a day or two. These people stayed in the cities to enjoy the solitude.

Everard Thorsen looked up at the digital numbers above the control panel to the right of the elevator doors. The increasing number meant they were going deeper below the Teton Mountain Range in Wyoming. This facility had originally been constructed at the height of the Cold War. During the intervening decades, the Army Corp of Engineers had strengthened and enlarged the complex. It was self-contained, and those housed could survive being cut off from the surface for years.

Ten minutes into the ride down from the surface, the elevator car began to slow. At level 112, the car stopped and the doors opened to reveal a well-lit lobby that could be found in any five-star hotel in the country. Potted plants graced the room, fine art decorated the walls, and comfortable chairs stood in one area of the lobby. There was even a water feature. Of course, this lobby was six hundred feet below the entrance level. The entire presidential complex was below a mountain in the Tetons, about thirty miles south of Yellowstone National Park.

"This way, Mr. President," said General Matsumo as he stepped out of the elevator and into the lobby. With Thorsen close behind, the general led the way through the room and into one of the corridors that branched off the lobby.

"Have we heard from the vice president?" Everard asked.

"A half hour before you arrived," Matsumo replied. "He's in Cheyenne Mountain. The other designated survivors have reported in from their secure locations throughout the country."

The two men walked the rest of the way in silence, each man absorbed by his thoughts. The sound of their footsteps echoed and reverberated in the empty hallway.

The door to the presidential bunker situation room opened to let Thorsen and General Matsumo enter. Electronic sounds and muffled talking greeted their arrival. A call rang out from one of the two guards by the door. "Commander on deck!" The assembled officers rose to their feet from their consoles, came to attention, and saluted the president.

"We don't have time for formalities right now," the president announced as he moved toward his station. "We've got to get our retaliatory strike against the Russians launched."

The officers and ratings looked at each other in confusion. There'd been no indication that an attack was incoming. Some glanced at the electronic map of the world that covered one wall, expecting to see tracks of missiles crossing the North Pole from Russia. There were none. Even more confused they turned back to look at the president.

"You heard the president!" roared Matsumo. "Get those orders issued!"

Startled by the shout, the stunned officers hurried over to the communications console assigned to their branch of the military. Messages began to go out.

Upon receiving their orders, SAC pilots opened their sealed packets. Moments later bombers loaded with nuclear cruise missiles left their holding patterns for Russian targets. In the lower forty-eight contiguous states, missile techs pressed buttons. Intercontinental Ballistic Missiles thundered from their underground silos, leaving white threads in the sky to mark their passage. Submarine-launched cruise missiles erupted from the surface of the ocean as they began the journey to add their destructive power to the holocaust intended for Russia. In the world's oceans American fleets launched missiles and planes to destroy the shadowing Russian fleets.

The only people in the United States aware that a nuclear war was being fought besides those in the military were those who lived near the ICBM silos. Before running to find what shelter they could, they watched the missiles disappear into the distance. More than one wondered what had caused the world to go mad.

President Berezin took his seat in the control room of his underground command bunker. While he'd never seen Thorsen's war bunker, Anatoly assumed it'd be much like his own. In the middle of the room were communication consoles manned by officers maintaining contact with Russian forces throughout the world. On the far wall, a bank of screens showed a map of the world. Cities, military bases, fleets, and command posts of allies and enemies alike were indicated.

Berezin watched as lights on the map began blinking. A voice came over the room's announcement system. "American fleets are attacking Admiral Kristoff's fleet in the Atlantic Ocean and Admiral Chaban's fleet in the Pacific. They are responding."

Another announcement came on the heels of the first. "American bombers approaching projected launch points."

Before any reaction to the news could be made streaks appeared on the electronic map and lengthened. Some started in the United States, where ICBM missile silos were known to be. Other streaks rose from various locations in the United States.

Surprised, Berezin stood and pointed at the map. "What are those?" he called. "Are those missiles? Where are they going?"

"Early warning system has American ICBM launches!" came the announcement on the heels of the president's questions. "Trajectories suggest Russian targets."

"They launched first," Berezin muttered in disbelief. "They said they would never launch first."

"The Americans are attacking, Mr. President," announced Field Marshal Orlov from his seat next to the Russian leader. "What are your orders?"

Berezin shook himself to clear his head. "Put our civil defense plans in effect Field Marshal," the president ordered. "Launch our weapons!"

At the sound of sirens, the civil defense plans for cities in Russia were put into effect, and people rushed for shelters. Factories that had been designed for just such an event closed to take in the families of workers who lived nearby. Within minutes of the sirens starting, all shelter exits were sealed.

As American weapons crossed Russian borders the command to launch reached silos and mobile launchers. The Russian version of the Strategic Air Command left the air space of their bases. Seconds later ICBMs cleared their silos. Regardless of their location, what remained of the submarine attack force launched their weapons. More ICBMs rose out of the ground from silos hidden in North Africa, North Korea, and Cuba.

President Thorsen and his staff watched the trajectories of incoming weapons on their large wall screen while the Russian president and his staff concentrated on the tracks made by the American weapons. Consternation and despair filled both command posts.

American intelligence hadn't learned about the ICBM silos in Cuba, Africa, or North Korea. Because of that the weapons of the SDN were concentrated for a strike from Europe and Asia coming over the North Pole. Missiles disguised as Russian weather and communications satellites dropped from orbit. When he saw that violation of international treaties, General Matsumo ordered all Russian orbital facilities destroyed as a precaution.

Thorsen did have some good news. Interceptors sent to stop the enemy bombers had been able to destroy all the aircraft before they were close enough to launch on the United States. The space defense was working. Most of the missiles coming from Russia were being destroyed. But each missile that passed through the defenses carried a minimum of ten warheads, in violation of several prior treaties.

As the head of a project, Rod was cleared for access to the control room for the observatory. When he and Tali entered the room, there wasn't much to see beyond people at their stations monitoring the facility's vital services and screens showing Earth. It took a few minutes of looking before the scientist found Colonel Harvey Christopherson, the commander of Copernicus. The two people walked through the control room to where the colonel was sitting. "What's going on, Colonel?" Rod asked.

Christopherson made a few entries on his console then looked up at the new arrivals. He spoke rapidly. "All we know is that a trans-lunar ferry had just completed offloading supplies and passengers at the MLB and was preparing for the return trip to the OTS when word came in that the United States was evacuating cities. The ferry was ordered to hold position, but beyond that, we've heard nothing. All communications have been cut. Military priority was the reason given."

"That's not good," said Tali. "Does that mean another war is being fought?"

The colonel shrugged. "All we can...."

"Oh, look at that!" A technician's shout cut off Christopherson's statement. Everyone turned to see what had caught the woman's attention. The silence that filled the room was interrupted only by electronic whines, beeps, or chirps.

There, on the large screen, was the magnified image of Earth with its blue oceans, brown and green land masses, and swirl of clouds. Small flashes of light were seen in orbit, which then began to appear on the land masses.

Tali gripped Rod's hand and leaned close. "What do those flashes mean?" she whispered, her eyes wide and frightened.

The Russians were not prepared for the multitude of missiles headed in their direction. Their plan had been based on the Americans retaliating after absorbing a first strike. That meant many of the missiles heading for the United States would destroy empty silos. Russian interceptors and air defense missile batteries were destroying American bombers, but most of the aircraft had already released their cruise missiles.

Major Mikhail Romanowski was strapped into his command seat and listened to the chatter around him. He was in command of the Kinetic Energy Weapon section of Russia's latest orbital station. He gave a grim smile. What the world knew about this orbiting station was that it was a research station helping battle climate change by monitoring sources of pollution. The Americans were in for a big surprise when its true purpose became known.

From his station across the room, Lieutenant Anton Popov keyed the link to his commander. "It's been confirmed, major," Popov announced when Romanowski answered. "The Americans have launched a first strike against Russia. President Berezin has responded by launching all our weapons. "One moment, sir," the exec said interrupting his report. "I'm getting another update."

A few seconds later Popov spoke again. "I'm sorry for the pause, major. We've just received authorization from General Elin to utilize our weapons."

"Did we receive any targeting instructions?" Romanowski asked.

"No, sir," Popov replied. "Targeting is at your discretion."

"Join me!" ordered the major and cut the link.

The lieutenant unbuckled his restraints and floated over to his commander's station. He saw that Romanowski had called a map of the world to his screen. Their station's orbital track was already identified.

"We're way out of position, Anton," the major said. "The plan had us over the American Midwest for our firing position. Instead, we're over the Pacific Ocean. My calculations have us reaching the enemy West Coast in less than an hour."

"Our main targets are only an hour or two beyond that," reminded the lieutenant.

"I don't think the Americans will give us that much time," commented Romanowski.

"But we're a research station!" protested Popov.

"That's our cover story," Mikhail said then shook his head. "But I'm not going to bet my life and yours on the enemy believing it," he said.

"Our attack plan includes taking out all their facilities in orbit—research or military. We also have nuclear weapons in orbit that are in violation of several international treaties. Once the Americans see those weapons dropping from orbit, don't you think they'll start taking out our orbitals as a precaution?"

Popov shrugged and seemed to want to argue but the major stopped him. "I'm changing our targeting!" he announced. Romanowski made some entries to his console, and a map of the western United States replaced the world map. "There are cities and military installations in California we could hit," he mused.

A sly grin came on his face. "Although there is something I've wanted to try since I was given this posting." Romanowski glanced at his exec. "How many weapons do I have ready for firing?"

"We have six KEWs in the launch tubes," Popov answered. "There are eighteen more in the armory."

"We'll only get the one launch," Mikhail said after a moment's thought. "Once we fire, the Americans will know we're armed and target us." He paused again, looked at his exec, then added with a wry grimace. "If we aren't a target already."

"We're going to be creative in our targeting for that very reason," the major continued. "There's a major fault line just off the coast of Canada's British Columbia and the State of Washington. I want one KEW to hit here and another here." He indicated the points on the map. "If we do this right, we can trigger a massive earthquake that will run the length of the coastline." His finger traced down the coast. "The event will devastate the entire American West Coast."

The lieutenant looked at the monitor in awe. "All those cities and bases with just two weapons. It might even trigger a tsunami that'd take out Pearl Harbor!" exclaimed Popov.

Romanowski nodded in agreement and continued his instructions. "Two more KEW's are to be staggered and take out the American leadership bunker in Cheyenne Mountain."

"And the last two, major?" asked the exec.

"I want them staggered as well to hit the Yellowstone supervolcano." Popov gave his commander a stunned look. "You can get the coordinates for those targets from the Internet," Romanowski said. "We launch in thirty minutes. When that's done, we get everyone into the escape capsules and leave."

The Greater Russian Republic was obliterated from the face of the planet first. The Americans had always anticipated making a retaliatory strike and programmed several warheads for a single target. Since they had launched first, most of their warheads reached their targets.

The detonation of the first warhead on Russia created a miniature sun. This sun's heat vaporized everything within ten kilometers. The shock wave generated by the explosion obliterated any nonhardened structures within the blast zone. Flaming debris blown outward set fire to surrounding buildings, grasslands, and forests.

Following warheads added to the holocaust. The heat became so intense that concrete and metal melted and ran like water. Those people who hoped to find shelter in reinforced factories were broiled alive from the heat radiating from the concrete ceilings. Paper, clothing, and wood smoked as skin blistered, then blackened. The concrete roofs melted, sagged, and collapsed, allowing the molten, radioactive mixture to pour in and end the suffering of the few who remained alive.

Missile silos and military bases were not just obliterated but turned into craters coated with blackened slag. The only survivors were those people who lived well outside the target areas.

Anatoly Berezin and the people in the Russian command bunker watched the missile tracks on the electronic map. Tension ratcheted up as the tracks closed on the projected targets. Then a missile struck Moscow. A trembling was felt as the shock from the explosion transmitted through the ground.

In building their own presidential bunker, the Americans had a good idea of how their enemy's command bunker had been constructed and designed weapons to take it out. A depleted uranium nose cone allowed the warhead to burrow deep into the ground before detonating. A total of ten weapons were targeted on the command facility and were staggered to let the explosion of the preceding weapon dissipate before another weapon arrived to extend the hole deeper. Eight made it through the Russian space defenses.

Less than a minute after Moscow had been obliterated the first missile targeted at the command bunker struck. Its armor-piercing nose cone pierced the camouflaging factories with ease and drove twenty meters below the surface. Then the warhead detonated. The explosion vaporized dirt and threw debris into the atmosphere as it left a crater sixty meters deep and a hundred wide. All communications with the outside world were cut off at that moment.

Hundreds of meters below in the bunker, the concussion shook the facility. The thunderclap was deafening. Equipment shorted out from the shaking starting fires; lights flickered, then grew bright again. Seconds later the shaking stopped, and people rushed to grab extinguishers to put out the fires.

Berezin shook his head and turned a stunned look on the field marshal next to him. A ringing in his ears was making it difficult to hear people talking in the room. The president saw the field marshal speaking to him but couldn't understand a word. "What was that?' he asked. His voice sounded thin and strange through his ringing ears.

Orlov repeated. This time he almost shouted. "I said we may have underestimated the Americans!"

Before Berezin could reply the second missile struck.

Impact after impact struck the ground above the bunker extending the crater deeper. It was as if a giant in his wrath was determined to root out a pest. People inside the bunker not in restraints were thrown around. Equipment tore loose to smash into its operator crushing and killing. Ceilings and walls collapsed. The repeated concussions killed everyone inside the bunker. When the missiles stopped falling there was a huge crater seven hundred meters deep where the command bunker had been.

The United States suffered as well. The entire eastern seacoast was vaporized in seconds by missiles launched from submarines off the coast of Greenland. Cities and military bases in Florida, the South, Hawaii, and the West Coast were destroyed by ICBMs. The heat from the explosions set forests and grasslands aflame countrywide. The Midwest and mountain states were left relatively untouched because of the space defenses. There was an exception: Nellis Air Force Base and Las Vegas, Nevada each received three missiles.

As nuclear explosions obliterated civilization, two KEW's plunged into the Pacific Ocean off the coast of British Columbia. The weapons, traveling at more than twenty thousand miles-per-hour, sliced through the water to reach the sea floor in mere seconds. Huge explosions from the weapons' impact released the pressure that had built up over millennia in the Cascadia Subduction Zone. Tectonic plates began to move. An enormous earthquake ripped along the fault line and triggered a tsunami a hundred feet high.

The result was better than Major Romanowski hoped for. The initial earthquake triggered others, which spread down the San Andreas Fault. A portion of land including Baja, California, was ripped from the mainland, creating an island chain several miles from the new coastline. Millions from Vancouver, Canada, to San Diego, California, died as the planet writhed in agony. The equilibrium that had been in place for millennia blew apart and more tectonic plates moved.

Water and molten rock fought for supremacy in the space left by the separating plates. Steam and ash were blown high into the atmosphere as the tortured planet rocked from man-made and natural explosions.

The tectonic movement upset the delicate balance that had existed in the Pacific Ring of Fire. Volcanoes all along the Ring erupted in an unprecedented manner. Those in Washington State literally blew themselves apart. The ash added an inky blackness to the already dark day for the dying world. Eruptions in the Aleutian Islands followed. The Hawaiian Islands saw a volcano on every island spewing molten rock. Japan was transformed into a contiguous range of volcanic mountains belching lava. Volcanoes in Antarctica erupted, starting a rapid melt of the southern ice cap. Sea levels began to recede as billions of gallons of water were vaporized in nuclear explosions or volcanic eruptions.

Two white-hot dots of light trailing lines of smoke broke through the expanding clouds of ash and smoke to spear toward the surface. One was targeted on Cheyenne Mountain, the other on Yellowstone. Some distance behind them followed two more.

Within a minute of its launch a Kinetic-Energy Weapon impacted Cheyenne Mountain. An entire mountain in the Colorado Rockies disappeared in a brilliant explosion. The concussion from the impact killed everyone in the bunker hundreds of feet below the surface. Ceilings and walls collapsed throughout the complex.

Seconds later a KEW struck Yellowstone. Thousands of tourists waiting for Old Faithful to erupt, resting in campgrounds, or walking along the boardwalks examining the hot pools and mud pots, were incinerated in the explosion. The shock waves killed still more people. Trees were shattered, fragments shredding people and animals. The forest was flattened for miles with trees, shrubs, and grass bursting in flames.

A second KEW struck Cheyenne Mountain. When the fireball dissipated all that remained of the bunker where the vice president and other designated survivors had taken refuge was a vast glowing crater.

Yellowstone National Park was wracked with earthquakes as magma in the huge underground chamber miles below the surface began to force its way upward through the newly fractured rock to the surface. New geysers erupted when water met the rising magma. Then the second KEW targeted on Yellowstone struck. The explosion broke open the immense magma chamber and the supervolcano erupted. An area more than one hundred miles in circumference was blown skyward as the intense pressure holding the magma in place released.

CHAPTER 8

Captain Norman Abrams was belted in at his command station and looked over the area spread out before him. The twenty-foot-square room located in the middle of the central shaft was the control room for the Orbital Transfer Station. His station was at one end of the room and elevated three feet above the rest, enabling him to get an overview of all the activity. Since they were in a no-gravity zone, his people had to belt in when they were at their stations. Most of the people in the room were dressed in the standard blue jumpsuits of the United States Space Force. Two wore the tan jumpsuit of the British Royal Air Force.

Along the wall to his left stood the consoles that controlled all the functions of the OTS. There was life support, the rotation and orbit of the facility, the reactor and power throughout the entire station, and so on. On the right wall he could see the station where the dispatcher and his people controlled the coming and going of transfer ships, orbital ferries, and the trans-lunar vessels. Next to that was the suite that monitored the satellites and other orbital facilities. The bank of screens attached to the far wall showed images of the planet as seen from those orbiting stations. In the middle of the deck facing Abram's command station stood the main communications suite. He could see the men at that post trying and failing to keep up with all the calls coming in.

It had started half an hour ago, when the first missiles exploded over or on Russia, and calls had come in one or two at a time. Within five minutes of the first detonations, hordes of missiles were crossing in orbit, and the calls coming in multiplied. The lieutenant responsible for the communications suite had called in two off-duty ratings to help with the tidal wave of calls. Even with all the stations operating, it was a fruitless task. It seemed everyone on the station and other facilities in orbit were calling in trying to find out what was happening back home and why. But Abrams had no answers to give.

He glanced down at the slip of paper his executive officer had just handed him. Commander Goldstein, of the RAF, was reminding him that every observation gallery in the OTS was filled with people. He was afraid that, with the shutters open and debris flying everywhere from the explosions, the station may be breached. The captain glanced over at the man who controlled the safety shutters of those galleries. Perhaps he should have the shutters closed.

He looked back to the bank of screens showing Earth. The ones over Russia and Europe still showed nuclear explosions in orbit and on the planet. Satellites over North America revealed a similar image.

A sense of despair came over him. There was no going home. They didn't have a re-entry vehicle, and, if there was one available, Abrams doubted there was a landing site left intact. Each orbiting facility had escape capsules that could deliver people to the surface. It wouldn't be an easy ride down, but they'd get to the surface. But he gave a brief shake of his head. Who'd want to drop into a radioactive wasteland?

The captain took a deep breath to clear his thoughts and came to a decision. He'd leave the shutters open for now. At least the people watching from those galleries weren't calling in, adding to the communications problem. Crumpling the paper, he placed it in the waste receptacle attached to his console, then turned to face the wall monitors again.

Without warning, one of the screens flashed, then showed static.

Abrams keyed for a link to a tech station along the right wall. "We've lost the link from R Beta Three," he said when the man responded. "How long to restore?"

"A moment sir," was the response. Off to the right, the captain saw the man begin to work his console. There was a brief pause, then the tech reported. "All circuits show clean, Captain. We're good from this end." Another screen disappeared in static on the heels of the announcement.

"We've now lost R Beta Six," said Abrams.

"It isn't our equipment, Captain," replied the tech, pointing at his console in frustration. The communications link couldn't mask the man's irritation. "Continuous diagnostics show green. The fault must be in those satellites." A third screen that had been showing Russia blanked.

Abrams leaned back in his seat after he cut the link and rubbed his eyes. "What is going on?" he muttered.

"Captain!" The voice of the communications officer came over Abram's earbuds. "Orbital Lab Bio-One reports seeing an explosion in the area of R Beta Six."

Abrams acknowledged, cut the link, and looked back to the wall screen. Another screen showing Russia and Europe went out. Something had happened to those orbitals. But. . . .

Then he realized what was happening. Not content to kill tens of millions of people with radioactive fire, the Russians were taking out everything in orbit that wasn't theirs. He paused as he considered the implications. Did they assume all allied orbital facilities were armed? Did that mean the Russian orbitals were?

Cursing, Abrams keyed for communications using a priority signal to jump to the front of the call queue. "All incoming calls are to be ignored," he announced when the lieutenant commanding the communications suite answered. "Send a general broadcast to all manned orbital stations. The Russians are taking out all non-Russian orbitals. Considering the current emergency, our communications are to be kept clear; all research is to be suspended; personnel are to prepare to be evacuated to the OTS. When the evacuation ferry arrives, all personnel are to enter. No personal effects beyond what can be carried in a small bag will be allowed on the ship. If a person doesn't want to be evacuated to the OTS, the escape capsules in their orbitals are available."

"Does this evacuation order include Russian facilities?" the lieutenant asked.

Abrams thought for a moment then shook his head. "No. It's the Russians who've started taking out the orbitals. I'm sure their military has plans for their own people in case we respond in kind."

When he finished with the communications officer, Abrams contacted the ferry dispatcher. "Get the ships currently docked with the OTS into space," the captain ordered. "We need to get the other orbitals evacuated to the OTS before the Russians kill them. Don't worry about the Russian facilities; they're on their own. Each person is allowed to bring only one small personal bag. No exceptions! I don't care if the extra item is an urn containing their favorite cat's ashes. Only one item goes onboard!"

The captain cut the link without waiting for a response, then turned to watch the wall of screens. Abrams knew the facilities nearing Europe were already doomed. The people in those orbitals would have to use their escape capsules if they wanted to survive. His hope was to save the people in orbitals over the United States and on the other side of the planet.

Within ten minutes of the captain's order, crews in the OTS rushed to their orbital ferries and received their routing instructions from the dispatcher.

A ferry making a regular supply run had just docked with an x-ray observatory over the Atlantic Ocean when the orders were received. The crew didn't try to unload their supplies. They just rushed the astronomers into the craft and cast off. Moments later all signals from that facility went dead.

Another lab in the same area, but at a lower orbit, had just been evacuated when a missile arrived. The explosion sent shrapnel from the destroyed orbital in all directions. Pieces tore through the unarmored hull of the departing ferry, shredding vital components and killing passengers. The people who hadn't been killed by the flying metal died from explosive decompression as atmosphere blew from the passenger compartment. The evacuation had been so unexpected that none of the evacuees had been able to get into environment suits. A power surge set off a steering jet, which threw the vehicle into a rapidly decaying orbit. Before matching orbits for another ferry could be computed and a rescue team sent, the hapless ship fell into the atmosphere to become another blazing meteor over the tortured planet.

Captain Abrams remained at his command post listening to the progress reports of the evacuation and watched screens blank. His fingers drummed a slow cadence on his console as he thought. The Russians had to know the satellites and labs weren't military but were destroying them anyway. Then a sudden realization came. His fingers rattled over his keyboard and opened a link to Commander Goldstein. "What's our current position over the planet?" he asked.

"Between Japan and Hawaii, sir" replied the exec.

The captain nodded. At least they had that. "Time until we reach Europe?"

Several long seconds passed before the answer came. "Six hours to England, Captain. Why?"

Choosing not to reply to his exec's question, Abrams cut the link then rubbed his face with both hands as he thought. Six hours was the maximum safe time he had. It was probably less. Reaching out, he used the keyboard to query the database. Two labs were left to be evacuated, and the dispatcher had detailed vehicles for pickup. That meant... he had twelve orbital ferries and two trans-lunar ships available to use.

Abrams cut in his override link, interrupting whatever his people on the command deck were doing. "I want everyone's attention," he said into his headset boom microphone. When the personnel on the deck looked at him from their stations, he spoke again. "In light of the current hostilities, we are evacuating this station. Everyone's going to the Main Lunar Base. If the Russians are taking out unarmed orbitals, they'll take out this station as well! I'm releasing the escape capsules." He nodded to the technician whose responsibilities included the capsules to confirm the order. "Those who don't want to go to the moon can use the capsules.

"All foodstuffs on the station are to be loaded onto orbital ferries. After a vehicle is loaded it's to be sent into lunar orbit." Abrams glanced over at the dispatcher, who nodded his understanding. That man and his people would have to plot the route for those ships. "Set the transponder for each vessel to squawk distress. Personnel on the station will be evacuated aboard a trans-lunar ferry. Those who are already on ferries are to head for the moon in those vehicles. We'll get them aboard the nearest trans-lunar during the trip out.

"Communications, let General Yamato at the MLB know we're coming, and why."

He paused for a moment to look around at his staff, then continued speaking. "We don't know what's caused the war back home, but our only hope for survival seems to be the moon, unless you want to take the escape capsules. Either way, the quicker we work the more people we can save."

The cargo crews aboard the OTS went to work like demons. Abrams sent Commander Goldstein to the transfer bay to make sure things went smoothly. As ferries docked, they were loaded with supplies, refueled, and sent off to the moon. Captain Abrams made sure everyone knew about the six-hour deadline. At the countdown mark of three hours, the first trans-lunar ferry left the station overloaded with personnel. At four and a half hours, all the supplies had been sent and the last trans-lunar ferry was being loaded with personnel. The majority of the station's population had taken to capsules, leaving just over a hundred people on the OTS. That was when one of the radar operators on the command deck noted three strange blips.

"Captain!" the officer called, "I have three missiles inbound. ETA is twenty minutes."

"Have the ferry cast off," Abrams ordered after keying his all-call link to his command crew. "They've got everyone they're going to get. Get them a course to the moon. Make a general announcement to the station about the missiles. Those not in the bay had better get to the remaining capsules." He turned to the technician monitoring the blast doors. "Seal off the transfer bay now! Cut the power to the airlock. No one else is getting in there." He glanced around the command deck. "That includes everyone in this room. Get to the capsules. Move!"

When the warning about incoming missiles sounded, everyone already in the transfer bay rushed into the trans-lunar ferry. Hatches were shut on the craft, moorings removed, and steering jets activated. Those trying to get into the bay found the airlock sealed and hammered on its metal hatch, screaming for someone to let them in. When they found the lock wouldn't open, everyone raced for the nearest escape capsules.

The process to undock the ferry took too long, and the missiles were too fast. The weapons arrived just as the ship was pulling out of the transfer bay. Pieces of the ferry and OTS fell into the atmosphere following a spectacular explosion that rivaled the sun.

General Sam Yamato commanding the main lunar base, stared at the monitor showing the MLB's wallpaper after the replayed message from the OTS had ended. "Coming here," he whispered and shook his head. "They're coming here. But why? There's nothing here but a slow death."

The general was a stocky six feet tall and weighed in at two hundred pounds. He worked hard to keep trim and fit, even in the lower gravity of the moon.

Yamato gave a slight shake of his head to clear his thoughts. Those people were coming here because there was nowhere else to go. He looked over at the monitor showing Earth. Eight hours ago, when the missiles were launched, he'd ordered a telescope to focus on the planet and the picture put up on the main screen.

At present the screen showed Europe and Western Russia. Occasional flashes of explosions could be seen, as missiles were still flying. But there weren't as many as before.

The magnified outlines of the continent were barely discernable through the haze. All the debris blasted into the air from nuclear detonations and volcanic eruptions was beginning to cover the planet. Then he remembered those who had chosen to return to the planet in escape capsules. Why would anyone want to go down into that?

A brilliant white flash, bigger and brighter than the others, appeared and shocked him from his thoughts. The planet seemed to quiver. "What was that?" the general asked.

"Unknown, General," came the immediate reply from the rating responsible for keeping Earth on the monitor. "All I can tell is that the explosion was in the area of Italy."

"If it's Italy, that could be another supervolcano erupting, sir. Just like the one in Yellowstone."

Yamato looked in surprise at Chloe Trinowski, who was standing nearby. "How do you know that?" he asked his chief of staff.

The blonde, blue-eyed, five-foot-ten captain shrugged. "Geology's one of my hobbies," she replied. "Geologists have been warning about a possible eruption of Campi Flegrei for decades now."

General Yamato continued to watch the screen. That brilliant dot of light had been replaced with an orange-and-black cloud, which was starting to cover parts of Italy, Switzerland, Austria, Greece, Romania, and Albania. "Are there any more of those things?" he asked in a low voice. "Are there any more supervolcanoes?" he asked in a louder voice to be heard.

"Besides Yellowstone?" the chief of staff asked. Yamato nodded.

"One or two, I think," Trinowski replied.

"Are they all going to erupt now?" the rating asked from his console.

The captain held out her hands to show ignorance. "Who knows?" she replied. "With all that's going on down there I wouldn't be surprised if they did."

"That's not good," the rating commented.

"Not good at all," agreed Yamato, then turned to his chief of staff. "We can't do anything about what's happening back home," he said. "But we've got to do something about the orbital shuttles loaded with supplies that are heading our way. We need a way to get to those supplies."

"That's possible," Trinowski said. "While those shuttles can't land on the moon, they're set up for docking in orbit. We've got a trans-lunar here. It's on the pad now. When the war started, I stopped it from leaving. That vessel should work to get the supplies."

The general nodded his approval. "That's good," he said with a grim look on his face. "But speaking of a trans-lunar ferry, we've got a second trans-lunar with eighty-five people coming here. We've got to find a place for all the additional supplies and people."

Captain Trinowski left her console and walked over to stand next to the general. "I don't see how we can do that, sir," she said in a low voice no one else could hear. "If we'd been able to move out the people who wanted to leave when Europe fell, we could find the room." She gave a slight shake of her head. "As it is, there's no way! All the space we've got is already filled with supplies, people, and their experiments."

"We will find the room, Captain!" Yamato said firmly. "We've got two weeks to get ready. Send what supplies we've got on hand overland to Copernicus. It's the closest facility and isn't being fully utilized. In fact, get a landing pad constructed near that observatory—immediately!" The captain started to make notes on a tablet as the general gave his instructions.

"As of right now, all projects are suspended." Yamato continued. "The equipment from those projects is to be dismantled. Any salvageable components are to be inventoried and stored for later use. Everything else will be thrown outside. That'll give us room for the additional people. We can spread them around the other facilities up here."

Trinowski looked up from her pad. "With what's happening back home, I don't think pictures of pulsars or novas are going to be in high demand," she said and shook her head. "There shouldn't be any complaints."

Sam nodded. "I'm glad to hear that, because right now our main concern is survival, not science."

The people on the moon and in the trans-lunar ferry were scientists. They could look at the pictures of their home and determine for themselves there was no chance of rescue from that planet. Projecting into the future, they saw no hope of survival long-term. The only prospect they saw was a slow death from starvation when the food ran out, or from suffocation when the life-support equipment failed. Colleagues would check on a friend absent from a mealtime only to find the person dead. The MLB reported six suicides within hours of the word spreading about the OTS evacuation.

A week before the trans-lunar ferry was to enter orbit around the moon General Yamato stood in a storage room watching a console being dismantled. The hatch opened, and Captain Trinowski entered. Motioning for the technicians to continue their work, the general moved off to one side with her.

"What've you got for me, Captain?" Yamato asked.

"We may have a problem, sir." Chloe answered. "We've been tracking the trans-lunar and ferries since they left orbit."

Yamato nodded his understanding. He'd given that order.

"We have several objects pulling ahead of the main grouping," the captain continued. "The bogies' speed isn't consistent with shuttles, nor are they squawking."

Cursing, the general slammed a fist against a metal wall. "Missiles!" he exclaimed. "Why are the Russians doing this?" he asked. "We don't have any military significance."

With some of his frustration vented, Yamato turned back to face his aide and asked, "What's the ETA for the bogies?"

"Three days," Trinowski replied. "That's assuming there are no alterations in course or speed."

"Three days," repeated the general. "Three days to evacuate."

"Evacuate? General, is that necessary?"

Yamato nodded. "After what happened to the orbital labs and the OTS? Get a message off to the incoming trans-lunar. It's to remain in lunar orbit until notified otherwise. While we're at it, the orbit of the *Mars One* is to be adjusted. If the Russians are shooting at us, they'll shoot at that ship. There's no point in wasting all that effort and material. It might prove useful."

"What about the other facilities, General?" asked Trinowski. "Do you think the Russian's will hit everything up here?"

"It's possible," replied Yamato. "There aren't that many targets up here after all."

"So where can we go?" Chloe wondered. "If there's no hope, why not commit suicide? Or just wait for the missiles? At least a nuclear explosion will be quick!"

Yamato considered the problem for a moment. "I don't think our situation's completely hopeless," he replied. "We may yet come up with something to save our lives. And until the time comes that I know for sure there's no solution I'll keep trying.

"Now, as to where we'll go. Copernicus is our best bet. It's the smallest facility up here and the least likely to be targeted. It's also in the mountains, which may make it a more difficult target to hit. We need to get everyone we can there."

"Will we fit?" Trinowski asked. "As you pointed out, that facility isn't very large."

"We'll have to," Yamato replied.

Over the next three days, a tense atmosphere pervaded the MLB and the two other lunar installations. Lunar Rovers filled with refugees and supplies left their facilities to race across the lunarscape for the Copernicus Observatory at speeds previously considered unsafe. A persistent cloud of dust hung over the mouth of the canyon leading to the observatory from all the vehicles passing through. Makeshift storage areas in the ravines outside the observatory were quickly constructed to provide shelter for the additional supplies being delivered.

The radar detected more missiles passing the ships on the way to the moon. The updated count was now up to ten. The news added intensity to the evacuation.

As an additional precaution, General Yamato ordered Copernicus to shut down all external and surface segments. That order included the magnetic loading rings. There were to be no electronic emissions coming from the observatory. Yamato was not going to risk the last shelter of humanity by allowing it to be an easy target.

Six hours before the first missiles were expected to arrive the evacuation was complete. People from the other manned lunar installations were crammed into the three levels of Copernicus. All electronics except for the reactor, lighting, life support, and the control room had been shut down; much to everyone's chagrin, that included the cafeteria.

PLRs were parked near the loading rings and shut down while discarded equipment and supply sheds lined the opposite canyon.

Getting everyone to the observatory was a feat to be celebrated, but there was one item that put a damper on any celebration. Before the last PLR left for Copernicus each facility's commanding officer and his executive officer conducted a final inspection. They found more people had committed suicide. Their bodies were left where they died. The incoming nuclear missiles would provide an adequate funeral pyre.

Even more depressing were the people who refused to evacuate. No amount of coercion or threats could get them to leave. None of the people who remained behind wanted a slow death of suffocation or starvation. Some had religious convictions that wouldn't let them suicide; others were too cowardly. At least the nuclear fires of the incoming missiles would be quick.

General Yamato, Captain Trinowski, and Colonel Christopherson were in the observatory's control room now watching three split screens showing rotating interior scenes of the evacuated facilities. Those installations had been left well-lit and broadcasting on every wavelength. Yamato wanted them to be perfect targets to draw missiles away from Copernicus.

The observatory didn't have the radar or other amenities of the MLB, so the progress of the weapons couldn't be tracked. All the people in the control room could do was watch the clock to get a general idea of when to expect the missiles. Observers had been placed a safe distance away from each facility to watch and report back.

A single monitor next to those with scenes of the evacuated facilities showed a countdown to the expected arrival of the missiles. As the numbers reduced, Yamato and Christopherson paced around the room. Several people were tapping on their consoles to relieve the tension. Everyone in the room wondered if all their precautions would work and Copernicus survive. Silence came over everyone when the count reached ten seconds. Tali reached over and took Rod's hand. He glanced at her and squeezed back. The console operator activated the facility intercom and counted down so everyone in Copernicus would know when the time was up. When the screen showed zero, the man stopped counting.

Everyone stared at the views of the abandoned facilities. Yamato held his breath as he waited.

Ten seconds passed, then thirty, with no explosion. Finally, after one minute, the general had to breathe.

Two minutes went by, and everything appeared normal. Christopherson turned to look at Yamato. "Were we wrong about the time General?" he asked. "Or has something gone right at last, and the missiles malfunctioned?"

Yamato looked over at the colonel and held out his hands in a show of ignorance. "Who knows?" he replied. "Those bogies on our screens weren't sensor ghosts and were going too fast to be manned. They had to be missiles."

People started to relax as the time lengthened without explosions. Three minutes had gone by.

"Maybe they were probes sent to see what's up here," Trinowski suggested.

"There were no secrets about these installations," Yamato replied as he shook his head. "Anyone was welcome to go anywhere up here at any time. That was in the UN resolution allowing settlements on the moon, and we've complied with every request for inspection."

"Then why haven't the missiles hit, General?" Christopherson persisted. He indicated the view screens showing the other lunar installations. It was obvious that the facilities hadn't been destroyed. "Our time estimates can't be that far off." He cocked his head as he considered. "Perhaps we were wrong about what the targets were, and we can move back."

"Perhaps," replied Yamato. "But there aren't any other targets to hit up here. I can't explain why the missiles haven't hit, so we'll wait."

"How long?"

The general didn't reply to the question. He just stared at the monitors.

Ten minutes after the deadline the people who'd stayed behind in the evacuated facilities started to appear on the screens. They'd left their rooms and were wandering the halls. Some looked disappointed to be alive. Others seemed to be talking to themselves.

Trinowski nodded at the screens. "It seems. . .."

One of the three screens flashed and went out. The other two followed seconds later.

"All transmissions lost!" the communications officer announced after she'd checked her equipment. "Cut at the source."

"Any word from our observers?" Yamato asked.

The observatory began to shake. People cried out in surprise and held on to whatever they could reach. Yamato almost fell but spread his legs like he was standing on the deck of a storm-tossed ship. Christopherson fell onto a nearby console, and Trinowski was thrown against a wall.

After what seemed an eternity, the shaking ended. Colonel Christopherson pushed himself to his feet. "Have we sustained any damage?" he called.

"Checking now, Colonel," was the reply.

"The observers?" Yamato prompted again.

"Coming in now, General," the communications officer answered. There was a slight pause, and then the officer continued his report. "All sites report multiple explosions."

"Colonel," Lieutenant Grace Gonzales called, getting Christopherson's attention. Her job was to oversee the operations of the observatory. "We can't find any damage from the shaking," she reported. "The reactor's in good shape, and there aren't any atmosphere leaks we can detect. The observatory's good."

"Thanks for the report, Grace," Christopherson said. "Have everyone keep checking though. I don't want anything to sneak up on us."

"Yes, sir," Gonzales said with a bob from her head.

Colonel Christopherson turned from the lieutenant to look at Yamato. "I guess that's it, General," he said. "Everything's gone except us." He shook his head. "With all the targets to choose from on Earth why order a strike on the moon? And those missiles were launched a week after the war had started. I'd have thought the missiles were gone after the first two days."

"I don't think it was ordered," replied Sam. "At least, not when the war began." He turned from looking at the image of Earth. "It was automatic. Once the war began, so did the launches; everything was taken care of by computers."

The general shrugged. "To avoid confusion in the initial launch, a priority list of targets was set by the brass in the Pentagon long before the conflict started. When seconds counted it would save time with the targets already in the computer. No one has to program anything. Once the button's pushed, everything's run by computers.

"I'm sure the Russians did the same thing. It's obvious they had enough missiles available to hit everything American, everywhere. As the missiles were launched, the computer simply went down the list. With no one to countermand the launches, they continued until the missiles were gone or the computer was destroyed.

"As far as the delayed launch?" Yamato shrugged. "Who knows? Maybe some of our missiles damaged the controlling computer and it took that long to fix. Or perhaps the delay was part of the program."

"So, what do we do now?"

"Let's see if there's anything to salvage," replied Sam. He turned back to the communications officer. "Have the observers move in," he ordered. "I want to know if we can get anything from the ruins."

The observer teams sent to each site found that the blasts had vaporized metal, plastic, and dust, creating a large crater. Sun-like heat had fused what remained into a molten surface, glowing orange. There was no way anything or anyone survived. The Russians had targeted three missiles on the MLB. Perhaps they were expecting anti-missile defenses or were allowing for guidance errors to send that many missiles. There weren't any problems and all three missiles hit the base. The other facilities also received three missiles each. The only evidence that humanity had reached the moon was found in the Copernicus Observatory.

Moving the *Mars One*, laborious as it had been, turned out to be well planned. Moments after the MLB had been destroyed a missile passed through the orbit where the ship had been.

Days later, when the trans-lunar ferry entered orbit around the moon, the refugees looked down at the still-glowing craters on the surface and wondered why they'd been singled out. Death and destruction seemed to follow them. With their long-term chances for survival nearing zero, more people committed suicide. Since returning the corpses to Earth wasn't an option, those who died in the ferry were pushed out of an airlock. At Copernicus, the dead were placed in bags and buried in the canyon outside.

Rod and Tali no longer went to the observation gallery. It was crowded with people trying to sleep or crying or talking. No one opened the shutters, because what they saw hanging in space above the lunar horizon reminded them of what they'd lost. Earth was no longer a jewel of stark blue and white. A dark grey cloud covered the face of the planet.

In the control room people monitored all radio frequencies. Most carried static. On occasion, the interference would clear long enough for a plea for help to be heard, but only for a moment.

Rod met Tali in the cafeteria after she'd come off her shift with the reactor. "How was your day?" Rod asked as they walked down the food line.

"Same as always," Tali replied with a slight shrug. "The reactors are still there producing electricity and heat." The engineer finished putting her meal on the tray then looked around the room for empty seats.

"Are you all right?"

Tali gave a curt nod. "I'm just tired," she said. "Fred didn't show up for his shift today so we sent someone to check on him." The engineer gave a sigh. "He's dead."

"Another one?" exclaimed Rod. Tali just nodded. "I'm sorry," the scientist continued. "What're you going to do?"

"We've got more fusion reactor engineers waiting," she replied. "We'll put them into the rotation."

"Where do we sit?" Rod asked, changing the subject. "I can't believe we've stuffed so many people in here." From what they could see, every table was full. There were a few empty chairs scattered about. Even with so many people in the room, it was quiet. If anyone was talking, they were whispering.

"Believe it," replied Tali and gestured with her tray. "It's wall-to-wall people."

"Take what seat you can," Rod suggested. "I'll do the same. We can meet after we've eaten."

Thirty minutes later the two people were walking the corridors dodging people.

"Want to go to the rec room?" Rod asked. "We can watch a movie or find someone to play cards."

Tali shook her head and looked at her watch. "No," she replied. "I want to go to my room. My roommate should be gone by now."

Rod grimaced. That wasn't what he wanted to hear. With so many people crowded into such a small area, they had to hot bunk. And when Tali went to her room, she'd see pictures of her family. That always set her off. "Are you sure?" he asked.

The engineer gave a curt nod. "There are too many people," she replied. "I guess I just need some alone time to sort things out."

Then Rod noticed the tears starting to track down her cheeks. He reached over to put an arm around her shoulders and pulled her close.

She leaned into his embrace. "It's so hard," Tali said. "What's happened to our families? Are they all right? Are they dead?"

Rod gave her a little squeeze but kept quiet. This wasn't the first time they'd talked about this, and he still had no idea of what he could say that would help.

Tali's family lived near San Diego, California, or had lived there. She wasn't sure if she wanted them to be safely evacuated before the bombs hit or to have died in the blasts. If they survived, they faced a harsh life filled with starvation, radiation sickness, and roving bands of desperate people looking for food and shelter. She hoped they didn't have to endure that.

And there was Max. The satellite hookup to the Nevada base had been knocked out in the first half hour of the war.

The worst part of all this was the uncertainty. Tali had no idea if Max or her parents or the rest of the family were dead or not. It was tearing her apart inside that she'd never know.

Rod's story was different. His father had been a fan of doomsday vids and anticipated a disaster, man-made or natural. He'd moved his family to the Rocky Mountains north of Durango, Colorado when Rod was a young child. Over the decades he'd prepared a bunker large enough for everyone in the family to take refuge. It'd been stocked with food, water, and medicine to last a year. His dad had installed air filters to keep the air clean. A nearby stream had been dammed and rigged with a water turbine to generate electricity with rooms inside the bunker filled with batteries. The power from the stream kept the batteries charged, and the batteries were in place for the few times a year the water wasn't running.

Once the family emerged from the bunker his dad planned to turn farmer with the non-hybrid seeds he'd preserved. The family would plant and grow crops that would produce food for the current year and enough seeds for future crops.

Rod had been taken on a tour of the compound when the construction had been completed, and he'd been impressed. His dad had thought of everything. Besides food, medicine, power, and water, there was an armory stocked with pistols, shotguns, and hunting rifles. In other rooms there was enough ammunition to fight a small war. There was no question his family would be able to hold off any roving bands of bandits trying to steal food. As a further security measure, their house and bunker were far enough into the mountains to be difficult to find. Rod had to admit his family's situation was much better than his at the moment.

When they reached Tali's room, Rod paused. "Are you sure you don't want company?" he asked.

She gave him a weak smile and nodded. "I'll be fine," Tali replied.

"You're sure?" the scientist persisted.

"I won't do anything stupid," she replied. "I'll see you at breakfast." Tali gave Rod a quick hug. "I promise."

With that, she disappeared into her room. Rod stood in the hall, looking at the closed door for a few minutes, debating what to do. He wasn't in any mood now to go to the rec room. There was nowhere else to go but his own.

Even though his room wasn't that far from Tali's, it took him almost ten minutes to get through the congested halls. It was with a sigh of relief that he let his room door shut out the noise of the hallway.

Examining the room, he saw his roommate had made the bed and hadn't disturbed anything on the bookshelf. The general had limited what could be brought from the other facilities, so Rod's decorations were the only ones on display.

There were the John Carter books and his scriptures. Rod took the scriptures from the shelf and opened the leather cover. He leafed through the pages, noting the passages he'd marked. Suddenly, Rod closed the book and went to throw it against a wall. How could a loving God; any God, have allowed this atrocity to happen? He paused, thought of his mother, then shoved the book into a desk drawer and slammed it shut. But he vowed he'd never read the scriptures or pray again.

Yamato walked the halls of Copernicus, his mind roiling over the problem of how to keep far too many people alive with limited supplies of air, water, and food. He moved down the left side of the hallway to avoid people using the other side to sleep on. Even with the residential rooms doubled up, there wasn't enough room for everyone. At times he'd have to wait to get through a clump of people trying to console another who was sobbing hysterically. He could see the tears running down the cheeks of those trying to comfort the other person. Other times he had to step aside for several people heading the other way.

Then there were the lines outside the bathrooms. They were at least twenty people deep. And that recalled another problem: recycling equipment. It was managing the unanticipated load for now. But the engineers couldn't guarantee how long that would continue.

Another delay came when he reached the side door leading to the outside. A group of six people suited up to go outside blocked the corridor. He waited respectfully as three corpses were taken through the airlock.

The ongoing suicides had helped ease the overcrowding situation somewhat but resulted in a demoralizing effect on the survivors. There was also a risk that vital people would suicide leaving the facility without needed expertise. Yamato made a mental note to meet with those valuable people. They had to live so the rest of them could.

At last he arrived at his destination: the lab where the suspension experiments for the *Mars One* had been conducted.

An hour earlier he and Captain Trinowski had been in the control room working with Colonel Christopherson on the problem of getting people down from the orbiting trans-lunar. That was when word reached him about one scientist who had not dismantled his equipment.

The general entered the reception area for the suspension project and looked around. It was empty except for a few pictures on the walls and one plastic, potted plant in a corner. There was no equipment which was good. The problem was no one was using the place to sleep or gather. He continued through the next door.

This time his reaction was different. While the room wasn't filled with equipment it was apparent that his dismantle order had been ignored.

Yamato saw a man sitting at a console in the middle of the room with his back to the door. It seemed the man was so engrossed in what he was doing that he hadn't noticed the general's entry. The general marched over to stand behind the man. "Why hasn't this equipment been removed?" he demanded.

The tech started at the near shout and looked back. Seeing the anger on the other man's face, he quickly stood to face the officer. "Carter" was the name printed on his name tag. "It was Dr. Carue, sir, "the tech replied. "He felt the maintenance of this equipment and retention of supplies was vital."

Yamato looked around the room again. This time he noted that about one-third of the room contained barrels and boxes stacked to the ceiling.

"I see. Why should this Dr. Carue think his project was exempt when all experiments everywhere were ordered ended?" Yamato's face had turned a deeper shade of red by the time he'd finished speaking.

"The way he put it, sir, was that before the food and air runs out, we can sleep."

"What?" asked the general, blinking twice. "What are you talking about?"

Carter hurried to outline the cryogenic suspension process and the test results to date.

Understanding came for the general. It seemed the load of worries that had parked on his back was being lightened.

"You know, general," said the technician as he ended his explanation. "Since the war, Xavi and I have been tossing an idea around."

"Who's Xavi?" Yamato asked.

"He's the other technician working with me on the project," the man replied. "We're in rotation maintaining the chamber.

"Anyway, as I was saying, we have this idea. There's the *Mars One* in orbit." He nodded at the ceiling, then waved at the boxes and barrels stacked along the far wall. "We've already prepared enough drugs for hundreds of people, and a lot of chambers have been constructed." Carter shrugged his shoulders. "Why don't we load up the *Mars One* and head for Mars? There are a lot of supplies and equipment already there."

Yamato stared at the technician for a few seconds, then asked, "How long can anyone 'sleep' as you put it?"

"Indefinitely, as far as I know," Carter answered. "Our tests have found no harmful side effects after a prolonged sleep." He gestured back to the console he'd been sitting at. "Our longest test to date has been for six months though," he added.

"Your idea just might work," Yamato said, then turned for the door. "Please have Dr. Carue report to me in the control room immediately," he ordered then hurried out of the room.

"Yes sir," replied Carter as he stared at the closing door.

After a two-hour planning session, Rod and Wes Chandra stood in the control room, where General Yamato was to make a base-wide announcement. The refugees orbiting the moon in the crowded trans-lunar ferry were included in the broadcast. When the links were in place and the introduction made General Yamato took over the microphone.

"The Copernicus Observatory is too small to house everyone," the general stated without preamble. "In addition to the overcrowding, we have a limited amount of supplies. It's estimated that the supplies we've been able to procure will last our entire population for almost nine months.

"If there are any people remaining on our devastated planet, they'll be concentrating on their own survival," the general continued. "We cannot delude ourselves into thinking a rescue from that source is possible. We're on our own.

"The problems I've just outlined aren't new to anyone who can hear my voice," said Yamato. "Anyone with any kind of intelligence knows our situation here is dire. I'm sure the consensus is that we're just fighting and kicking on the way to the execution chamber.

"I'm very happy to announce that that is not the case."

People stopped talking and doing what they were doing to look at the speakers or monitors as the general resumed his announcement. "Our salvation has three parts. One part is in stationary orbit over the observatory. The *Mars One* is almost complete. I've met with Westin Chandra, the ship's lead engineer, and he assures me that, with a little effort, we can complete its construction."

Rod nodded silently at the engineer.

"The second part is Mars," Yamato continued. "For the past several years NASA has been shipping supplies and equipment to Mars in anticipation of setting up a colony on the red planet. This is our chance for survival. We're going to go to Mars in place of the selected colonists.

"The third part will answer the question most of you are having about this time. We know the trip to Mars will take close to a year, based on the current position of the two planets, and we have neither the supplies nor room to get everyone there in a conventional manner. NASA's plan covers that problem, as well. Dr. Rod Carue and his staff have been here at Copernicus for the past couple of years testing specialized equipment and his process. It's been confirmed that this process can place people into suspended animation long enough for the journey to Mars. I repeat, this process has been successfully tested on humans. There have been no observed side effects associated with the suspension process.

"We're going to complete the ship. While that's happening, we're going to ensure we have sufficient suspension chambers to transport everyone to Mars. Then we're going to load up and travel to that planet. Once there, we will use the supplies and equipment already in orbit to colonize Mars!"

"Captain Trinowski, in conjunction with Wes Chandra and Rod Carue, will be making assignments for the work crews. I am asking everyone listening to my voice for their cooperation. You have the skills required to pull this off, and I need your best efforts if we're going to survive."

Under the engineer's supervision it took only two weeks to finish the ship because the work was mainly cosmetic. The cryogenic chambers that had already been constructed were propelled into orbit using the magnetic catapult. Work crews collected the chambers after they floated up from the surface and installed them in the *Mars One*. Rod and Xavi followed the installation technicians through the spaceship and ran diagnostics to see if any flaws in the circuitry had developed in the electronics during transit. When each capsule passed the diagnostics the drug reservoirs were filled.

Carter remained at Copernicus to oversee the construction of new chambers.

Toward the end of the chamber-installation process, it became apparent that there was a problem. While sufficient room could be created for the needed suspension chambers by sending redundant equipment to the lunar surface, there was a limit to the power. Eighteen people would have to be left behind.

Rod entered the undecorated room General Yamato was using for an office. With most of the preparations complete for the journey to Mars, the scientist was curious why he'd been summoned. He saw Yamato sitting at a table, with Captain Trinowski just off to his right. The two officers looked up from the tablet they'd been reading with grim faces as the scientist walked through the door.

"Have a seat, Rod," Yamato said and gestured at an empty chair. By this time, military procedures and protocol had been dispensed with for the three.

"What's going on?" Rod asked as he sat down.

"You're here to help us come up with a method to select who goes to Mars and who remains behind to die," Trinowski said.

"I don't think we have to be so morbid about this," the scientist replied.

"What are you talking about?" asked Yamato. "Assigning people to a slow death is not something to be considered lightly." He held out his hands. "Oh, we can leave enough supplies to sustain life for some months, but those who remain behind are under a death sentence." He shook his head and dropped his hands onto the table. "We need to face this problem realistically and develop a plan for an equitable lottery, or we'll have fighting."

"We could have a lottery for those who remain behind, but no one needs to die," replied Rod. "I thought the solution was self-evident."

He scooted to the edge of his seat. "It's simple, really," the scientist announced, holding out his hands. "All we have to do is install chambers here at Copernicus." A stunned look appeared on the officer's faces as Rod continued. "There's plenty of power to run the few chambers that would be needed to house the excess people." Rod gave a little nod of his head. "Those who remain behind can sleep until the ship returns to pick them up. In fact, I'll volunteer to remain behind and wait for the next taxi."

Trinowski and Yamato looked at Rod, then at each other. As realization came, so did smiles.

Yamato closed his tablet and stood. "Why are we sitting here wasting time when there's work to be done?" he asked.

Two storerooms on the second level of Copernicus were chosen to house those who remained behind. A third room just off the elevator was selected for a single chamber. That solitary device was for Rod, and he would be the sentry for the other Sleepers. 'Sleepers' is what the people who were remaining behind were being called. The scientist had decided to be suspended in the chamber used for the run-up tests.

Programmers set up a link between the observatories' main computer and the sentry chamber. The idea was that the computer would activate the base and start the sentry's revival process if the proper code was received via radio transmission. If the procedure failed, the person would be revived if the facility were powered up. The reverse was also prepared for. The observatory would reactivate if the sentry revival process were initiated.

As an added precaution Tali and the other fusion engineers checked and serviced the fusion reactor for the observatory. They didn't anticipate needing it, but enough fuel rods were placed in the feeder machinery of the reactor to guarantee ten thousand years of continual, full use. Of course, with the facility shut down, the demands on the reactor would be reduced. That would extend the life of the reactor even further.

The number of rods needed for that safety margin was well outside the standard allotment for Copernicus' reactor, but additional rods had been transferred to the observatory from the other lunar facilities during the evacuation. There wasn't any concern about replacing any spent rods while the people slept. The reactor had been designed to automatically remove and replace the rods without human intervention.

As the orbital shuttles were emptied of supplies, they were sent back to Earth, where they'd burn up in the atmosphere. The general didn't want anything to be in the ship's way when it departed for Mars.

Within a month of Yamato's announcement, the preparations for the journey to Mars were complete. There was no ceremony or celebration to mark the occasion, just a regular shuttle service that ran up from the surface to move people and the final supplies to the ship. Those in the orbiting trans-lunar ferry were to be suspended first. Rod was in the first group taken to the ship, now officially renamed the *Ark*, to help place the soon-to-be colonists in suspension.

The scientist moved from hold to hold where the chambers were placed wishing people good luck and supervising their suspension. Carter and Xavi went along to help, which meant they could put three people into suspension at once. Yamato tagged along to observe.

Eight hours after the suspension process began, the small party was alone and went to the room where General Yamato and the chamber technicians would be suspended. Xavi and Carter had wanted to remain at Copernicus when they learned Rod and Tali were going to stay, but the scientist insisted that the technicians go with the ship. If they remained on the moon there wouldn't be anyone with the necessary skills or experience to revive the passengers when they reached Mars.

Xavi went into his chamber first. Then Carter. Before injected with the sedative, Carter looked up at Rod from his pad. "I'll make sure we come back for you."

"I'm sure you will," Rod replied and pushed the button to start the process.

After Carter's chamber was sealed Rod turned to face the general. "It's your turn, Sam," he said. The scientist nodded at the last chamber.

"Carter's promise isn't empty," Yamato said. "If we make it, we'll come back to get you."

"You'll know where to find us," Rod responded with a smile and held out his right hand. "We won't be going anywhere."

They shook hands carefully in the low gravity, and Rod helped the general lie on the chamber pad, then strapped him down. After the IVs were inserted and the monitoring leads attached, the lid was closed. Rod pushed the button to start the process. As the drugs flowed into Yamato's veins the scientist scrutinized the gauges for any sign of trouble. It was very important that there be no problems with this chamber and its occupant. The general was, quite possibly, the only person on board the *Ark* who could keep the new colony from destroying itself.

Rod knew that despair could lead to suicide. He'd seen enough of that since the war. That meant that once the *Ark* reached Mars, any suicide would rob the colony of desperately needed genetic material and technical skills. A death would also create a morale, problem which could spread and destroy the entire colony. Yamato would be able to keep everyone focused on the future and too busy to dwell on what had been lost.

The scientist kept a careful watch on the console gauges as the cooling process began. An hour later the equipment confirmed that General Yamato was in suspension, with all lights showing green. A double check showed Xavi and Carter's chambers still in the green. With his task complete, Rod made his way through the mile-long vessel. At the docking bay he climbed into his environment suit then went through the airlock to the shuttle that would take him down to Copernicus.

"How'd it go?" asked James Warren, the shuttle pilot, as Rod settled into the co-pilot seat.

"Everyone's in suspension," Rod replied and began to buckle his restraints. "We're ready to go."

"Gotcha!" Jim replied and reached out with a gloved hand to start flipping switches. A moment later he checked a few readouts. "*Ark* seal is good," he announced. "Shuttle seal confirmed. Releasing clamps." He reached over and flipped another switch. Two clunks were more felt than heard. "Now!"

Using maneuvering jets, the pilot backed the shuttle away from the ship, then matched orbits a safe distance away. Jim looked over at Rod. "We're in position," he announced. "It's your show."

Rod nodded his acknowledgment and took a deep breath. "Well, there's no point in waiting," he said then adjusted the radio to a specific frequency. "*Ark*, this is Control One, acknowledge," the scientist called, using his helmet boom microphone.

The radio interfaced with the ship's AI master computer. Rod's call was received and analyzed. When the computer recognized the sequence of words, a response was routed to the voice synthesizer. Micro-seconds after Rod's transmission, the computer controlling the ship responded, "*Ark* acknowledging."

"Take my people home," Rod relayed.

Again, the computer responded, "Acknowledged."

Satisfied with the response, Rod cut the link and settled back in his seat. Both men looked through the front viewscreen, waiting to see if the ship's programming responded as expected.

After receiving the appropriate codes, the master computer sent electronic commands along miles of fiber-optic conduit. As essential relays and circuits were checked, non-essential functions were shut down. All the lighting was turned off. Life support was discontinued, with all inner pressure doors closed and sealed.

When the preflight diagnostics were complete, the reactor's output was adjusted, and the main drive flared into existence. The *Ark*, carrying almost four hundred people, began to move slowly at first then gathering speed. Its programmed trajectory was to swing around the dark side of the moon, then drop into a close orbit with Earth, where gravity would help sling the *Ark* on its way. There was a calculated risk in using this method of gaining enough speed to reach the fourth planet. Any automated defense station that had survived the war and its aftermath might identify the ship as hostile and open fire.

Rod watched the flare of the *Ark*'s drive dwindle in the distance. Depression started to come over him, only to be replaced with anger.

Billions of people should be sitting in their comfortable living rooms watching this ship depart for a new planet.

Instead, some insane men had turned the event into a desperate attempt at survival, with only two observers instead of billions. Possibly, no one would ever know of this attempt to find a new home. Cursing silently, Rod had Jim take them back to the observatory landing pad.

Tali met Rod and Jim as they came through the hatch leading to the parking garage. She gave Rod a hug and a little smile, then nodded at Jim. The scientist acknowledged by giving her a return hug.

"What's next?" Tali wondered.

"We are," replied Rod. "We go into hibernation and shut down the base completely."

"That sounds 'bearable,'" joked Tali.

Rod and Jim groaned but the scientist's mood had lightened a little. "That was 'grizzly,'" Rod said.

Then it was Tali's turn to moan.

Smiling, the three people went to the control room. Along the way Rod kept looking for people, he'd gotten used to the corridors being crowded. Muffled sounds of their footsteps echoed down the corridors, emphasizing the point that only a few people remained in the entire facility.

Rod met the other fifteen people in the control room. In a few days, the *Ark* would be at its closest point to Earth, gathering speed for the outward journey. "Do we hear anything from home?" he directed his question to one of the radio technicians who manned the consoles.

Alivia Anderson looked up from her equipment. "Nothing," she replied.

"How about radio or television?" asked someone else.

Livy looked frustrated. "Same problem," she replied. "Every electronic board on the planet is useless by now. I doubt if there's any electricity being generated anywhere down there."

"Any sign that the *Ark* is being targeted?" asked Rod.

"We don't have the equipment to know that," replied the woman. "We won't know if the *Ark's* been destroyed or if it's safely on its way to Mars."

Nodding, Rod looked at the group of people. He saw their sagging postures and drawn faces. The impact of the empty corridors, coupled with the sight of the devastated planet, rested heavy in the facility. They were dwelling on dead families and lost opportunities. If he didn't act now, there might not be anyone left on the moon to be rescued. "All right, people," he said. "We're burning daylight. Let's get to our chambers."

A few people started to leave the control room but Sean Simmons, an astronomer from the MLB, spoke up. "Why? What's the use? Humanity is dead!"

Those who were leaving stopped at the door to look back at Rod, as did everyone else. Before he'd left for the *Ark,* General Yamato had announced that the scientist would be the leader for those who remained behind. Tali moved up next to Rod and held his right arm with a light touch. He gave her a slight smile.

"We're kidding ourselves," Simons was saying. "There's no one left on the planet to build a civilization that'll be able to get us." He gave an emphatic shake of his head. "There's not going to be a rescue."

"Maybe not from Earth," replied Rod with a slight shrug, "but we will be picked up. The *Ark* will return for us after a colony has been established." Rod glanced at all the survivors, remembering his depression when the Ark left.

"Although our civilization is gone, we still have hope and intelligence," he continued. "We've come this far using that hope and intelligence." Rod waved at the ceiling. "The *Ark's* on its way to Mars because of those two virtues. Humanity has faced catastrophes before and survived. We'll survive this one. When the colony has been established, they'll come back and get us." Simons went to say something else, to continue arguing, but Tali spoke before he could. "You heard Rod," she said and glared at the astronomer. "Let's go." The engineer cocked her head. "Unless you'd rather save time and trouble by stepping out of an airlock?" she asked.

When there was no reply from Simons the eighteen people left the control room.

In the first chamber room, Rod began by reviewing the suspension process with the other seventeen people. Arnold Ericson, who'd been a subject for an earlier test, confirmed that the process was safe and painless. He'd been in a chamber for six months before the war. "It's just like falling asleep for the night," he explained. "Although I don't remember dreaming."

Rod motioned for Simons to climb onto a chamber pad. "Let's get you in first," he said.

"Are you sure this is safe?" the man asked.

"Weren't you listening?" Rod asked.

"But what if the automatics don't work?" Simons persisted.

"You're an idiot!" Tali exclaimed. "Get in there! You're holding everyone up."

"Then you go first!" argued Simons, glaring at Tali.

Arnold pushed the astronomer out of the way and stepped forward. "I'll go first," he said and glanced at Sean. "Anything so I don't have to listen to this moron anymore."

An hour later the process was complete, with the chamber control panel showing green. Tali took Simons by the arm, moved him up next to the console, and pointed at the green light. "There!" she said. "He's suspended with no problems. He'll be fine for the few years it'll take for the general to get us. Now, it's your turn." The rest of the group muttered their agreement.

"It'll take hours for all of us to be suspended," Simons said. "It's late, and Rod's tired. He's just finished putting those on the Ark into their tubes. We can do this tomorrow when he's rested."

Rod glanced over at Jim and gave a slight nod. The shuttle pilot who'd moved up behind Simons reached around and pinned the man's arms to his sides. While Simons squirmed and yelled curses, Rod injected the sedative into the man's arm. A moment later, Simons stopped struggling and slumped into the pilot's arms.

"Why don't we dump him outside," suggested someone from the back of the room. Rod couldn't tell who. "He's been a problem the whole time he's been at Copernicus."

"We're not that kind of people!" Tali replied. "He'll play nice once the general gets back. And when we get to Mars, we'll need his expertise and genetics."

Rod and Jim lifted the unconscious man into a chamber. The scientist inserted the IVs into Simon's veins and attached the monitoring leads to the man's throat, chest, and arms. Then he activated the process.

"Who's next?" he asked as the lid swung shut.

One by one, the remaining survivors were placed into suspension. Rod didn't wait for each process to be completed before starting the next person. He just called for the next person to climb into an empty chamber. Tali checked the tubes that were in process to make sure nothing was going wrong. When the tubes in the first room were full, the remainder of the Sleepers went to the second. Tali insisted on helping the scientist place people into their chambers.

Three hours after starting the suspensions, only two people remained awake in Copernicus. "Now," Rod smiled at the engineer and said, "let's get you to bed."

Tali gave him that smile, and Rod knew he was in trouble, so he pointed at the last unoccupied chamber in the room. "No talking. Just get in."

Laughing, she climbed onto her chamber pad and arranged herself so she was comfortable. Rod swabbed her arm and inserted the IV. "This won't take long," he said as he started the sedative. "Try counting down from one hundred. I bet you won't make it to seventy-five."

She looked up at him. "Rod, do you really think the general will come for us?"

"I didn't lie to get Simons into a chamber," Rod replied. "General Yamato and the *Ark* should be back in about four or five years." He gave a little shrug. "It could be ten, twenty years, at the most, if they want to get the colony really up and running before they come to get us."

"And Earth?" Tali looked concerned.

"I worry about Max too," he replied, knowing what she was really asking. "Our Nevada base wasn't a target, but Nellis Air Force Base and Las Vegas would have been. The test site is almost a hundred miles from Vegas so there's a good chance our people survived."

"Survived for what?" Tali slurred her speech and was struggling to keep her eyes open as the sedative began to take effect.

"He could go into suspension like we are, or maybe he'll help rebuild," Rod answered. He watched as she gave a slight nod of her head. Then the engineer closed her eyes and her breathing slowed.

The scientist leaned forward to give her a light kiss on the lips. "See you in a few years, Sleeping Beauty," he whispered.

Leaving the second chamber room, Rod moved through the silent, deserted corridors of the observatory to conduct a final inspection. During the walk his mind went back to a conversation he and Tali had when they were at the OTS. That was when she'd told him about the nuclear winter theory. From what he could see of the devastated planet, it wasn't a theory anymore. He gave a little shake of his head. That conversation seemed two lifetimes away.

Before going to his chamber, Rod went to the observation gallery for a last look at the ruined world. There were no continents, no seas, and no white storm formations to be seen. The entire planet was covered by a single dirty, gray cloud. Occasionally a yellow-red spot flared up from a volcanic eruption.

Sighing, he closed the protective metal shutters over the observation windows and returned to the control room. Pulling a paper from his jumpsuit's right breast pocket, he went down the checklist. He confirmed that all lights would be turned off and life support dropped to a minimum when his chamber completed the suspension process. The exits were already sealed. He also made sure that all unnecessary equipment had been powered down.

Satisfied that everything was prepared, Rod returned to the sentry room and stretched out on the chamber pad. He inserted the IV and placed the monitoring leads where they belonged. Then, reaching over, he pushed the button on the control panel set nearby to begin the process.

Rod relaxed on the padded cushion, watched the lid close, and felt the sedative enter his bloodstream.

An hour after the computer confirmed suspension, the remaining lights in the observatory went out, and the life support system hummed off.

NOTE TO THE READER

Thank you for reading this work. I hope you've enjoyed it as much as I did writing it for you. Please take the time to provide a review (a glowing review would be much appreciated if appropriate). Thanks again,

    E. Wayne Stucki

ABOUT THE AUTHOR

E Wayne Stucki lives in St. George, Utah, with his wife, Franece. They have been married for forty-five years. Together they have five children and fifteen grandchildren. Wayne has a number of hobbies. He enjoys playing basketball, hiking, and camping in the nearby mountains or boating at Lake Powell. He reads all kinds of genres, including mystery, military, science fiction, and fantasy. What he enjoys most is spending time with his family.